In
the Key
of
Us

In the Key of Us

Mariama J. Lockington

FARRAR STRAUS GIROUX
NEW YORK

Farrar Straus Giroux Books for Young Readers
An imprint of Macmillan Publishing Group, LLC
120 Broadway, New York, NY 10271

mackids.com

Our books may be purchased in bulk for promotional, educational, or
business use. Please contact your local bookseller or the Macmillan Corporate
and Premium Sales Department at (800) 221-7945 ext. 5442 or by email at
MacmillanSpecialMarkets@macmillan.com.

Library of Congress Cataloging-in-Publication Data is available.

First edition, 2022
Book design by Mallory Grigg

Printed in the United States of America by LSC Communications,
Harrisonburg, Virginia

ISBN 978-0-374-31410-1 (hardcover)
10 9 8 7 6 5 4 3 2 1

For my heart, Vanessa

Don't play what's there. Play what's not there.

—*Miles Davis*

I may make some mistakes.
I may have to learn on the go,
but I'm open to this journey.

—*Janelle Monáe*

This book contains depictions of
self-injury, anxiety attacks, and grief
associated with the loss of a loved one.

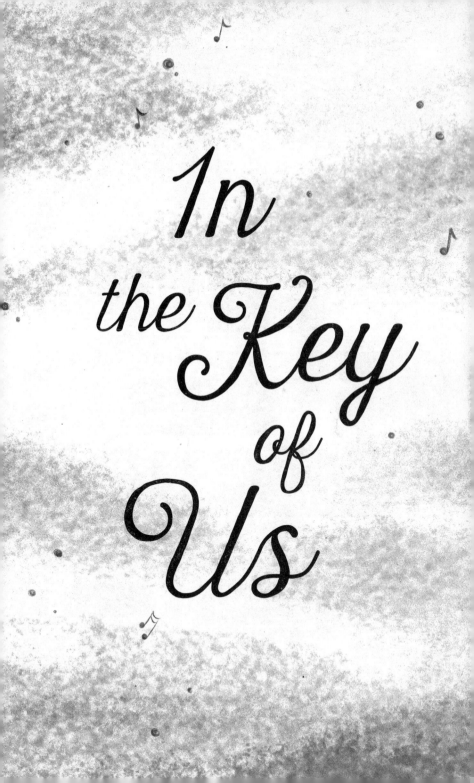

Harmony Music Camp

I get lonely   too
Especially during the long winter months
When the lake freezes over
And all I can see for miles
Are the little hills of white snow
Heaped on the cabin roofs
The amphitheater chairs
The kayaks and canoes at the dock

I get lonely   too
And count the days until the ground thaws
And broken blue eggshells
Litter the sidewalks
Up above, in hidden nests
Baby robins learn to sing

The music always starts soft:
The *drip drip drip* of icicles melting from gutters
Lake water unfreezing at the edges
And then the *slap*   *slap*
Slapping of small waves
Relearning the sound of the shore

The chorus of robins grows stronger
The trees yawn and stretch their branches green

Someone comes to open all the windows
To remove the cobwebs from each corner
To *sweep sweep sweep* the dark cherry floors
A quartet of light playing on each cabin's wall
A familiar rhythm thrumming

I become myself again
A place people return to
A summer home   full of birdsong, brass
        Eager voices
June brings them by the hundreds
Campers flood my sunlit rooms, stone practice huts
My campus full of nodding tulips and tall white oaks

I open my grounds to all of them
I listen I listen   I listen
Until my listening becomes a prayer
I creak and sag and hold the weight of their dreams
Until their music is everywhere—
In the concrete of each foundation
In the nails holding up rafters
In the soft dirt of each pathway
Until I am so full of harmonies
I remember:

        As long as there is song
        I am alive

WEEK ONE

Andi

BLACK IS MY
FAVORITE COLOR

My name is Andrea Byrd, but everyone calls me Andi. Black is my favorite color. Every day I wear black: black T-shirt, black jeans, black Chucks. Black reminds me of Mama. Black is Mama's smile—a white swan gliding across a dark lake. Black is Mama wrapping me in her thin-strong arms before school. Black is her huge, fluffy Afro, absorbing all the visible light—a colorful dark—a rainbow crown on her head. Black is the smell of Mama's strong coffee in our Detroit apartment. Black is Mama's paint-splattered hand waving goodbye to me that first Friday of school last August. Black is the last time I saw her smiling.

"Andi!" Aunt Janine screams from downstairs. "You're going to be late."

Black is me under my covers, on my deep-space memory planet, not wanting to get up to face another day without her. *Whir whir whir crunch crunch crunch chug chug chug.* I hear Aunt Janine start the blender in the kitchen. It's probably full of flaxseed, kale, and other nastiness. Full of healthy stuff Mama would never make me eat. But Mama is gone, ten months gone. I live with Aunt Janine and Uncle Mark in Grand Rapids now. It's summer, again, the first one without her. Seventh grade is over, and I am headed to camp. I slide down my bed, out of my covers, and onto the floor because I am a slime-person. I used to be a girl, but now I am a blob disguised as a girl. A blob-girl named Andi Byrd. I don't have wings, just a few shiny black feathers hidden in my heart.

"I'm up!" I yell downstairs. My attic room looks like it's been raided by zombies. Every drawer in my dresser is thrown open, crumpled school papers and pieces of sheet music all over the floor. A green army duffle sits at the foot of my bed, overflowing with black jeans, tees, and hoodies— but mostly ugly khaki shorts, light-blue collared shirts, and, get this: light-blue KNEE SOCKS. Not even a blob-girl should have to wear knee socks. I groan just looking at Harmony Music Camp's uniform, the socks balled up like Smurf poop in my duffle.

Harmony Music Camp hadn't seemed like a terrible idea back in February when Aunt Janine and Uncle Mark presented me with the information. The fall months right after Mama died had been rough. I was angry, and Aunt Janine and Uncle Mark were the enemy. I barely left my room except to go to school, therapy, or mandatory family dinner. But then, in December, they'd told me they were having a baby, due in August.

"You're going to be a cousin!" Uncle Mark beamed.

I didn't know how to feel about the news, but I knew I had to at least try harder to fit into this new version of my life. I had to try to be a normal kid again, and maybe applying to some nerdy music camp wasn't the worst thing. I liked music.

Uncle Mark filmed me playing "Tightrope" by Janelle Monáe on trumpet, and Aunt Janine helped me with my application essay. Then we sent my audition packet off. To be honest I forgot about it after that. I forgot until a big envelope arrived, a big envelope with a "Welcome, Camper!" letter and a whole folder full of information and packing lists.

"You got in!" Aunt Janine screamed. "This is one of the most prestigious music camps in the country!"

"Good job, kiddo," Uncle Mark said, patting me on the arm.

"I didn't think I'd make it," I said.

"Nonsense," Aunt Janine said. "You're very talented, Andi. That's something your mom and I always agreed on. She'd be so proud of you!"

When Aunt Janine said that, I felt a light brushstroke of a tickle in my throat. Mama loved the way I played trumpet. *Like you're painting a picture with your notes, Andi.* But the truth is I don't play like that anymore. Not since Mama. Now, when I play, I play like a rusty bike. I seem like I'm keeping up, but all the notes in my head feel squeaky and choked. Aunt Janine and Uncle Mark can't tell—they've never played a musical instrument in their lives—but I can tell. I've lost my soul-sound, my pizazz, my magic. Now I'd have to find it again, stumble my way back to the notes that tell a story. Now I'd have to do it in front of a bunch of other kids who were the best in their school bands or orchestras, all while wearing stupid knee socks. *What kind of camp makes kids wear uniforms in summer?!* An injustice, I tell you. Extra, extra stupid. I tie up my duffle, throw on a pair of black shorts, pull on a black tee and my Chucks, run a soft brush through my fade, and look at myself in the mirror. I like to keep it clean and simple—short hair, no jewelry, no makeup. My brown eyes stare back at me, my narrow face and blackberry-plump lips full of shadows. Sometimes I look in the mirror and I see Mama in my face. Other times, like right now, it's just me looking back.

When I get to the kitchen, Aunt Janine is waiting in her light-pink workout suit, keys in her right hand, nasty green juice in her left. Her box braids are pulled into a tight bun on her head. Two pearl studs catch the sunlight on her earlobes. Saturday mornings are Aunt Janine's Zumba time, and now that she's pregnant (seven months, to be exact), she walks the track afterward with a group of expecting moms. Aunt Janine's life is full of planners, gym schedules, and rules—so many rules it is exhausting. Aunt Janine is

Mama's younger sister, by three years, but she's the bossiest person I've ever met and also the fanciest.

Everything in Aunt Janine and Uncle Mark's house is tan—tan couches, tan curtains, tan pillows, and tan walls. Even their dishes are plain: Every one of their mugs matches, and there are none with pictures or words on them. Me and Mama's apartment overflowed with secondhand furniture, our kitchen shelves jammed full of mismatched mugs. I keep a bundle of Mama's paintbrushes in the Diego mug on my desk now, but the hummingbird mug stays empty. I'm going to drink coffee out of it when I finally get grown enough to actually *like* the taste of coffee. Coffee, with a splash of coconut milk and a dash of cinnamon, just like Mama made it. Aunt Janine doesn't drink coffee—only green tea. I don't really understand how two sisters can be so different; all I know is that before I came to live here last September, we only saw Aunt Janine on holidays.

"It's better this way," Mama used to tell me when I'd ask why, if Aunt Janine lived so close, we only ever saw her on special occasions. "Your aunt has never supported my choices in life, and I can only take so much of her looking down on me. It's not my fault I started a family before her. She's had so many blessings, but not a baby. She's never forgiven me for that."

Mama and I didn't have much, but we always had enough. Plus, Mama was an artist—mixed media and paint, so she was forever finding scraps and turning them into treasure. Our apartment was full of her painting-sculptures, dangling wind chimes, pieces of fabric stapled or glued to canvas, bright metallics and neons. Our home was a collage of everything beautiful but forgotten. Now it's like I'm stranded on a blank canvas. There are no bright colors: only Aunt Janine in her tan nurse scrubs or pink workout gear, and Uncle Mark in his white dentist's coat or polos with khakis. And me, in my all-black everything.

"You and Uncle Mark need to get on the road; you don't want to be late for check-in," Aunt Janine says, handing me a variety box of granola bars.

"Are there any chocolate-chip-marshmallow ones in there?"

"No. This is an all-natural brand, Andi. No chocolate, but there is a cinnamon-raisin one made of real oats and honey. They even have a little protein. I thought you might like to try them."

I grimace. "I'm good."

"Andi, you have to start trying new things. God doesn't like picky."

I shrug and walk toward the pantry. (A) I don't believe in God, but that's none of Aunt Janine's business, and (B) I'm not picky. I just know what I like. Mama let me cook and eat what I wanted. I take down a family-size box of Honey Nut Cheerios that I convinced Uncle Mark to get for me on our last shopping trip and pour some into a Ziploc bag. "This will work!"

"You know you're just eating straight sugar. That's how folks get diabetes. Food companies are out here killing us slowly with that processed junk."

"Let the girl live a little, Janine," Uncle Mark says, coming in from the garage, where the car is running. "Andi's young. She's healthy. There's way worse cereal she could be eating." Uncle Mark winks at me, but I keep quiet.

Aunt Janine throws Uncle Mark one of those looks that adults like to throw over kids' heads, one of those looks that means STOP UNDERMINING ME! Then I feel Uncle Mark throw back a look that means GIVE HER SOME SPACE—HER MOM DIED! They do this a lot, communicate over my head, silently, with their eyes, as if I am a toddler, instead of an almost-fourteen-year-old. Mama never treated me like a baby, even when I was one.

FAMILY IS COMPLICATED

*A*unt Janine has always been my aunt, but now that she's my legal guardian, everything is different. Aunt Janine went to nursing school at the University of Michigan and then met Uncle Mark, a dental-school student, her junior year. By graduation she and Uncle Mark were planning their wedding, which Mama didn't even go to because two months before the wedding she got drunk and told Aunt Janine that Uncle Mark was a "safe, basic white dude," so Aunt Janine un-invited her.

Mama didn't do anything easy or safe or predictable. Soon as she graduated high school, she was done with school. She bought a beat-up minivan and solo-road-tripped her way across the country. She'd camp in national parks and meet up with Outdoor Afro folks to hike and enjoy nature. She spent a year like that, living in parks out west, then she came back home to Detroit to work on her paintings and be part of the art scene. Then when she was twenty-eight, she got pregnant with me, on her own. She didn't even tell Aunt Janine until I was almost born. That was another fight they had. I know, because Mama was always telling me about fights they had. "I love my sister," Mama would say, "but I don't have to like her all the time. That's just how it is with family sometimes. Just because you're blood related doesn't mean you're the same."

Mama didn't believe in baby talk or shielding me from "adult things." My whole life she just told me the truth. When I came home from school in first grade and asked her why I didn't have a daddy, she sat me down at our kitchen table with a file full of paperwork. "You know, Andi," she started. "There are lots of ways to be a family. I wanted a baby, but I didn't want a husband or a partner. So, remember when I told you that to make a baby you need an egg and sperm?"

I nodded. She'd explained the basic biology of how babies are made just weeks before. I knew all the anatomically correct names for things, even if I didn't fully understand how it all worked.

"Well, I found a sperm donor so that I could make you. You don't have a dad in your life, but there is a man who you're biologically related to."

"Can I meet him?" I asked.

"Maybe one day, when you're a little older, you can try. That's what this file is for," she said, resting her hand on top of it.

"But why don't you want a husband?" I continued.

"Because I have my art, a roof over my head, and you. That's all I need." She'd kissed me then, and left me sitting at the table with the file and some pizza. I was too little to read most of its contents, but I flipped through the pages anyway as Mama turned up the music in her studio, closed the door, and went back to painting. That night, when she tucked me into bed, I threw my arms around her tight. She smelled like paint and sweat. I squeezed her tightly and she kissed my cheek. I wanted her to know that she was enough.

"Good night, Andi Byrd."

"Good night, Mama Byrd."

"Have big, wide dreams, okay?"

"Okay."

Then she left and shut the door to my room. I heard her pour a glass of water and return to her studio. Most nights, Mama didn't sleep much. It was her "big, wide dreaming" time, and the only time she had to paint, since during the day she worked full-time as a manager at Whole Foods on Mack Avenue. Mama didn't believe in selling her art in fancy galleries or online. "Art is for the people," she always said when Aunt Janine would complain about how her "li'l art projects" didn't even make enough to feed us.

"We eat just fine," Mama would say, waving Aunt Janine's worries away. "Plus, if you ever came to an art walk or to a street show, you'd understand. It's not all about profit."

I loved going to art walk nights in the summer and fall. Mama would lay out her pieces against the curb and talk with folks. Sometimes she didn't even take money but would barter instead: a painting for three huge tubs of shea butter or a set of handmade cloth earrings. "Everyone should have access to free art," she'd say to me as we sat and watched people take in her bold-colored portraits painted on scraps of metal, wood, and plastic. "Let them look. Let them enjoy it." Sometimes those nights made me feel proud to be her daughter; other times, I bit my tongue and glared as she spent hours talking with some stranger about her inspiration, telling them things she never told me.

It was just me and her then.

And then it was just me.

And now it's me, Aunt Janine, and Uncle Mark—and an unborn baby the size of a cantaloupe.

I don't know if I fit in this picture. But I'm in it.

"You can't wear that outfit at this camp, you know?" Aunt Janine says as she and Uncle Mark stop their adult eye-talking.

"I know," I say, crunching on another handful of cereal.

"Why don't you go change real quick. We'll wait."

"No, thanks. I'm not putting on that uniform until I have to."

Uncle Mark clears his throat. "I think that's fine. It won't get all wrinkled on the car ride that way, Janine. Are you ready to roll, Andi? Your very first Harmony Music Camp adventure awaits you! Here, let me take your things out to the car."

Uncle Mark grabs my duffle, sleeping bag, and backpack. He'll be driving me to camp, since Aunt Janine has to work an afternoon shift at the hospital today. At least the car ride will be quiet. Uncle Mark doesn't talk nearly as much as Aunt Janine.

Aunt Janine downs the rest of her green drink and then stands in front of me. Before I can slip away, she's hugging me tight, her belly jutting out and poking mine.

"Be good. Stay out of trouble," she says, pulling away. "And here, we got you something." Aunt Janine pulls a little wrapped box from a nearby drawer and hands it to me.

I open it and find a small MP3 player with a pair of AirPods.

"So you can still listen to your music, even if you don't have your phone."

"Why wouldn't I have my phone?"

"Andi, chile. Details are not your thing, huh? Camp policy says no cell phones; they collect them when you get there. But you can have MP3 players. I called about that. As long as you don't let it interfere with rehearsal time, you can listen to your music whenever you want."

Another injustice. No phones! "Thanks," I say. I'll have to spend the car ride adding my favorite albums.

"Let us know if you need anything while you're there? I know you don't think you're going to have any fun, but I just know you will. This will be good. For all of us."

For all of us. The words ring, and I feel that drop in my gut. *They want me gone because I'm messing up their new family.*

I swallow hard. "I will."

"Don't forget—this is a big opportunity, Andi. You earned this. Don't waste it," Aunt Janine says, back to her business tone. "I know it's been a hard year for all of us, but you're so talented. If you're having a tough time, just communicate through your music. You've always been good at that."

Aunt Janine gives me one last smile, and waves goodbye. I listen to her sneakers squeak their way outside and into her car before she drives away to Zumba. I shove a final handful of Cheerios into my mouth and crunch down hard. My whole head fills with noise, and for a moment I close my eyes and disappear into the loud darkness of my mind.

Aunt Janine and Uncle Mark got custody of me last September, a month after the accident. They'd been just as surprised as I was to find out that Mama had listed them as emergency guardians, but then again where else would I go? Mama and Aunt Janine had been raised by their father, my grandpa Bill, and he'd passed just before I was born. I had a grandma too, Grandma Liza, but nobody had seen her for years. She'd divorced Grandpa Bill and left Mama and Aunt Janine with him when they were in elementary school. She never really came back, and Mama and Aunt Janine never talked about her except to say "We didn't want her around anyway." That was at least one thing they agreed on.

"Sometimes I think me and your Aunt Janine fight because some part of me reminds her of your grandma," Mama told me once, "but I always come back. Even when I go on adventures of my own, I always come home."

But this time, Mama is not coming back. That's something I couldn't wrap my head around last fall. How one moment someone can be your whole world, and then they can be gone. My whole world was Mama and music. I played for Mama, and she painted. We made things together. Moving in with Aunt Janine and Uncle Mark had felt like falling off that spinning globe we'd created. Uncle Mark honks the horn, and I come out of the darkness behind my eyes. On my way out the door, I pick up my trumpet case. It's a shiny black case, black like mama's face lit up by the streetlights when I used to play for her at night.

HARMONY
MUSIC CAMP

*H*armony Music Camp is beautiful. When Uncle Mark and I pull up to the main lodge a couple of hours later, he whistles. "They don't make camps like they used to in my day," he says with a grin. Then he jumps out to grab my things from the back. I tilt my head suspiciously as I look out the window. I watch as a camp employee with a clipboard walks over to greet us.

"Checking in?" she says.

"Sure are! This here is Andrea 'Andi' Byrd," he says, pointing to me in the front seat.

"Welcome, Andi!" the woman says, marking off my name. "We're happy to have you. Once you grab all your stuff, you can stand in line over there by the main lodge entrance to get your cabin assignment and name lanyard."

I nod through the open window as the woman starts to go over a detailed map of the campus with Uncle Mark. The air smells like spruce trees and also French fries, which must be coming from the nearby dining hall. When Mama and I used to go camping, the lodge was a dingy little cabin where we paid our twenty-five-dollar fee. Then we'd get our campsite number and set up our tent on a bare-bones plot deep in the Sleeping Bear Dunes National Lakeshore. Harmony Music Camp's lodge is a huge green-and-white building with two stories and a large wraparound porch filled with rocking chairs. Outside the front entrance hangs a huge banner that reads WELCOME, CAMPERS! There's already a line of people that snakes around the porch and down the side stairs into the parking lot. From the car I count at least a half dozen cello cases, a few French horns, a harp, and some smaller cases that must hold flutes, clarinets, or oboes. Almost all of the campers are already in their uniforms, and besides a small brown boy hauling a trombone case almost as big as his body, everyone in line appears to be white.

I sink down into the passenger seat and poke my right thumb through the hole in the cuff of my hoodie. Ever since I left Detroit, I've been one of the only Black faces anywhere I go. I'm not used to it—Mama always made sure I was surrounded by people like us—Black people. I miss how when I used to come home from school and Mama was still at work, Mrs. Greene from down the hall in our apartment building would come check on me and bring me a slice of her fresh-baked pound cake. Then on weekends, we'd sometimes drive Mrs. Greene over to her grandkids' house or pick up her prescriptions at the drugstore. It wasn't until I left that I realized not everywhere is like this. Aunt Janine and Uncle Mark barely know any of their neighbors, and everyone keeps to themselves. The kids in line at Harmony Music Camp look like the kids back at my school in Grand Rapids, the kind of kids who don't understand a girl like me. The kind of kids who always get everything they want, who have never lost anything or anyone they loved.

"Andi?" Uncle Mark is peeking inside my window now. "You ready?"

No. I am not ready. Not at all. Take me home, I want to yell. But I don't mean to Aunt Janine and Uncle Mark's house, I mean home to me and Mama's little apartment with the cabinets full of random mugs and the rooms full of mismatched furniture.

I squeeze my eyes shut and take a deep breath. *Remember, you earned this.*

"Andi," Uncle Mark says, softer now, "it's okay to be nervous. Why don't we take a walk after you get settled in your cabin? So you can see some of the campus, and I was just told that the dining hall is open for families to stay for lunch today. How about it? Are you hungry?"

I open one eye and then the next. Uncle Mark smiles at me with his lopsided grin. I haven't eaten anything since this morning's dry Cheerios, and the fried smell in the air makes my tummy rumble. I nod and slowly climb out of the car.

Uncle Mark and I get in the line, which is moving faster than it looked like from the parking lot. The brown boy I saw lugging the huge trombone case is in front of us, accompanied by a petite woman with long black hair that flows down her back like a river. He's smaller than she is, and like most kids in line, already in uniform. He clutches his informational Harmony Music Camp folder to his chest, and I can tell by the worn corners he's read it a thousand times.

"Christopher!" she scolds. "Tuck in your shirt. I will not have you out here looking sloppy on your first day of camp."

The boy, Christopher, nods and tucks in a small flap at the back of his shirt that was sticking out. His belt is the same light blue as the knee socks, which means he's also in the junior division. The junior division girls wear light-blue knee socks, and boys wear light-blue belts. The high school division campers wear light-yellow belts (boys) and knee socks (girls). I don't know why they can't just let us choose based on what we are comfortable with rather than assigning boys one thing and girls another. I'd much rather wear a belt.

"Hi. I'm Christopher!" the boy says with an outstretched hand and a narrow but friendly smile. "Christopher Flores." His face is as round as an apple, and his spiky black hair falls over one side of his face. His voice is a little squeaky but much stronger than I imagined. I take his hand and he shakes mine firmly. "And you would be?"

"I'm Andi," I mumble.

Uncle Mark and the woman (who turns out to be Christopher's older sister) introduce themselves and then launch into a friendly conversation about the camp's perfect landscaping.

I shuffle my feet. I've never been good at small talk.

"Is this your first summer at Harmony Music Camp?" Christopher asks.

"Yep. You?"

"Me too. I can't believe I got in, to be honest. I mean, I really wanted to, and getting to attend a prestigious camp like this is part of my plan to get into the best college I can, but I didn't think they'd accept my scholarship application till maybe I was older. What about you? You play the trumpet, right? That means we will be in the brass section together. Most excellent."

"What grade are you in?" I ask, wondering why he's already talking about college and using phrases like *most excellent* when he looks like he's barely a middle schooler.

"Going into eighth," he says. "I know I look young, but that's because I still have these delightful baby cheeks. I'm really an old soul. Plus, it's never too early to start thinking about college, if you ask me."

"I guess," I say, and then, remembering his other questions, reply: "I play trumpet. And no, I've never been here before. My aunt and uncle made me apply."

"Well, you must be good. I've applied the last two summers and finally got in this time. We should practice together, if you want to?"

"I'll think about it," I say.

Christopher shrugs. "Well, it won't be hard to find me in this crowd."

I laugh a little at that, and nod. "True."

"It would be to our advantage to form an alliance, Andi. We cannot be out here in the woods, Black and brown as we are, and not be friends."

"Hey, we're next!" Christopher's sister interrupts us, ushering him away.

"See you later, Andi!" Christopher waves, hoisting his huge trombone case at his side. "Don't be a stranger."

"See you," I say, giving him a small smile and a wave.

"See that!" Uncle Marks says. "You've already made a friend."

"I don't even know him."

"Well, I bet by the end of camp you will be best buds."

I stop the eye roll I feel coming on, and instead start to pick at the I TOOT sticker on my trumpet case.

The line moves, and soon I have my cabin assignment in hand. Christopher and his sister wave bye to us as they head over to the junior boys' division.

"All right, Andi! You're in cabin four, in the junior girls' division, which is just a short walk across the main entrance road, past the dining hall, and toward the band shed. Your cabin counselor will greet you when you get there," the man checking us in says with a big smile. "Welcome to Harmony Music Camp! I think you're going to like it here."

We'll see, I say to myself. *It's too early to tell.*

CABIN FOUR

*C*onsidering how fancy the Harmony Music Camp lodge is, I'm expecting cabin four to be the same, but it's not. It's more of a tent than a cabin, with a dark-green canvas roof and matching canvas sides that sit on top of a sturdy wooden platform. A long stake stuck in the ground outside has the number four burned into it, and the front two flaps of the tent-cabin are tied open. Through the open front flaps, I can make out a few shadowy bodies and rows of narrow bunk beds lining the inside walls.

"Well, isn't this cozy!" Uncle Mark puts on his happy voice again. "Why don't you go ahead and claim your bunk. Then we can walk around and go get some food. I'm going to stay out here and call your aunt. Let her know we arrived safely."

I adjust my duffle on my shoulder and then grab my sleeping pack and backpack from Uncle Mark. I walk up the three wooden stairs and duck into the cabin, letting my eyes adjust. A few metal fans are clipped to the wooden rafters in the corners of the cabin, and they blow a strong, warm breeze into my face.

"Hello!" A youngish-looking white woman with the

curliest black hair I've ever seen appears in the center of the room. She's wearing a staff uniform—white shirt, khaki shorts—and clunky brown hiking boots. A blue ID lanyard swings from her neck. "I'm your counselor, Joanna. And you, let's see . . . ," she says, looking down at the tablet in her hand. "And you are?"

"Andi."

"Well, now, I don't see an Andi . . ."

"It might be under Andrea. Andrea Byrd?"

"Gotcha! Yes, here you are. Cool. Let's get you settled in, huh? You're one of the first few to arrive, so you can have your pick of whatever bunk isn't claimed yet. You get three shelves on the bookcases between bunks to put your things, and then there's a cubbyhole in the back of the tent for you to leave your shower things. I used to be a camper here as well, so if you have ANY questions, I'm your girl."

I nod. "Thanks, Ms. Joanna."

"Call me Joanna. We're on a first name basis here. Plus, 'Ms. Joanna' makes me sound so old. I just finished my sophomore year at the University of Michigan."

I nod. Mama taught me to always greet adults with respect, but I guess camp rules are different. I scan the space. There are three sets of bunk beds on each side of the room, but the one in the front-right corner is where Joanna sleeps. She apparently gets both the top and the bottom bunks, which means that there will be ten girls total sharing the remaining bunks. *It's extra cramped in here*, I think, suddenly missing my huge attic room at Aunt Janine and Uncle Mark's as I head to a bottom bunk in the far-back left corner near the shower cubbies. At least with a bottom bunk there's a little more privacy.

"Good choice!" Joanna smiles, handing me a piece of yellow card stock cut into the shape of a star. "This is for you to write your name on and decorate. You can tape it to your bunk when you're done. There are a bunch of stickers and markers in the middle of the floor for you to use. Don't be afraid to get creative and silly with it!" She giggles then.

"What's up with the star?" I ask, my throat tightening like a string. The shape reminds me of Mama. Her full name was Augusta, but she always went by Star.

"That's my theme for our cabin this summer! For this next month, you all are my little constellation—ten stars, shining bright!"

Gross. I hate pet names, unless they're coming out of Mama's mouth. I take my star and write ANDI in big black letters in the middle—no stickers—then I tape it to my bunk, free my ash-gray sleeping bag from its cover, and stuff my pillow into my favorite black pillowcase. I line up my other high-top Chucks, my Vans, and one pair of Nike slides—all black—under my bunk and start to unload my clothes onto the waiting shelves. When I look up, I notice that there are two other campers in the cabin.

On the top bunk next to me, an athletic-looking girl with long blond hair is setting up an elaborate pillow and stuffed-animal display on top of her floral comforter cover, which I guess is taking the place of any kind of sleeping bag. I glance at the star on her bunk, which she's decorated with flowers and gracefully scrawled her name on, Channing, in cursive. She looks more like a volleyball player than a musician, if you ask me, but I keep my mouth shut.

"Channing, have you met Andi?" Joanna says, skipping over to us.

Channing looks down at me with flushed cheeks and waves. It's a friendly wave, but I see her green eyes quickly assess my minimalist bunk decor and my all-black outfit.

I give her a nod back and force a smile.

"You two are both trumpet players! Isn't that cool?" Joanna continues. "I bet you can learn a lot from one another."

Channing's expression turns stony as she hops down from her bunk and walks over to me. "How long have you been playing?" she asks. "I haven't seen you at camp before. Is this your first year?"

I gulp. *Be cool.* "Yeah, I'm not really a camp person," I say. "My aunt and uncle wanted me to apply, so here I am. I've been playing the trumpet since I was seven, though."

"Well, I've been playing since I was six, and I'm first chair in my youth orchestra back home."

"Where is home?" I ask, ignoring her stuck-up comment.

"Louisville, Kentucky."

"Like where KFC is from?"

"Girl, you would ask me about chicken," she says, rolling her eyes.

"What does that mean?" I shoot back, the tips of my ears on fire. And since when were we close enough for her to be calling me *girl*?

"Oh, nothing," Channing says quickly. "What are you going to play for your seat audition?"

"My what?"

Channing gawks at me. "Your seat audition. You know, like, to determine what chair in the trumpet section you'll be?"

As she registers my blank look, her eyes go wide.

"Oh, bless your heart. You better get to the practice huts real quick. We have to audition for our seats each week on Sunday. That's, like, tomorrow. I plan to be the first-chair trumpet every week, so good luck."

Before I can fully register what Channing is saying, the other girl, who has been setting up her bunk across the room comes over. "Hi, I'm Julie!" she says, her thick black hair pulled up into a high ponytail.

"This is Andi," Channing says before I can answer for myself. "She's new this summer."

"Welcome to Harmony Music Camp!" Julie says cheerfully,

without any of the suspicion in Channing's voice. "Were you guys talking about seat auditions? I'm so nervous. I've been practicing my piece all week."

"Yeah, well," I say, "if it makes you feel better, I haven't prepared at all."

Julie raises a thin eyebrow, and Channing giggles. "That's exactly what my face looked like when she told me."

My ears burn hot. *Why, why didn't I read the entire Harmony Music Camp packet closely?!* It's probably still next to my bed collecting dust.

"Well," Julie starts, "I'm sure you'll do great, and even if you don't get first chair, you can try again next week. I'm hoping to make it into the first violin section this year. Last year, I stayed in the second violins the whole month."

"Well, like I said," Channing says, walking back over to her bunk, "I'm planning on being the first-chair trumpet all month. So if you're lucky, Andi, you might get to be second chair."

Julie rolls her eyes in Channing's direction and then leans in to whisper in my ear. "Don't pay attention to her. Channing's, like, the most competitive person I know. She doesn't mean to be rude. She's just super serious at first. She'll loosen up as the summer goes on; I promise. We were in the same cabin together last year too."

"Cool," I say, inching toward the doorway. "I gotta go meet my uncle outside. See you later."

"Andi!" Joanna yells from the back of the cabin. "Don't forget to be back here by four o'clock. That's when we have our first official cabin four orientation. You'll need to be in your uniform by then too."

My watch reads 1:30. Should be enough time to eat, figure out what I'm going to play for my audition, and get into stupid uniform. I wave at Joanna and then burst out of the cabin into the sunshine. Uncle Mark is still on the phone, pacing back and forth near the bathrooms. He looks upset and is waving his hands around, so I lean against a nearby tree to wait until he's done. My stomach growls, but I push the feeling aside and watch as more girls arrive at cabin four. Most of the girls squeal when they see each other and run up for big hugs. All seem to be carrying actual comforter sets instead of sleeping bags, and many have big trunks decorated with stickers that they drag up the front steps. Everyone is in uniform, with the bottoms of their khaki shorts rolled up and light-blue knee socks displayed proudly. Most of the girls wear sandals with their knee socks, which, if you ask me, is a really awful fashion combo. I plan to only wear my Nike slides to the showers and back; otherwise I'll be in my Chucks or Vans.

You're judging. Mama's voice appears in my mind so clear that I startle and look over my shoulder. She does this sometimes, pops up into my head, her voice ringing through my whole body. It's just a memory, but it feels real. Like Mama is speaking from somewhere deep inside me, and if I just stay still enough, close my eyes, she might appear from my rib cage and walk right out into the sunlight.

What if I don't belong anywhere?

You do belong. Mama's voice echoes up and out of me.

And that's when I open my eyes and see her, not Mama but someone else, rolling a big purple trunk up the stairs of cabin four, her locs pulled up into a high bun, small gold hoops in her ears, and skin so brilliant black it glimmers like jewels in the afternoon heat.

"ZORA!" A group of girls, including Channing and Julie, come running to the entrance to greet her.

"I'm here, ladies!" Zora calls, walking into the cabin like a song.

LUNCH

"*Y*ou ready to eat, kiddo?" Uncle Mark says, off his phone call with Aunt Janine.

I tear my eyes away from the cabin doorway, which that girl Zora has disappeared into, dragging her bright-purple trunk and talking a mile a minute. *At least I won't be the only Black person in the cabin.*

I nod. "I could eat."

"We'll have to make it quick, because I need to get back home. Your aunt had a little scare at the gym today."

"Is she okay?" I ask, my heartbeat quickening.

"Everything is fine, she just got light-headed during her class. I think it's just too much for her right now. The stress . . . of everything . . . ," Uncle Mark says, trailing off.

I don't ask Uncle Mark what he means, because I know it's my fault Aunt Janine is stressed out. I know I lost my mom, but sometimes I forget that Aunt Janine lost her sister and then gained a kid she never expected to have to raise. I haven't exactly been the easiest niece to deal with, especially with all the drama that went down in the last week of school, all while Aunt Janine was working long shifts at the hospital, getting me set for camp, and decorating the baby's room. *No wonder she made Uncle Mark drive me. She must need a break. I'm always letting my temper get the best of me, hurting the people I love.*

We make a beeline for the dining hall, which is in a stone building across from the main lodge. When we step into the front doors, I see big round tables full of campers and family members. Christopher waves from a table in the middle of the room, where he sits with his sister. I wave back as Uncle Mark and I walk toward the buffet line. I pile my plate with lasagna and breadsticks, skipping over the tray full of broccoli and the bowl of mixed greens. Uncle Mark doesn't say anything, and I notice that he only puts a few small pieces of broccoli on his plate before making his way to get a large glass of pop from the nearby machines.

"You're drinking pop?" I say with a smirk. "Won't that 'rot your teeth,' Mr. Dentist?"

Uncle Mark's cheeks turn a little red, but he shrugs. "One glass won't kill us. Don't tell your aunt."

"Deal," I say, filling my glass to the brim, then we find a seat at a table by the window and dig in. We don't speak for five minutes solid as we stuff our faces.

"So." Uncle Mark clears his throat. "How are you really doing, Andi? I mean, that last week of school was rough."

Understatement of the year. The last week of school was a nightmare. All because of my archnemesis, that bully Amy Vandenburg, aka Amy Vanden-Vampire.

I shrug again. "I'm fine." I peel a piece of cheese off the top of my lasagna with my fork and pop it into my mouth, making sure to avoid eye contact with Uncle Mark. *Why is he bringing up the last week of school now? We'd made it a whole two-hour car ride without talking about anything too deep and now, in our final moments together, he's got questions?*

Uncle Mark shuffles in his chair and takes another swig of pop. "Do you think maybe you'd like to start seeing Dr. Raynor again? When you're back from camp, I mean. It sounds like some of the things going on at school were worse than your aunt and I imagined."

Now it's my turn to squirm in my chair. I am exhausted. I just want to go to my bunk and sleep.

"No. I'm good," I hear myself say.

"Well, your aunt and I think it would be good for you to have a session or two again. So, we set one for you in August when you're back. Just a check-in, Andi. We know that this year has been hard, and we're worried about you. It might help to talk to someone about things. You know, about your mom, and anything else that might be on your mind . . ."

"Like what?" I say, looking Uncle Mark straight in the eyes now.

"Oh, I don't know. We know that kids at school have been saying some pretty offensive things to you . . ."

"It's not fair!" My whole body trembles, and I can feel

myself heating like a volcano about to explode. I take a deep breath. "Why did you ask me if I *want* to see Dr. Raynor if you've already made the appointment?"

"Please don't get upset, Andi. We're just worried about you, and with the baby coming we want to make sure you feel like you have a home with us. You're going to be a big sis . . . I mean, a big cousin soon. We all need to be at our best, for this baby."

When Uncle Mark says that last part, I feel all the heat drain from my body. I tried to be my best self for Mama, to love and support her no matter what, but when it counted the most, I failed. I put my fork down and stare at my plate. I ball my fists up. I didn't ask for any of this. I didn't ask for my mom to die. I didn't ask for kids to be jerks, I didn't ask for this fancy camp experience, and I sure didn't ask to be a big cousin-sister. I feel a few tears escape.

"I'm done eating," I say, my voice trembling. "I need to practice for some seat audition I didn't know about."

"Andi, I'm sorry. I didn't mean to make you upset. You know we want you to be happy, right? We just . . ."

"I know," I say. "You just want everything to be perfect for the new baby. I get it."

"And for you," Uncle Mark says now, catching my eye.

"Sure, whatever," I say.

SOME KIND OF BLUE

*U*ncle Mark hugs me in the parking lot, and then I watch him drive off. Seeing him go makes my chest turn to rock. I take a gulp of air as all the tall trees seem to lean in and tower over me. *Not now, not now, not now.* I rush back toward the junior girls' division, hoping nobody will stop to talk to me. Once inside cabin four, I grab my trumpet, CeCe—I named her after CeCe Peniston because Mama and I loved that song "Finally"—my MP3 player, and the map I was handed at check-in and make my way back across campus to a row of practice huts near the main entrance. I pick a room all the way at the end and shut the door. Instead of taking out CeCe, I sit on the cold concrete floor of the room and press my back against the cool stone walls.

My anxiety attacks started when Mama died. The first time it happened was about a month after I started living with Aunt Janine and Uncle Mark. It was early October, and we were eating dinner. Uncle Mark reached across the table for more asparagus and asked me what I wanted to do for my thirteenth birthday, which was coming up in November. I froze right in the middle of chewing a bite of rice and couldn't swallow. I'd forgotten all about my birthday. Mama normally let me invite my one friend Delia, from down the hall, over the night before my birthday for a sleepover and scary-movie marathon, and then on my actual birthday, she'd take me out for a slice of fancy cake at Good Cakes and Bakes bakery. The thought of turning thirteen without Mama was too much, and Delia and I barely talk anymore—after I moved, she stopped texting. So right there at the dinner table, the whole world began to close in, and it felt like I wasn't ever going to be able to get enough air. Aunt Janine took one look at me and snapped into nurse mode. She helped me slow my breath. The next week I started weekly talk therapy with Dr. Raynor, and spent the next five months working with her. At first, I didn't know what to do or say, but after a while she started to help me a lot. Now when I feel my chest go hard like a rock, I try to remember what she taught me:

1. It's okay to feel your feelings, but sometimes your feelings can betray you and make you *think* that you can't breathe, that the world is ending.

2. When you feel an anxiety attack coming on, find a quiet spot and focus on taking deep, long breaths. If you can, try saying to yourself *I can breathe. I can breathe.*

3. Closing your eyes can help you focus better on
   your breathing.
4. Anxiety attacks are often caused by triggers—try to
   identify your triggers so you can manage the intensity
   of your anxiety attacks.

I think about Uncle Mark speeding off. I think about the last time I saw Mama and the warm spot on my cheek where she kissed me before sending me on my way into school. I think about the back of her head, her big Afro like a halo as she zoomed away in our maroon Subaru. Every memory of her is an aching in my body as I remember what I did later that day. How she would have hated me for it. You don't get second chances when someone you love is dead. I breathe in *1, 2, 3, 4* and out *1, 2, 3, 4*, in *1, 2, 3, 4*, out *1, 2, 3, 4* and soon the rocky cliff that is my chest crumbles away. Soon I hear the robins outside the practice hut and the whispers of trees bending toward one another. I wipe an escaped tear away, and put in my AirPods. I hit play on *Kind of Blue*, my favorite Miles Davis album, and let the music continue to calm me down. I hear those first curious notes of the first track, "So What," the piano tiptoeing out of the shadows and the bass following, then the speed picks up and the *ting ting ting* of the drums starts, followed by the horns, and then finally Miles begins his trumpet solo and takes us for a smooth ride. Before I know it, I am bobbing my head along and breathing slower and tapping my hands against my knees.

"Eh-hem."

Someone is pressing lightly on my shoulder. It's Christopher. Christopher Flores.

I take out my AirPods. "Hey."

"Hi, Andi. I saw you through the window. I knocked, but you didn't hear me."

"Hi," I say again.

"I brought over these to share with you." Christopher holds out something wrapped in foil. "My sister made them so I wouldn't get homesick on my first day. May I join you down there on the floor?"

"What is it?"

"Lumpia!"

I stare at him with a blank look, and he laughs.

"It's a Filipino spring roll that's filled with ground meat and veggies and deep-fried. I can eat, like, a whole tray of these things."

"I'm kind of a picky eater . . ."

"Do you like egg rolls?"

"Yes . . ."

"Then you'll like these. I promise. Lumpia are smaller than egg rolls and have a thinner wrapping, so they get really crispy. They're better hot but still scrumptious when they're cold."

Christopher sits down next to me, unwraps the foil, and hands me a lumpia. Before I can even taste my first one, he's chomping on his second.

"Soooo delectable, so gour-met!" he says, pronouncing the hard *T* in *gourmet* and air-kissing his fingers like a chef as he crunches down. "Going to miss these."

I take a small bite, and it's pretty good. A flavor bomb of goodness. So, I take a bigger one, and another till I finish it. "Thanks. That's actually really good. Can I have another?"

"Told you so. My sister's a phenomenal cook. Top-notch," he says, handing me more.

"Are you always like this?" I ask.

"Like what?"

"Extra friendly, and you talk like a walking dictionary."

Christopher smiles and nods ferociously. "Yep. This is just me. I've pretty much been extra my whole life. My sister is always calling me a show-off, but so what if I like to use big words and experiment with my language? It's what makes me unique. Does it bother you? It bothers kids sometimes, but I'd rather speak like the king I am than be boring."

I laugh. "*Boring* is not a word I'd use to describe you, and no, it doesn't bother me. I'm just . . . I'm the opposite. When we first met, I wasn't sure what to say to you. I didn't think you'd want to hang with me after that . . ."

Christopher shrugs, quiet for the first time since I met him. He hands me another lumpia, takes the last one for

44

himself, and then balls up the foil. I watch as he eats it, slowly, as if he is trying to make it last forever or remember what love tastes like. When he's done, he looks down at his hands and says, "It seemed like you were missing home too, and plus, I need quieter friends to balance out my loud. I had a feeling we'd get along."

"Oh, that makes sense," I say, releasing the last of the worry in my chest. "I am missing home; this place is really overwhelming."

"Don't I know it," Christopher agrees. "It's terrifying, but in a good way. I'm going to learn a lot here, but I'd be lying if I said I wasn't nervous."

I take a deep breath and nod. "Can I play my seat audition piece for you?" I ask, rising to my feet.

"That would be superb," Christopher says, jumping up and dragging his trombone case into the small hut with me and CeCe. "And then I can play you mine."

"Cool."

"Cooler beans."

And just like that, I have a friend.

ORIENTATION

"All right," Joanna begins as we all sit in a tight circle in the middle of the cabin floor. "Now that we're all here, I can officially welcome you to the awesomeness that I know will be cabin four this summer. First things first, if you haven't done so already, please hand over those cell phones. You won't be needing them here. It's time to unplug!"

There are a few soft groans, but nobody protests. I add mine to the plastic tub without much fanfare, because I'm distracted by something on my collared shirt stabbing me in the back of my neck. I twist my arm around to try to reach it and jostle Julie, who is sitting next to me.

"Your tags are still on," Julie whispers.

I tear them off and give her a thankful shrug. I only had a few minutes to change after Christopher and I practiced till our lips went numb. I can already tell this uniform is out to get me—the knee socks feel like death on my calves.

"Great!" Joanna continues, snapping the lid closed over our phones. "Now, let's all go around and introduce ourselves—our names, where we are from, what we play, and some fun fact! I'll start."

Turns out Joanna is a brass head too. She plays trombone in the U of M marching band; she is studying to become a middle-school teacher, and this is her second year as a counselor. "I'm going to learn so much from all of you this summer," she says. "Oh, and my fun fact is that I love every flavor of Doritos equally."

"Even Cool Ranch?" Channing asks.

"Yep. Even Cool Ranch. All right, who is next?" Joanna says, searching the circle for someone else.

Fun fact? I don't have any fun facts, I think, as Channing starts to introduce herself. I miss everything she says, until she gets to the end.

"Oh, and, y'all, I have a horse named Skittles. I ride him in competitions sometimes. Riding is my other passion."

After Channing, a cellist from Brooklyn named Cooper shares. Cooper looks extra cool, with three piercings in each ear and a long, brown, messy braid.

"Hi, I'm Cooper or Coop. I use they/them or she/her pronouns; don't really care. I'm just Coop. This is my first time here, but I've been to other camps before. I play cello. I guess my fun fact is that I once swam with dolphins on a family vacation to Hawaii."

"Thanks, Coop," Joanna says. "Dolphins! How cool."

Coop shrugs and then looks at me. I give a small nod and a smile, but also, I am aware that some of the girls are whispering nearby: *They/them . . . What does that even mean?*

It means exactly what Coop said, I say to myself. Mama always taught me to be more open than other kids: "Some people in this world don't know how to love themselves, let alone people who are different than them. You're going to have to learn how to value yourself and stand tall in who you are; stand up for what's right. When people tell you who they are, believe them, listen, and love them. That's all that matters. Just like I believe in and love you for you, Andi. Just the way you are."

I believe Coop. They seem cool to me.

Two cousins from Chicago named Beks and Jori go next. Beks is Star Wars obsessed, which she didn't need to tell us because she's wearing Baby Yoda earrings and her viola case is covered in BB-8 droid stickers. Beks has a cute brown bob and a super-freckled face. Jori, who is sitting next to her, also has freckles but wears thick black eyeliner around her eyes, is taller, and has her long pitch-black hair tied up into two pigtail knots on her head. She drums her fingers on her legs as she talks. "I play percussion—timpani," she says, "and I'm also into giving people Sharpie tattoos, if anyone wants one." Jori holds out her arms then and shows us a bunch of designs she's doodled on them. They're not bad. Then Jori, unprompted, also shares that she can burp the whole alphabet, and the circle erupts into giggles as she starts to demonstrate.

Then it's my turn. I shift so that I am sitting on my hands, and can feel the full weight of my body pressing all the blood out of them.

"I'm Andi," I start. "I play trumpet. I'm from Detroit, Michigan but I live in Grand Rapids, Michigan, now. I don't have a fun fact."

"It can be anything, Andi," Joanna coaxes. "A hobby, something you did this past year. Of course you can always pass, but I bet you have something unique to share with us."

- Fun fact: My mom died last summer!
- Fun fact: I got suspended from school in the last week!
- Fun fact: My aunt's having a baby and I'm in her way!
- Fun fact: I can't seem to play my trumpet like I used to!
- Fun fact: I'm not like most girls!

"Pass," I say.

"All right then," Joanna says, a little less cheery. "We look forward to getting to know you better as the first week goes on, Andi. Julie, you're next."

I barely hear Julie's share, or the next two girls', Angie (a French horn player from DC) and Arya (a harpist from Seattle), because I've lost all feeling in my hands, and I am instead working on moving my fingers one by one to get the blood flowing again. But when a violinist from New Mexico named Ivy finishes, I look up and find that Zora is speaking.

"Hi, friends!" she says with a voice full of purpose. "As most of you know, I'm Zora. Zora Lee Johnson. I'm a flautist, and I'm from Ann Arbor, Michigan, which is right here." Zora holds up her right hand to represent the mitten shape of Michigan, and points to a spot near the bottom of her thumb. "And fun fact: I have a sausage dog named Ginny, who is basically me in dog form. Oh, and I've been coming here forever, so if you need to know where anything is, feel free to ask me."

"That's great," Joanna interrupts. "I'm sure Andi wouldn't mind someone to show her the ropes. Since you two are bunkmates, it's a perfect match. And, let's see, who can help Arya and Coop get acquainted with camp . . . ?" Joanna continues, looking around the circle and enlisting returning campers Julie and Angie to help out as well.

Bunkmates? I look over at my bed, and for the first time notice the transformation the top bunk has undergone. Purple everything, and twinkly lights blink at me, and a collage of pictures of Zora with friends and family is plastered on the wall. I force my gaze back to the circle and watch as Zora's smile shrinks, but she makes eye contact with me anyway and nods a little too forcefully. "I'm happy to answer any questions you have," she says to me.

But I get the feeling she's not. And that's fine by me. I can already tell that Zora Lee Johnson is a teacher's pet, know-it-all kind of person.

"All right!" Joanna says a few moments later. "Since all of you have shared, it's time to go over the cabin rules and expectations, and then we'll all head to the dining hall together for our first cabin four family dinner.

"Every morning at six a.m.," Joanna begins, "a bugle will sound to wake you up. Then before you get dressed, we'll head outside by six twenty and line up at the flag in the middle of our junior girls' division for morning announcements. I don't ever want us to be the late cabin, so I expect all of you to get up and out as fast as possible. You don't have to be fully awake, but you do need to be present.

"After morning announcements, you all will have until seven thirty to shower, get dressed, make your bunks, and complete cabin chores. The chores will rotate each week and are posted at the back of the room by the shower cubbies. If you don't know how to complete your chore, please come see me before bed tonight and I'll give you a crash course.

"Breakfast is from seven thirty to eight fifteen in the dining hall, and by eight thirty I expect each and every one of you to be in your seats for full orchestra rehearsal in the band shed. Harmony Music Camp does not tolerate tardiness, so I'd encourage you to get there five minutes early."

"Ain't that the truth!" I hear Jori say, giving some of the returning cabin four campers a knowing look.

"Lunch is from noon to one o'clock," Joanna continues,

"and then the afternoons are reserved for either your sectional rehearsals or individual practice time. In the evenings, before dinner, you'll get some free time, and that's when you can opt in to elective classes, the Craft Shack, waterfront sports, or quiet cabin time. Occasionally, there will be special master classes during this time, and then of course we have tons of weekend fun lined up for you, including our two-night camping trip in week three, and mixers."

At the mention of mixers, the whole cabin starts to talk at once.

"I can't wait for the first mixer! When is it?" Angie from DC almost screams. She pulls out a lip gloss and smears it all over her already shiny lips.

"That," Joanna says, with a twinkle in her eye, "has yet to be revealed."

"What's the big deal with mixers?" I lean over and ask Julie.

"It's just Harmony Music Camp's way of saying *dance*. It's when we get to hang out with the junior boys' division, and there's always a DJ and you know, it's, like, when all the love connections happen."

"A dance? Sounds like my worst nightmare. Plus, don't we get to hang out with the boys all day during orchestra?" I say quietly.

"Oh, yeah, but this is different. We don't have to wear uniforms. It's like a whole social event. It's fun! You'll see. And you don't have to dance—they have other activities too, like Ping-Pong or soccer or croquet."

"What the heck is croquet?"

Julie starts to laugh then. "Oh man, Andi. You're going to learn so much this summer."

I give her a small smile and then look back down at my hands. *I guess I am.*

UNICORNS

I sleep so hard my first night of camp that I barely hear the morning reveille sound. *Reveille*, I learned, just means "to awaken," and it's normally delivered on a bugle, which is like a trumpet except it doesn't have valves and the tone it produces is lower, darker. It's not a bad way to wake up, and as I stretch in my sleeping bag, I notice that the top bunk, Zora's bunk, is sagging more than usual.

"Isn't he cute?" I hear Beks say above me, and when I stand up, I see that Beks and Jori are piled on Zora's bed with her, staring out of the cabin windows.

"If you like that kind of nerdy scruffiness," Jori says, sounding like she's still half asleep.

"What are you looking at?" I ask.

"Davy Edwards." Beks sighs. "He's so beautiful."

"Who?"

Zora elaborates: "He's in the high school division, but he earned the honor of playing reveille this year. Beks has had a crush on him since he was in the junior division with us last year."

"Uh, cool," I say, sorry that I asked.

Zora jumps down from her bunk while Beks continues to drool out the window at Davy.

Jori slides down next from Zora's bunk and slinks across the room back to her bed. I watch as she grabs her comforter, wraps it around herself until she looks like a burrito, and then, without putting on shoes or sandals, makes her way outside to the flag for morning announcements.

"I know," Zora says, registering my confused look. "Jori doesn't really believe in shoes."

"But it's all dirt out there. Her feet are going to get so nasty," I say.

"Trust me; it's gross. I always wear shoes. Even in the shower."

"Me too!" I say, giving her a small smile.

I notice then that Zora is already fully dressed in her uniform. Last night after dinner and more cabin bonding games, it was finally time for bed. Zora had thrown on a matching PJ set, with a loose T-shirt top and cotton drawstring shorts. There were small rainbows and unicorns all over the fabric, and the glitter lettering on her shirt read STAY MAGICAL. I'd started to roll my eyes at the sight of the unicorns (I'm team vampire), but I stopped myself when Mama's voice appeared in my head again: *Stop judging, Andi.*

"What are you staring at?" Zora had asked, wrapping her hair back into a silk scarf.

I was already in bed and I realized, in horror, that I'd been staring at her chest.

"Uh"—I quickly averted my eyes and started scrolling through my MP3 player for a track—"nothing. Your shirt is just . . . really glittery."

"I like bright things," Zora shot back.

"I can tell," I said, motioning to her bunk, which was lit up like a fairy tree house. It sounded harsher than I meant it too, but my hands felt sweaty, and I didn't know how to fix my tone.

"Well," Zora said then, observing me with a puzzled and slightly hurt look on her face. "Good night, Andi."

"Night," I'd mumbled, slinking down into my sleeping bag.

And that was it. That was how Zora and I ended our first day of knowing each other.

Today, Zora is fresh-faced, wearing gold hoops, and she seems to have forgotten about our awkward exchange before bed. Her locs are pulled back halfway so that some cascade over her shoulders. She looks nice. I feel very exposed in my soft black Miles Davis sleep tee and black shorts. It doesn't help that now Zora is staring at me in a way that makes me feel, well, weird. Without saying another word, I rush to my cubby and grab my uniform clothes. There's no time to go to the bathrooms to change, so I jump into my sleeping bag and wriggle into my shorts, sports bra, and shirt. When I've managed that, I shed my sleeping bag like a snake skin, and pull on my knee socks, then I scrunch the knee socks down around the tops of my high-tops.

"Make sure you pull those up before rehearsal," Zora says, grabbing her bag and flute case from her bunk. "You'll get in trouble with Mr. London."

"I'll risk it," I hear myself say. "Why are you taking all your things with you anyway? Don't we have another hour to get ready before breakfast?"

"I like to get an early start," she says, tucking in a loose end of her shirt. "I practice a little before breakfast if I can. You know, some of us have to work harder than others just to be recognized."

"Right," I say. "That makes sense."

"The practice huts get unlocked at six a.m. Pro tip—if you need to practice early too," Zora says as she heads out to flag.

Was that an invitation? Or a challenge?

When I get outside it's a whole scene. I don't really understand the tradition of making us listen to announcements *before* getting dressed, but it's how things work around here. Every cabin stands in a line, around the flag at the center of division. Some campers, just like Jori, have dragged out their bedding with them, and lean on one another in various states of half sleep. Most campers are in robes and flip-flops, and then there are a few of us fully dressed in uniform. Cabin six is the last cabin to arrive, so not us, and Joanna nods with approval.

"Good morning, campers! You all did a pretty good job of getting out here on time. Let's keep it this way for the rest of camp. Just to make sure everyone is awake, let's shake out some of those sleepies." Morning announcements are delivered by our junior girls' division lead, Aubrey. Aubrey doesn't look that much older than Joanna, but she's definitely not as bubbly. She holds a clipboard and a mug of steaming coffee and yells at us in a voice louder than necessary.

Oh no. More forced bonding.

Aubrey leads us through a game called Go Bananas! where you lift your arms up and down like you're peeling yourself, and then at the end you get to "go bananas" and dance. Finally, Aubrey runs through the day's agenda and dismisses us. My stomach growls as I grab CeCe and my bag and head out for the day. As my feet move along the gravel path toward the dining hall, I focus on their rhythm. *Crunch, crunch, crunch, shuffle, shuffle, shuffle.* Anything can be a song if you just listen.

SEAT AUDITIONS #1

*A*fter a bowl of cereal at breakfast and a quick practice session, I'm slipping into a seat in the band shed. The Junior Orchestra rehearses here, because we have fewer members than the High School Orchestra. High schoolers rehearse in the amphitheater across campus. We'll also get to play there, but not until the final showcase. At least the band shed has walls, so if it rains we don't get too cold. The amiptheather is only partially covered.

Channing is already sitting first chair in the trumpet section even though we haven't auditioned yet. She gives me a tight-lipped smile as I take the seat next to her. I look down the aisle and make eye contact with Christopher in the trombone section. He gives me a thumbs-up and then takes out a pen and notebook.

Was I supposed to bring a notebook? Nobody has their instruments out yet, so I push CeCe farther under my seat and sit back. Mr. London, a short white man with a shiny bald head and dark-framed Coke-bottle glasses steps onto the podium. He's dressed in the faculty uniform of khaki pants and a white collared shirt, and he's tied a gray sweatshirt around his shoulders. "Good morning!" Mr. London starts. "Welcome to Junior Orchestra meeting. We've got quite a challenging repertoire planned, normally played by high-school-level musicians, but this is Harmony Music Camp, and you all are some of the brightest and most talented musicians from around the country. I have no doubt you can pull this off, with focus, practice, and collaboration."

Mr. London pauses to take a swig of coffee.

My throat feels dry, and my lips are cold. I catch Christopher's eye again, and raise my eyebrow. He grins at me and starts to scribble in his notebook.

"All right," Mr. London continues. "Your folders for this week are getting passed down each section, with your sheet music and my group expectations. Please read over the group expectations and sign the last page to return to me. If one of us is off, all of us are off. Being a member of this orchestra, no matter what chair you are, is a great accomplishment and responsibility. Once you've turned in your sheet to me, you are free to head to your auditions. My assistant conductors will be supporting your progress and working with you in sectional rehersals. Mr. Wright is overseeing the woodwinds and brass, and Ms. Gilly will be overseeing the strings. I will audition percussion. You can find your audition time posted on the wall on your way out. Your seat assignments will be posted by lunch in the dining hall, once auditions are done. Good luck, play well, and see you in the afternoon for our first official rehearsal."

Everyone jumps up at the same time to see the audition list. I watch as Channing pushes her way to the front and then high-fives Zora across a sea of heads. Zora catches me looking at them and gives me a too-big smile, pointing to what must be my name on the list. I duck my head down and flip through my folder. The sheet music looks complicated. I'm definitely going to need Christopher's help. Reading music has never been my strength—I have a good ear and like to feel my way around to the right notes. I read and sign my expectations sheet. I'm not about to get run over. When the crowd thins out, I walk my signed paper up to Mr. London, who is talking with Beks about something. I leave my paper on his music stand. I'm halfway back to my chair when I hear him clear his throat.

"Excuse me, young lady—um, Andi, is it?"

I turn slowly to face him.

"You forgot to sign your last name. I need a full, formal signature to know you are fully committed."

Is this dude for real? I never sign my full name. I like the way *Andi* looks by itself, and I scrawl it in cursive with a big *A* and the *n* inside the *A*, then I add a small bird squiggle at the end to represent my last name. Mama always told me a true artist has to have their trademark, and one afternoon when I was eight she helped me come up with mine. It's never been a problem for anybody before. Lots of people sign their names like this. Uncle Mark's signature is just one long squiggle that you can't read even if you try.

"It is my full name."

Mr. London looks down at my paper and pushes his glasses up on his nose. "I only see your first name and what appears to be a mustache?"

I hear a few snickers from behind me and turn to glare at a couple of girls still in the viola section.

"That's a bird," I say, "and it's a symbol for my last name. It's my original signature."

Mr. London continues to look at my paper, then he looks at me, and pushes his glasses up.

"And this is your first year here, I presume?"

"It is."

"And have you ever been in a youth orchestra?"

Why is he asking me all this? I don't see him bothering anybody else.

"No, but I'm in an advanced band at my middle school, and I've been playing since I was seven."

"You're on scholarship, I presume."

Now this dude is making me extra mad. Not that there's anything wrong with being on scholarship, but I know Aunt Janine and Uncle Mark paid a bunch of money to get me here.

"Your presumption is incorrect" is all I say, my fists balled at my sides.

I watch a small shadow cross Mr. London's face and then vanish. "Well, Andi Bird-Symbol. Since it is your first year here, I'll give you a pass on your uniform today, but when you come back this afternoon, please have your knee socks pulled up like the rest of the girls. Welcome to the big time," Mr. London finishes, and then shuffles the stack of papers and steps down from his podium.

I feel something crack inside my rib cage, and then I feel my chest start to harden. I lean down and roll my knee socks up and grimace as they pinch the backs of my calves. *Deep breaths, Andi. Deep breaths*, I say to myself as I walk back to my chair, snatching up CeCe, my backpack, and my folder. My heart feels like it's in my ears, and my skin feels like it has a million itchy welts all over it. I'm so heated that I almost forget to check my audition time, which is, of course, in fifteen minutes. I book it out of the band shed and make it to the rec hall with five minutes to spare. Channing, who has just finished, appears from inside one of the small audition rooms, beaming confidently. "Nailed it," she says to me, and then adds with a smirk, "Break a leg in there, Andi. And don't stress if you don't get the chair you want. There's always next week."

Dr. Raynor gave me a word for what I feel next.

Depersonalization. It's when I start to feel removed or detached from what's happening in the moment and all of a sudden my vision and world get really small. When I step into the audition room with CeCe and stand in front of Mr. Wright, it feels like I'm not actually there. It feels like I am looking down from above. I watch myself put CeCe to my lips, and the punchy notes of "Tightrope" blast through the air, but they are not loud. It sounds like I am playing underwater. Like I am deep in the middle of Lake Michigan, screaming through my trumpet but making almost no sound, barely a ripple. I must get through the full piece, because then Mr. Wright is nodding at me and scribbling in his plain black notebook. Through the murky water in my ears I hear him say, "Thanks, Andi. That was certainly a creative arrangement. Seat assignments will be posted by lunchtime."

Then I am stepping out of the room, and walking down a long hallway until I am outdoors again. My ears unclog, and I am not underwater anymore. At lunch, I'm not even surprised to learn that I'm fourth-chair trumpet. *Dead last.* I'm pretty sure that's how it's going to be all summer. Might as well get used to it.

LANYARDS

*A*t Harmony Music Camp, the "work week" begins Sunday with seat auditions, and then Friday and Saturday are when general weekend activities happen. The first days of camp blur together into a string of very long days of orchestra rehearsal, brass sectional rehearsal, practicing with Christopher or on my own in the practice huts, eating huge meals of whatever I want in the dining hall, and then finally rolling into my sleeping bag at night to fall into a hard slumber. Mr. London and Mr. Wright are strict, and more than a couple of times in rehearsal I get called out for not reading the music and adding my own flair.

Channing is not a team player, even though that's the whole point of being first-chair trumpet, but the other two trumpet players in my section try to help out as much as possible. Jacob sits second chair and is from North Carolina, and Anna from Ohio sits next to me in third chair. They're nice, and I feel bad making them work harder to cover up my mistakes. Sometimes when Anna leans over to explain something to me, she gets that tone that people get sometimes when they think I'm stupid. She speaks slow and uses small words like I won't understand her otherwise.

Christopher never talks to me like that, and we hang out whenever we can.

"Don't take this the wrong way, Andi," Christopher says to me on Wednesday afternoon, as we haul our instruments and bags toward the Craft Shack after a long practice session, "but we need to take a break. It feels like you're forcing it, and I've never practiced so hard in my life. I'm utterly exhausted."

"I knoooooooowwwwww," I whine, following a few steps behind him on the path. "The music this week is confusing."

"Well, that's why we need a different kind of creative therapy," Christopher says, beaming up at the building in front of us. "We're here. The most glorious place ever. I read ALL about the Craft Shack online and in my welcome packet. I just know I'm going to love it. I've been waiting years for this moment. Come on!"

The Craft Shack is not actually a shack. It's a two-story studio by the main lodge, where you can paint pottery, weave baskets, make jewelry, tie-dye T-shirts, and more. Everything costs money, but there are some projects that are more affordable than others. Inside, I run my hands over a few baskets tightly woven with bright colors and intricate patterns.

"Forget basket weaving. I read it costs fifty dollars and it takes forever," Christopher says, all businesslike. "My sister put enough money on my fun account to do some of the smaller projects here. Do you have money on your account?"

"Yeah. I think so."

"Most excellent. Let's head to the 'yarn barn' corner and get to work. I'll teach you how to make a lanyard."

"I don't know what a yarn barn is, but sure."

"Oh, don't you worry, Andi, darling. We're going to find out together."

I laugh.

The yarn barn corner is impressive. It reminds me of the big shelf in our living room where Mama used to keep all her paints. Stuffed into what look like big paper towel tubes are a number of different balls of yarn, in all different colors. Hanging from a pegboard next to the yarn are long pieces of plastic colored string used for making lanyards. I follow Christopher's example and pick out two colors: black and a metallic silver. Christopher picks out a sunset orange and a teal. Then we record our items with the staff member at the front of the Craft Hut and find a table to ourselves, under a sunny window. Christopher shows me how to start the lanyard, knotting the two pieces of string onto a metal ring and then weaving the strings together to create a cool box-stitch pattern. It takes me a few tries to get used to the awkwardness of my fingers, and how slippery the string can be, but soon we settle into a focused silence as we work. Christopher is much faster than me, and before I've even made it halfway through mine, he's starting another one, this time in purple and yellow.

"That was your uncle, right?" Christopher says after a beat. "The white man who dropped you here?"

I nod. "He's married to my aunt Janine. I live with them."

"Do you like living with them?"

I squirm. Nobody my age has asked me this before. Most kids just assume I must be so grateful to have been taken in by family they don't even wonder if I'm happy. Or they just straight up ask why my mom is dead, and then I get all mad because that's an extra-rude way to ask that question. It's none of their business why or how she's dead. She just is. So I don't offer an explanation to Christopher about why I live with my aunt and uncle, and he doesn't ask.

"It's fine," I say, and it's some of the truth, "but it doesn't feel like home, really."

"Indeed," Christopher says then. "I like living in Chicago, but I think home is more about people than places. I was born here, in the US, and I've only been to the Philippines once when I was eight, but it felt nice to be there. I played on the beach with my cousins—some I'd never even met before then—and we'd go get halo-halo."

"What's halo-halo?"

"Oh, it's divine. It's a colorful dessert that is layered with a mix of ingredients, including fruit, shaved ice, and condensed milk. My favorite way to eat it is topped with *ube halaya*, which is purple yam paste. It's soooo delicious. I wish we had some right now, Andi. It's so refreshing and just *mwah*!" Christopher air-kisses his fingers.

I laugh. When Christopher tells stories, I can see the colors, shapes, and places he's describing.

"The way you talk reminds me of a painting," I say.

"Do you paint?" Christopher asks.

I shake my head. "But my mom did."

Christopher looks up from his lanyard now to study my face. Then he tilts his head to the side and says, "If you don't mind me asking, where is your mom?"

"Gone." I wait for Christopher to ask me more, to get that glazy look that people get in their eyes when they don't want to deal with anything sad. Or even worse, the way people smile at me with a fake expression full of pity. But Christopher doesn't do any of this. He just nods.

"I bet you miss her a lot."

"I do," I say, looking down at my hands. "How did you learn how to make these?" I change the subject, swallowing hard.

"My sister and I taught ourselves. You know you can learn anything on YouTube if you just apply yourself?"

"So you and your family are extreme crafters?" I tease.

"Very amusing," Christopher says, smiling. "Not really . . . It's just me and my sister in Chicago. She takes care of me now."

This catches my attention, and I snap my head up. Maybe Christopher and I have more in common than I thought. "Where are your parents? If you don't mind me asking."

Christopher does not look me in the eye for once.

Instead he shrugs, and then lets his shoulders sag into a slump. "They live in the Philippines, in Manila."

"So, they just left you guys here? By yourselves?"

Christopher's eyes meet mine, and they are full of fire. "No. They didn't leave us. That's what everyone always thinks. My goodness."

"I'm sorry— I didn't—"

"They had to leave the country," Christopher says, almost in a whisper now.

"You don't have to talk about it if you don't want to."

Christopher meets my eyes again, and I smile. I watch his face relax, but there's still a sadness in his expression.

"Can I tell you the truth? And you'll promise not to share it?"

Even though we just met, I sit a little taller, trying to make my body an extra layer of protection between the Craft Shack walls and the outside, where other campers are hustling by.

"I promise. Cross my heart."

Christopher nods, and then shakes the hair out of his face. I watch him weave a few more layers of his lanyard while I wait in the thick silence.

"Sixth grade was the worst year of my life. I came home after school one day in October and instead of my parents being home, my sister was there waiting for me. She was supposed to be at her college dorm, studying, but she told me that our mom and dad had been . . . detained, and that they weren't coming back."

"Detained like deported?" I whisper, beginning to understand.

Christopher nods again. "Yes, that. I had to spend the next couple of weeks in foster care until the paperwork allowing my sister to become my legal guardian came through. She was only nineteen. She had to move home from college and everything to take care of me."

Christopher takes a deep breath, and then lets the next part tumble out like he's been keeping it bottled up forever. "But the worst part is that my best friend, Samantha—she told some of the kids at my school what my family was going through, even though she promised not to, and so kids started hissing 'Go back to China like your parents!' every time they walked by me in the halls."

"Well, that's just ignorant on so many levels," I almost yell, my face heated. "I hate kids like that. I'm sorry."

"Indeed. Vile creatures. And after that Samantha and I, well, I couldn't trust her anymore." Christopher ties the end of his completed lanyard and then bites the ends off.

"I bet you miss your parents."

"Yes, very much," Christopher says. "Anyway, I had a lot of time to myself that year. At first, learning to make things on YouTube with my sister made me feel less alone, and then I found a whole community of kids online who were doing the same. In seventh grade I made my own channel where I offer tutorials—I have like a few hundred loyal subscribers."

"That's pretty cool."

"Yes," Christopher continues, "I like it. I can teach you to crochet if you want—next week, perhaps?"

I nod. "Sounds good."

"And, Andi?"

"Yes?"

"I don't need everyone here knowing all my business."

"You can trust me," I say. "I get it. Same."

"So," Christopher begins, his second lanyard almost complete, "tell me an embarrassing story. Since we're friends now."

"An embarrassing story?"

"Yes. I'll tell you one too."

"Um . . ."

"I'll go first."

"Okay . . ."

"Sometimes, I . . ." Christopher leans in and starts to whisper, "Well, allegedly, I fart in my sleep. My sister tells me they are deadly. I'm really nervous I'm going to fart-bomb my whole cabin without knowing it, and . . ."

I'm laughing so hard that Christopher doesn't even finish his sentence.

"Did you just say *fart-bomb*?" I finally manage between breaths.

"Yes, yes I did. And I realize it's funny, but if you could refrain from laughing for a moment, I'd—" Christopher can't even keep his face together, and soon we are laughing together.

"I won't tell anyone," I say when I catch my breath. "That's definitely something you should keep to yourself. If it happens, you should blame it on a skunk or something." I'm still giggling.

"Okay, now that I've mortified myself, it's your turn."

"I mean, I don't have any fart secrets," I say. "But, um, well. When I found out this place had uniforms, I considered running away. I'd really like to burn these knee socks."

Christopher laughs then. "Well, I enjoy wearing a uniform. It means I don't have to worry about having brand-name clothes, like I know some of the kids here probably wear."

"I guess I hadn't thought about it like that . . . And, well"—I find myself blurting out a secret I wasn't planning on sharing—"I love playing trumpet, but I just haven't been playing as well since . . . my mom died."

We go quiet then, and it feels like the bright coziness of the Craft Shack leans in to hug us.

"It'll be a year this August," I continue. "The same month my aunt and uncle's new baby is due. Did you have a hard time playing when your parents got deported?"

Christopher stops weaving his lanyard and furrows his brow. "It was the opposite for me. I couldn't stop playing and practicing. I was afraid my parents would be disappointed in me, like they'd think I wasn't working hard enough. And kids at my school were calling me lazy—and saying that my family didn't deserve to be in this country. But my parents work harder than anyone I've ever met. So I wanted to work just as hard as them."

"But you're still a kid . . ."

"I know. That's what my parents finally told me. My sister had to sit me down with them over Zoom so they could help me come up with a healthier practicing schedule. Now I set a timer for myself and don't let myself practice more than four hours a day. Also, my sister takes my trombone away at night so I don't get up and play when I'm supposed to be sleeping. And I take breaks to do crafts and other kid things."

"Well, you're really good at trombone and crafting," I say. "I'm glad you're here."

"And you're really good at trumpet, Andi," Christopher says. "I just know you'll get back to playing how you did before. And in the meantime, we can help each other stay on track!"

"For sure," I say.

Christopher smiles. "So, you're going to be a cousin."

"I guess so."

"Babies are delightful. They poop a lot. But they're cute."

I laugh. "Yeah. I can't really imagine my aunt Janine dealing with all that baby poop—although I guess she is a nurse. Their whole house is just so clean. I can't picture a baby in it, making a mess. I feel bad when I forget my dish in the sink or leave my trumpet lying around. And, like, if this baby ever brings home less than an A grade, Aunt Janine will freak out."

"If I bring anything less than an A home, I'll lock myself in my own room," Christopher shrieks.

"You're silly," I say then, glad for a friend who can be serious one moment and then make me laugh out loud the next.

"Sir Fart-Bomb, at your service," Christopher says, bowing deeply.

SHINE BRIGHT

It's Friday morning, and I'm already awake and dressed, sitting on my bed, before Davy even sounds the first note on his bugle. As Davy starts, Beks runs from across the room and joins Zora up top. Jori is over the obsession and snores loudly through the cabin.

"He's Kylo Ren to my Rey, Zora. The force is strong between us. I can just tell," Beks swoons.

Beks's drooling sessions over Davy Edwards have become a sort of new normal.

"You know you can't date him. It's against the rules," I hear Zora say.

"I can't date him *yet*," Beks corrects her. "But next summer, when we're all in the high school division, I can. He's only two years older than us."

"But do you really think an eleventh grader is going to date a freshman? Sounds suspect to me . . . ," Zora trails off as Beks ignores her and sighs a deep, longing sigh out the screen windows above.

I shake my head and sit up just as Zora is swinging her legs down. Two blue-socked feet hit me lightly in the face.

"I'm sorry!" Zora yelps.

I stand up and wiggle my nose like a bunny. "All good."

Zora jumps down and we face one another, both of us fully dressed and ready for the day. Zora's locs are pulled back into a tight ponytail, but a small one up front has escaped and falls into her right eye. Without thinking, I lift my hand to fix it.

"Can I . . . You have a . . ."

"Oh, sure . . . Thanks," Zora says, looking surprised but not mad as I tuck it softly behind her ear.

"How's orchestra going?" Zora asks me then, even though she's been there every day with me, sitting only a few sections away.

"It's fine."

"You know, Mr. London can be kind of . . ."

"OH MY GOD!" Beks shrieks from Zora's bunk, ducking down from the window and rolling off the bed to a standing position. "I think Davy just looked at me. Do you think he can see me through the window? He looked right at me, right into my soul."

Zora laughs. "Probably."

"For sure," I say.

Beks turns bright red, but she's smiling like a goof head, and before Zora can finish what she was saying to me, Beks drags her to the other side of the cabin to whisper more Davy-related gossip.

It's exhausting to be a girl sometimes.

After flag, I complete my chore (I'm on front-steps-sweeping duty) and then head to the dining hall. I fill my plate with hash browns and a few mini-muffins, and then find Christopher in his usual spot in the middle of the room.

"Why do you always sit here?" I grumble as I put my plate down and dump a whole heap of ketchup onto my hash browns.

"Well, good morning to you too, Andi," he says, taking a sip of his tea (what eighth grader drinks tea?!) with his pinky up.

"Good morning," I say with my mouth full. "Sorry, I guess I'm stressed about rehearsal today."

"You know I don't enjoy sitting in corners. This way I'm in the middle of everyone and can feel their energy." Sitting up a little straighter and clearing his throat, he says, "Pray tell, is that all that's the matter?" in what has to be the world's worst British accent.

No, it's not the only thing that's wrong. I'm still think-ing about Zora and how our conversation got interrupted. How she smiled at me with her eyes when I tucked her hair behind her ear. How I wanted to hear what she was going to say about Mr. London, and Beks kinda ruined the moment. All I say to Christopher is "Please stop that."

"Whatever do you mean, m'lady?" he continues, with a wicked glint in his eye.

"That terrible accent."

"I have no idea what you mean."

I throw a napkin at him, and just as it lands there's a commotion at the front of the dining hall where the doors are.

Aubrey and a counselor from the junior boys' division I don't recognize start parading around the dining hall. The junior boys' counselor is shaking a tambourine as we fall into silence. "Junior campers, come one, come all!" Aubrey yells into a megaphone. "Tonight's the night! Mixer, seven p.m., in the rec hall." Then she grins wide and drops the weird, formal voice she's doing. "Are there any questions?"

Angie is sitting at the table next to ours and shoots her hand up.

"Yes?" Aubrey says, squinting at her.

"Do we have to wear our uniforms for the mixer?"

"No, no uniforms for the mixer. But please wear your name lanyards. You'll all meet with your divisions at six forty-five tonight, and then head over to the rec hall. Don't forget to prepare your intro dances."

"Our what!?" I lean in and whisper to Christopher, my stomach flipping.

"Shhh. I'm trying to hear the rest. This is most exciting."

Is it? I listen in horror as Aubrey explains that at the first mixer of the summer, each cabin gets one minute to do a short intro dance or cheer as an icebreaker before the actual dance part of the mixer begins. There's a prize for the cabin that comes up with the most original act.

I groan. Christopher claps with glee, and already I see Zora waving members of our cabin together for a huddle as Aubrey finishes and leaves us to our breakfast.

"Yes!" Christopher whoops. "Our first mixer, Andi. What a delight."

I gawk at him, and Christopher reaches over and taps the bottom of my chin until I close my mouth.

"This is a disaster. I do not like dances, and now we have to do some coordinated dance routine. Something horrendous like that stupid 'Jingle Bell Rock' scene in *Mean Girls*?" I gag.

"You've seen *Mean Girls*?" Christopher teases.

"Haha, yes. I have. My aunt really likes that movie for some reason. Whenever it's on TV, we have to watch it all. I normally have AirPods in, but I've seen what I need to see of it."

"You're more of a dark, twisty movie type, aren't you?"

"I guess. Stop changing the subject. You're actually *happy* about this mixer situation?"

"Oh, yes! I love to dance. Before I got really serious about trombone, I took jazz and tap for years."

"Of course you did."

"Look, it's going to be fine, and I'll be there to cheer you on." Christopher stands up and starts to stack the empty dishes on his tray.

"Practice-hut time?" I ask.

"I don't think so, Andi. Look around. Everyone is gathering with their cabins right now. Mixer prep, I assume. I gotta go find mine!"

Christopher leaves and I look around. Sure enough, Zora is surrounded by most of my cabinmates, and when she sees me looking, she waves impatiently for me to join.

I walk over slowly, eyeing the exit for an escape.

"Good, we're all here. Let's talk about what we want to do for our intro dance," Zora starts.

Who made her the boss? I cough. "Um, hi," I say. "Can I just sit this out? I don't really dance."

Channing scoffs. "Of course you don't. It's not a big deal. You can be in the back—just follow along the best you can. It's more about the energy than being good."

"But we also want to be good," Zora butts in. "Like, we want to win the trophy. And everyone from the cabin has to participate—that's the rule."

Stupid rule, I think as I kick the floor with my Chucks. I can tell there's a big scowl on my face.

Zora ignores me and continues: "Since Joanna calls us her stars, I was thinking it would be fun to use that Chloe x Halle song 'Shine Bright' for our dance."

My ears perk up at the mention of Chloe x Halle. Before I can stop myself, I'm shouting into the group, "I can play that on trumpet, if that will help the routine?"

Zora's gaze snaps toward mine.

"Actually," Jori says, "that would be really great. I mean, normally people just play music on the speakers, but it would be low-key cool if we had live music."

A few others nod in approval.

I gulp. *What did I just get myself into?*

"Are you sure you can keep up?" I can always count on Channing to second-guess me. "I mean, no offense, but you're kinda struggling in orchestra."

I force myself to keep my head up. "I can do it. I play that song all the time."

"I believe you," says Zora. "Plus, this way you're included, but you don't have to dance. Since you said that's not your thing?"

"Right."

"So this is good. Andi will play the trumpet, and the rest of us will sing and dance. Nobody gets left out, everyone gets to be great. Done and done. Now, let's meet to practice after lunch. I've already thought of some fun moves."

ARETHA FRANKLIN

*T*he last time I really danced hard was with Mama. It was early February of last year, and a snowstorm so thick and full of ice ran around covering Detroit in frozen silence. I didn't need to turn on the TV to know school was canceled, but I did anyway just to confirm, since we hardly ever get snow days in Michigan. Halfway through my bowl of Cheerios, I saw the blue ribbon of school cancellations slide across the screen.

"Yes!" I shouted into the cozy, dark nest of our living room. "That's what I'm talking about."

Mornings in our house were the opposite of mornings at Aunt Janine's. For one thing, I was always the early riser. Mama kept our shelves stocked with food I could make, and even though I don't drink it, I'd learned how to start the coffeepot so that by the time I knocked on Mama's door to wake her up, it was hot and waiting for her. Plus, I always liked the way her coffee made our apartment smell like faraway places and the earth after it rained.

That morning, I finished off my cereal and then started on her coffee. After that, I put on my coat and boots and went outside to start digging out Mama's car. Even though

I didn't have school, I knew Mama had to be at work at nine a.m. We didn't have a garage, and Mama thought it was stupid to waste money on one of those covered parking spots.

"We're Michiganders!" she always yelled. "We don't let a li'l snow stop us."

I like shoveling snow because I get a lot of thinking done. It's the kind of task that wakes me up, and the cold air hitting my cheeks with a fierceness reminds me I'm alive.

When the car was all dusted off and I'd removed the big piles of snow from around the wheels, I stomped up the stairs to our apartment, shaking all the ice off my coat. Inside was just as cozy as I'd left it, and it was time to wake Mama up.

I know it sounds weird, that a child would be the one to wake up her mom, but that's just how it was for as long as I can remember. Mama was never like other mothers. She was always expecting me to be independent. Most nights, Mama stayed up late painting, sometimes till two or three in the morning. I always waited until the last second to wake her, knowing it would only take her about fifteen minutes to get her teeth brushed, throw on a coat and some boots, grab her coffee, and then take me to school.

But this morning was different. I peeked my head into her dark room, watching the lava lamp on her dresser for a few moments. Neon pink and purple bubbles separating from one another like droplets of blood. The one time Aunt

Janine came to visit, she made a huge stink about the lava lamp.

"Really, Star? A lava lamp. What is this, a college dorm room?"

Mama had just waved her hand in Aunt Janine's face and continued giving her the five-minute tour. "I don't know when you go so uppity, Janine. You act like we didn't grow up poor."

"Daddy always made sure we had enough," Janine had shot back then, "but is it a crime that I want better for you and Andrea?"

"She prefers Andi—you know that, Janine—and we are doing just fine. Just because we don't have a big fancy house and live with stuffy white folks in the suburbs doesn't mean we're struggling. At least I'm not trying to be somebody I'm not."

That ended the tour—and Aunt Janine's already short visit. I loved that about Mama, how she didn't let anybody shame her into being anybody but herself. I hope I can be like that one day.

"Good morning, baby!"

Mama had caught me staring at the lava lamp. She rolled over on her side, adjusting her bonnet and peering at the time on her iPhone. "Give me fifteen! Then I'll be ready to take you," she said, her voice a sleepy crackle.

"School's canceled," I said. "Snow day. Too cold outside,

but I cleaned off your car anyway. So you can get to work on time. Roads will probably be bad."

"Well, get in here then and let me snuggle you!" Mama had said, pulling up the covers and scooting over to make room for me in her bed.

I laughed and crawled under her blankets. Mama was in a sharing mood. I liked when she let me in like this. Mama turned over so that I was the big spoon, and all that cold that had seeped into my bones digging out the car disappeared with a quickness.

"So," she said after a beat, "who should we be today?"

"I thought you had to work?"

"I did. But all of a sudden I'm feeling kind of sick." She fake-coughed, and then giggled.

"You don't have to skip work just for me."

"I know. But I want to. It's been too long since we had one of our days." With that, Mama rolled over and sent a couple texts. "Easy as pie. I hardly ever miss a day," she said, turning back to me.

"Let's be people who have breakfast in bed," I said. I'd already had cereal, but I had room for more.

Mama laughed into the darkness and snuggled closer to me.

"That sounds like a good plan. But let's stay here for a little bit longer?"

Sometimes when I feel my brain spiraling into panic,

I imagine that I am back there, in Mama's bed, huddled against her thin back, under a mountain of blankets, the smell of snow and coffee tangling with my dreams. Neither of us meant to fall back to sleep, but before we knew it, the light was shining in brightly through Mama's windows and it was almost ten o'clock.

"How about waffles?" Mama said then, sitting up and stretching like a cat.

"Sure," I answered. "How many do you want? I'll fire up the toaster?"

"Oh, no," Mama said with a gleam in her eye. "I'm talking homemade."

Mama wasn't much of a cook, not like Aunt Janine with all her clean-eating recipes, but she could make a really good waffle. We wrapped ourselves in her blankets and shuffled into the kitchen.

"Look and see if we have sugar!" Mama ordered, snapping into motion like the most confident of cooks, pulling out bowls, measuring cups, the waffle iron, and a fresh carton of strawberries she'd brought home from work yesterday. As she began to stir up all the ingredients, snow began to fall again outside the window. Big, fluffy flakes that were bound to stick.

"Will you put on some jams?" Mama said, stirring the eggs into the batter.

I didn't even have to ask what kind of jams she was in

the mood for. I nodded and then turned on our portable speaker and hit play on the "This Is Aretha" playlist on
Mama's phone. Aretha's voice filled up the whole apartment,
and Mama yelled, "Turn that up!" and so I maxed out the
speaker. "Chain, chain, chain," Aretha's voice crooned as
Mama threw her head back and began singing into a wooden
spoon.

I shed the blanket from Mama's room and stood at the
counter, slicing strawberries, swinging my nonexistent
hips from side to side, doing a little shuffle, while Mama
lip-synched practically the full song word-for-word, still
managing to get the first spoonful of batter onto the siz-
zling waffle iron.

"Andi, baby! I know you got more than that. Let loose a
little! Nobody is watching but the snow."

I shook my head and continued my tentative two-step,
but Mama came over and grabbed my hand with her floury
ones. She pulled me into the living room right as Aretha's
version of "I Will Survive" began to play. Then Mama
shoved the spoon mic into my hands and yelled, "Take it
away, Andi!" And maybe it was the smell of syrup in the air
or the fact that days like this with Mama were rare, or maybe
I really was feeling the music in my body, my smile, but I
laughed and started to yell-sing along with the track. My
movements became bigger and bigger, until I surrendered
and just danced my way around the room with Mama, not

even caring how silly or uncoordinated I looked. Dancing, it turns out, can feel like flying. And that's what we did that morning; we flew around our little apartment. Eating, singing, dancing and swooping around as if we were weightless, while outside the snow fell heavy and full of hope.

"Andi," Mama said, after we got back into her bed with our plates and stuffed our faces with waffles and fruit, "as long as you are being your most true, most authentic self, that's all that matters. You don't dance to impress other people. You dance because something inside needs to be set free, because it makes you feel alive. Didn't that make you feel alive?"

It did. Dancing with Mama made me feel bigger than our little apartment, bigger that the whole city of Detroit, bigger than this universe. But I'd just shrugged in reply.

Mama shook her head. "Well, I hope you don't think we're done dancing for the day. Once this food settles, we're gonna 'turn up' as you kids say."

"Nobody says that."

"I low-key don't care. It's gonna be lit," Mama teased.

I giggled and popped another strawberry into my mouth. It tasted like summer, and love.

MIXER

$\mathcal{B}$y six thirty p.m. it's mixer time. Cabin four is a disaster of body spray, lip gloss, and heaps of clothes thrown on top of bunks. In the back of the cabin, girls crowd around three small mirrors, adding neon eye makeup to their looks or pulling their hair up into a variety of different styles. I'm wearing a pair of black jean shorts, a black tank top with small white polka dots, and my high-top Chucks. I sniff under my arms to see if they are funky (which they are, so I put on some more deodorant). I gag as Angie sprays down Beks with a cloud of nasty perfume. Whoever decided that cucumber and melon are two scents that go together is a monster. At 6:45 sharp, Joanna lines us up, counts us off, and then we join the other cabins outside and walk over to the rec hall in one big group.

The rec hall sits on the edge of Lake Harmony. It has two stories, with a great hall up top and then small game and audition rooms downstairs. It looks out over the dock and waterfront, where campers can swim and kayak during free time. I'm expecting the great hall to be all decorated like dances at East Hills, but it's pretty much just a big open space. All the chairs and tables have been stacked and pushed to the side. On a small portable platform stage someone has set up speakers, a mic, and a computer. Next to the computer, I see the trophy Zora mentioned. It's not really a trophy at all, but a pie tin that has been decorated with streamers, glitter, and flowers and then glued onto a wooden stand.

"That's what we're competing for?" I nudge Jori, who is in line next to me.

"A true masterpiece of trash, right?" Jori says, rolling her eyes. "Some people really care about the trophy, but winning is more about bragging rights. You'll see."

Joanna leads our cabin to a spot up front, and we all sit. I put CeCe in my lap and drum my fingers against the floor to keep still. Once everyone is inside and seated with their cabins, the "fun" begins. Aubrey emcees, and the boys' junior division head, Ben, aka DJ B, spins the tunes.

"Welcome, junior campers, to Harmony Music Camp's annual opening mixer!"

The room fills with loud whoops.

"As you know, we like to get things started here with a quick dance from each of our cabin crews. Now, I know you all have been preparing your routines, and I'm sure they will be great. While there is a prize for the best routine, a reminder that this is all in fun. Please be supportive during all the performances and stay within your one-minute limit."

I look around and see that cabin four is not one of those

"let's just have fun" cabins. Almost every one has that "we got this in the bag" look in their eyes, except for maybe Jori, who is doodling on her hand with a Sharpie, looking unimpressed.

"All right, let's get this party started!" DJ B yells into the mic. "We drew cabin numbers from a bag randomly, and it looks like the boys' division will start us off. Cabin two, you're up first, and then . . ."

There are six cabins in the junior girls' division, and four in the boys'. I wait and wait for DJ B to call our cabin, but we're the last cabin he draws. I gulp, and sit on my hands to keep them warm. I'd rather have gone first. Now we have to watch everyone else. There's always extra pressure on the closing act.

The performances begin. Christopher's in cabin one, and his cabin (I'm pretty sure at his suggestion) does a really funny dance/song to an old Beyoncé song called "Countdown," counting down the ten ways they are the best. Another girls' cabin, cabin three, does a bad hip-hop routine, which is low-key offensive because they all wear bandannas and gold chains and pose like they are in a music video. It's not good. Somewhere in the middle of everything, I hear Zora lean over and whisper to Julie, "Oh, we got this. Nobody has live music."

I shift my weight off my hands and stretch out my wrists. It's only fifty seconds of a routine. Then it will be over. *You know this song. You got this.* I close my eyes and imagine Mama and me in our apartment. I imagine her in her studio, and me in my room, sheet music thrown to the floor, just the two of us feeling our way through the songs and the colors. It's funny—these days I always remember us like this, but Mama rarely painted with her door open. She was extra private about her work. I guess when people die, memories get all mixed up, and right now—I need to hold on to the good, to the few times when everything was perfect and Mama let me be close to her.

"You ready, Andi?" Beks taps my shoulder. They've called us up to the front.

"I guess so."

We take our places, and everyone gets into their poses. Some boy whistles, and then the room erupts in nervous laughter. I'm in the front corner of the stage, standing close to the DJ station.

"And now for our final act," Aubrey says, "the Cabin Four Stars!"

Zora snaps the tempo, and I press my lips to my horn and take a deep breath. Right before I begin, I make eye contact with Christopher. He smiles and gives me two thumbs up. I close my eyes and start to play from memory. I feel the floor moving with the footsteps of the others as they begin to dance, but I keep my eyes shut and just groove with the notes in my own head. It feels good to be playing something

I know so well, a song that I just feel in my whole body. I am not outside of myself; I am inside of myself. I am home, and for a few moments I forget I'm at camp, I forget about Mama, I forget that what comes after this is a stupid, awkward dance, and I just blow and blow all my breath, all my uncertainty into CeCe. I must really be in it, because before I know it, I don't feel anyone else around me moving. In fact, the whole room feels still. But I can't stop playing yet. This feels too good. I open my eyes just as I am improvising a really big run to close out. Christopher is beaming at me as I add on more and more notes.

"Andi!" I hear Zora hiss, from somewhere behind me. "Andi, you're gonna make us go overtime. Wrap it up."

But I close my eyes again, and then finally, I end with all the power I can muster.

The room cheers, and I open my eyes to a partial standing ovation. Then someone in the girls' division starts chanting "Four! Four! Four! Four!" I grin, and then turn to face the rest of my cabinmates, but instead of grins, I am met with steely eyes. We filter off to the side of the room.

"Andi, that was epic. Didn't know you had it in you, but girl. You killed it," Jori says to me.

"Thanks," I say. "Did we go over?"

"I'm pretty sure we did."

"Oh no. I didn't mean to—Are they really strict about it?"

"They are. It's stupid. But the one-minute time limit is to keep things fair."

Oh no. Oh no, oh no, oh no. I watch as the judges huddle in the corner, reviewing their notes. That's the best I've played in a long time, but nobody cares how good I sounded if we don't win. Zora is sitting in front of me, her back and neck extra tall and stiff. I really messed up.

"All righty, campers!" Aubrey stands up front with her clipboard. "That really was a great show. Thanks for giving it your all. This was a tough call. The competition was fierce, and we had to disqualify a cabin for going overtime, even though they gave an outstanding performance. So, before we announce the winners, let's give a big round of applause to junior girls' cabin four for their effort!"

There are a few cheers and claps from other campers, but nobody in our cabin moves.

"And now, your mixer champions are: junior boys' division cabin one!"

I watch as Christopher and his cabinmates storm the floor. They lift the stupid pie-tin trophy over their heads while chanting "One! One! We're the best! One! One! We're the best!" Then DJ B cuts in with music and the floor starts to shift and clear for the actual dance.

I put CeCe into her case and follow my cabinmates outside. Coop leans in and whispers, "That was amazing. They can't be mad for that long." Then they fist-bump me.

"Thanks," I manage. At least Coop and Jori are on my side.

I look up and face everyone, now circled up. "I'm really sorry. I didn't think I went that much over . . . I got carried away. I love that song."

"We know," Channing starts. "We get it. You're, like, an improv genius. Too bad you don't play that way in orchestra."

"Channing, come on. It's not that big a deal . . . ," Coop begins.

"Yeah," Julie pipes in, "I mean, I think everyone knows we really won. We just lost on a technicality."

I give Julie a small smile.

"That's not how winning works," Zora's voice cuts in. "I mean, no offense, Andi, but that was really selfish. Didn't you hear me telling you to stop?"

"Like I said . . . I just got lost in the music. I mean, you must get that?"

"No." Zora again. "No, we do not get it. What we know is that we had that whole routine planned perfectly and you just went off track. I know you're new and everything, but that's not how we do things here."

"I . . ."

"It's done now. Congrats on your solo, Andi. Let's just all enjoy the mixer, okay?"

With that, everyone scatters. I walk back inside to find Christopher. There's a mess of kids dancing now, and I spot him in the middle of them. He waves at me with flushed cheeks to come and join, but I shake my head. For the rest of the night, I sit on a rust-colored couch downstairs and watch people play Ping-Pong. A few kids come up to say how amazing my solo was, but mostly I fade into the background. That's fine by me. You won't catch me putting myself out there like that again.

Harmony Music Camp

I love every inch of my grounds
Every cobwebbed corner
Every crack and tear and, yes,
Even the crooked steps outside of each cabin
Even the tangled swim lines
Bobbing carelessly in Lake Harmony's water

I love the vacuum of clashing noise
From the amphitheater and band shed
As campers warm up their instruments each morning
I love the *crunch crunch crunch* of happy feet
On my pine needle–dirt paths as they stomp
For cold treats and gossip at the Cavity Cave

I love the thick curve of trees
That line the highway and entrance
I love the sound of Ping-Pong balls
Bouncing across tables in the rec hall

But most of all, I love the Craft Shack
A camp is not a camp
Without a lopsided cabin
Bursting with yarn, beads, clay, and string
A warm, sunlit space with big wooden tables

Walls lined with watercolor paintings
Dangling from clothespins

I love listening to the secrets
Friends tell one another as they
Busy their hands with making
As they let their minds wander
Away from any outside pressure

Every bracelet or necklace that's tied shut with a knot
Every lopsided woven basket
Every messily tie-dyed T-shirt
        Is an artifact of love
A promise that friends make to one another
To never grow up or stop imagining

Like this year, the boy with the big vocabulary
The girl with the music all tangled in her sadness
They braid their hopes and dreams into one another
They think they are weaving bracelets
But they are also weaving a place in time

Soon, they'll be too old for this joy
On to big and bright futures
But for now, they are laughing
And folding every beam of sunlight
Into the dark middle of their rainbow lanyards
And I am here   in every corner
        To remind them
They belong exactly where they are

WEEK TWO

Zora

QUEEN OF CAMP

*Z*ora. *Zora. Zora. Zora. Zora. Zora.*

If I say my name out loud and fast enough, it sounds like bees humming. Most people are afraid of bees, of getting stung, but their sound has always been soothing to me. *Zora* means "alive," and that's how the sound of bees makes me feel—like I'm living. Whenever I start to feel out of control, I close my eyes and focus on the clear hum of my name. I imagine I'm back home in Ann Arbor, walking among the blooming peonies in the arboretum with Mom and Dad. I think about the busyness of bees, how each bee has its own specific job, a routine and schedule to stick to, all in service of the queen. I think about the neat hexagons that make up the honeycomb, how each chamber contains larvae, honey, or pollen. I picture all the parts of me that I don't understand yet having a place inside the honeycomb. I close my eyes and pretend that all I have to do is put things in order, work harder, and everything will be all right.

This is what my brain is doing Saturday morning after the mixer. Getting organized. I've been at camp for exactly one week, and while this is normally a place where I feel in control, this year is different. To start I had a big fight with my best friend from home, Kennedy, right before I left, and now I'm sharing a bunk with the only other Black girl in my cabin, a girl who makes me feel all out of order. To make matters worse, we got disqualified from the mixer competition and I said all the wrong things to Andi. I should have said, "I loved the way you lost yourself in that song. I wish I could do that." But instead, the worker bee in me, the person who hates it when plans change, told her she was selfish.

In the coziness of my bunk, I burrow into my covers and quietly say *Zora Zora Zora Zora* over and over again, trying to prepare myself for the day. I hear Andi shuffling below me, and all the feelings I just organized in my body fall out of order again. The thin frame of our bunk squeaks and sags as Andi wrestles into her uniform in the dark. I don't know why she has to get dressed like this—nobody is even awake to see her change. I always go to the back of the cabin, where it is dark and I can at least stand. That's another thing that's out of order: I'm used to being the only one up at this time. I like to get ahead of the day, to listen to the crickets sing the sun into the sky. Mom and Dad are always telling me that I'm going to have to work ten times harder than my white peers to be recognized as the talent I am, and since the two of them are convinced I'm going to get into Julliard one day, I try not to disappoint them, or myself. Getting up early at camp is how I stay ahead of the game. Plus, it's when I get a few moments to stretch and breathe and put on a smile for the day. A few moments where no one is watching my every move, where I can just be. But now I have to share it with her—Andi Byrd—a girl who is the opposite of me in every way.

I sense Andi's presence emerging from her sleeping bag, and then feel the weight of her as she sits up on her bed and starts putting on her shoes. From under my covers, I force a big smile on my face (sometimes you have to fake it till you make it) and then emerge from my beehive and throw my legs over the side of the bunk.

"You done?" I whisper to her.

"Yep."

I jump down, and then grab my uniform from my shelves. From the corner of my eye, I watch Andi smooth out her plain gray sleeping bag, and plump her black pillow. The girl literally brought, like, three things with her to camp, and they are all black. Her bunk decor is so minimal, it makes mine look overdecorated. But having to sleep right above her is what I get for showing up late on check-in day.

Normally I get to camp as early as I can on the first day so I can get the best bunk. But this year, my dad had insisted on a family walk in the arboretum before our traditional pre-camp breakfast at the Fleetwood Diner. I wasn't much in the mood, since Kennedy and I had fought the night before, but Mom and Dad are super obsessive about staying active. Family walks are not optional. Most kids my age spend their Saturday mornings watching TV or playing video games, but not in the Johnson household. In our family, Saturday mornings are reserved for outdoor adventures. "It's Fam Bam time!" my dad likes to yell down the hallway to my room bright and early, so early that I don't even bother to set an alarm clock. He's so corny. It really is torture to grow up the only child of morning people. I am *not* a morning person, but I've learned to fake it so I can be great. Still, it would be nice to have parents who understand that as a rising eighth grader I need my sleep and my space.

"My brain is still growing, you know!" I grumble-yelled when Dad's booming voice had made its way down the hall at 7:30 a.m. last Saturday.

"Fresh air is good for growing brains!" he'd replied. "Plus, it's your last day home. We're going to miss you, ZoZo."

For the record, I hate being called ZoZo. At school, I'm just Zora. Zora Lee Johnson: twelve years old (I'll be thirteen in September), valedictorian of my seventh-grade class, flautist, one of the youngest members of the Ann Arbor Youth Orchestra, best friends with Kennedy (the only other Black girl in Youth Orchestra), and the only child of University of Michigan professors Dr. Douglas and Dr. Carla Johnson. ZoZo makes me sound like a baby, but Dad insists on it even though these days my body is anything but baby-like. Somewhere in between sixth and seventh grade, my body "blossomed" (as my mom likes to say). All of a sudden, I was five-six, none of my training bras fit, and getting my full hips and thick thighs into a pair of skinny jeans without stretch just wasn't an option. I'm pretty much the opposite of my mom, who is a petite, flat-chested, light-skinned Black woman with an obsessive need to run or walk after every meal. "Some people *like* curves," I repeat to her most days at the dinner table when she tries to limit the amount of butter I put on my roll.

"Well, of course people like curves, Zora." She sighs. "I'm just trying to make sure you take care of yourself. Everything in moderation."

Mom never says it out loud, but sometimes I think she's mad that I look more like my dad. His side of the family is dark, thick, and tall. They live in Kentucky and put butter on everything. When we visit during the holidays, I pile my plate high with biscuits, fried chicken, greens, and all kinds of delicious food. Mom picks her way down the table, barely eating any of it. But Dad and I, well, we like ourselves a good down-home meal. Mom keeps us both in check when we're at home, but on vacation she's outnumbered.

"What people see on the outside, Zora"—Mom had started lecturing me the morning we left for camp—"is what matters most when you're out in public. It doesn't matter how smart you are, how talented you are, how kind; people will make snap judgments based on your appearance and attitude. And, Zora—because you're a Black girl, people are always going to be looking for ways to judge you unfairly. That's why it's so important to show well—do better than your best in orchestra. Don't even give them a chance to judge you or tell you that you don't belong."

She said this as we were waiting to be seated in the corner of the Fleetwood, a small diner in downtown Ann Arbor, famous for its twenty-four-hour service, bare-bones waitstaff, and a dish called Hippie Hash made of hash browns, veggies, and feta cheese. When we got to our table, Mom took out a bunch of sanitizer wipes and wiped everything on its surface down, including each individual condiment bottle.

I slid into my chair as the grumpy waiter came over to take our orders. My stomach flipped at the phrase *Don't even give them a chance to judge you.*

"What can I get you?" the purple-haired waiter had asked then.

"I'll take the Hippie Hash, with a side of extra-crispy bacon, please," I said. It was my favorite dish, and a delicacy that Mom only tolerated me ordering on special occasions.

"Are you sure you need bacon too?" Mom couldn't help asking.

"Yes, I'm sure." And then, just to make her squirm even more, I ordered a fried egg as well.

Mom pursed her lips and looked back down at her menu while Dad ordered a western omelet and hash browns.

"And for you?"

Mom flipped the menu. Finally she looked up and said, "I'll just have the oatmeal, a side of wheat toast, and some coffee, please."

"Make that two coffees!" Dad chimed in.

"And an orange juice!" I added.

"Is your orange juice fresh or made from concentrate?" Mom jumped in.

The waiter gave her a crooked smirk, and then pointed to a pop machine over by the front counter and register. "It's whatever kind of juice comes out of that."

"So from concentrate," Mom confirmed. "She'll just stick with water then. Thank you."

I started to play with the tray of sugars, but I kept my mouth shut. I didn't need to get into it with Mom, especially since I was already fighting with Kennedy. Plus, Mom let me get away with the bacon and fried egg.

"Zora, sit up straight, please. We might not be in the fanciest of establishments, but we are certainly not at home. Don't slouch."

"Yes, ma'am," I mumbled, rising to a seated position more to her liking.

"Now, as I was saying," Mom continued. "We're so proud of all that you have accomplished this year, Zora, but just because it's summer doesn't mean you can lose focus on your goals. We invest in Harmony Music Camp because we know it's going to make you a more competitive candidate when you start applying for colleges in a few years."

"In four years, you mean," I interrupted. "I still have four years left."

"Well, yes, of course. But it's never too early to start planning. You know that, Zora. Now, let's go over your camp goals one more time and then, I promise, no more business talk," Mom said, giving me a small smile.

I sat up straighter and took a deep breath. "Goal one: Earn first-chair flute in my seat auditions and maintain first chair in orchestra each week. Goal two: Always hit the practice huts before the crafting activities or the lakeshore. Goal three: Make connections with the conductor, in order to build my portfolio of adults who could give me recommendations."

Mom nodded approvingly as I finished. "That's my girl," she said as the waiter dropped off our steaming plates of food.

"AND?" Dad said, looking expectantly at me. "I think you forgot one."

"No, I didn't," I said, pouring a large glop of ketchup onto my Hippie Hash.

"Goal four: Have fun!" Dad said then, a twinkle in his eye.

"Oh right. Of course."

I know that these kinds of speeches from my mom are

meant with love, but it's a lot sometimes. All of a sudden, what was supposed to be a celebratory breakfast at my favorite spot turned into something else. I pushed my Hippie Hash around on my plate, my appetite gone.

"Why so gloomy, ZoZo?" Dad had said after our meal as we walked back to the car.

I shrugged. "Just going to miss you guys, that's all."

Dad grinned and pulled me into a bear hug. "ZoZo, we're going to miss you too." Then he motioned to Mom. "Get over here, Carla. What we need is a Johnson family hug right now."

I groaned, but my groan was muffled by Dad's enormous chest and big arms. I felt Mom join us with a tight squeeze, and then we just stood there for a minute, in front of the restaurant, looking ridiculous. I wiggled, and then wiggled some more and then slipped out from under their embrace. "Okay, okay!" I yelled, catching my breath. "Let's not get all clingy. People are staring at us."

"Let them stare!" Dad said, and then he dramatically opened the back door on the passenger side and ushered me in with the flourish of his hand. "Time to get you to camp!"

We didn't even get on the road until ten, and by the time we made the almost-four-hour drive up north from Ann Arbor, most of the other girls in cabin four had already arrived.

As soon as I rolled my purple trunk up the cabin front steps, Channing, Julie, Beks, and Jori burst out from the cabin and pounced on me.

"You're heeeerrree!" Jori had squealed. Jori, true to her punk-rocker style, was wearing her uniform but sporting heavy black eyeliner and twin messy buns.

Beks's Star Wars charm bracelet jingled in my ear as she gave me a quick hug next. Channing and Julie jumped up and down, and then Channing leaned in and said, "There's a new girl. And she kinda looks like she could be your sister!"

"Why?" I'd said, already not liking where this was going.

"Oh, never mind," Channing backtracked.

I ignored her and dragged my trunk across the cabin floor. Channing is someone I tolerate. Beks, Jori, and Julie are my real camp crew.

"And you must be Zora! I'm Joanna, your counselor."

"Hello!" I said, standing straight and extending my hand politely just like Mom taught me to. "Zora. Very nice to meet you."

"Looks like there's only one bunk left," Joanna said, motioning to the left corner of the room. "And, well, isn't that nice. It's right above Andi's bunk. I just have this feeling you two are going to get along."

I shrugged. At least the bunk was in the back corner of the room. More privacy. I rolled my trunk over to the bunk and swiftly made note of the new girl's decor, or rather, her lack of decor: no pictures on the wall next to her bunk, no stuffed animals, just a single black flashlight hanging from a tack in the corner. *Who is this person?* I'd thought. *She's super gloomy. Cleary, she's never been to Harmony Music Camp.*

I unbuckled the straps on my trunk and opened it. Inside, everything was in the order I'd packed it: eight pressed and folded light-blue collared shirts, five pairs of seven-inch khaki shorts that I fully intended to roll up and make shorter, some light sweaters and my raincoat, a nest of light-blue knee socks rolled into perfect balls, and of course my "Stay Magical" PJ set, my Chaco sandals, shower shoes, and hiking boots. Finally, I got to the bottom, where my bedding was. I pulled out a set of royal-purple sheets and my matching purple-and-white polka-dot comforter. I climbed up onto the top bunk and expertly made my bed. When I was done, I tacked a bunch of pictures to the wall next to me: pictures of Mom and Dad, and Ginny, and then a few of me and Kennedy all dressed up at the spring Youth Orchestra concert. Nobody needed to know we were fighting, or about what I'd confessed to her. Then, for the final touch, I strung a bunch of battery-operated fairy lights around the headboard and side rail. I clicked them on and jumped down to make sure everything looked perfect.

"Whoa!" Julie said from across the room. "Nice touch, Zora. You always have the best bunk. I wish I'd thought about fairy lights."

I smiled, already feeling more like myself. "Thanks. I just need to make my bunk label." I grabbed a star and sat on the floor, surrounded by markers, making sure to write my name out in clear, flowery purple letters, and then I started to add a bunch of unicorn, rainbow, and heart stickers around my name. When I was done, I taped it to my bed and stood back to admire my work. I quickly snapped a picture of my bunk, and then texted it to my parents.

Me: All set up & ready to be great!

Mom must have been driving, because Dad responded.

Dad: 😱😊♥ Knock em dead, ZoZo! We just know you're going to be first chair flute every week this year. You're a star.

Me: Thanks. Love you!

This was the first year I'd been able to convince them to let me find my cabin and get settled alone. The years before, they'd come with me, introduce themselves to the parents of each one of my cabinmates, and hover like helicopters. This year, by some magic, they'd let me get away with a teary (on Dad's part) goodbye outside the main lodge in the parking lot. I know Dad filmed me rolling my trunk down the path to the girls' division, so I turned and gave them a small wave before disappearing around a bend. After the final text sent, I turned my phone in to Joanna.

"Oh," she said, "are you sure you don't want to hold on to it? I'll be collecting everyone's phones later. You can have a couple more hours connected to the outside world."

"No, it's okay. You can have it now. I don't need it."

I didn't tell her that I was glad to be free of my phone. Free from my life back home. The thing I love about Harmony Music Camp is that for a whole month, I get a break from the Johnson family unit.

Zora, Zora, Zora, Zora. You got this, I repeat in my head, now fully dressed in my uniform and ready to start the second week of camp.

"Good morning, my stars. Time to shine bright and start your day," Joanna says, rolling out of her bunk and flipping on the cabin lights as the sound of Davy's horn blares through division.

A collective groan rushes around the room, and from deep in her covers I hear Jori yell, "I demand an extra hour of sleep after that mixer!" But she should know, just like I do, that Harmony Music Camp waits for no one. Even though it's technically the weekend, we still have flag and breakfast waiting. Hopefully, I can take a nap later, after I practice. Beks jumps out of her bunk and scrambles over to mine to catch a glimpse of her crush. I watch her press her face to the window and shake my head. I've got more important things to worry about than Davy. I smooth my shirt and check my knee socks. Then I head outside to line up for flag. Behind me, I feel Andi following. I should just turn around and tell her the truth. *I'm sorry I snapped at you. I'm not mad. Your solo just surprised me. It was really good.* But my tongue feels swollen and heavy. So, I don't say anything. Not yet.

PRACTICE HUTS

"*Z*ora!" Julie pleads with me over breakfast. "Why don't you come to the waterfront with us for the early-bird swim this morning? It's so fun. You can practice for seat auditions afterward—it's the weekend after all."

I am eating a bowl of steaming oatmeal dotted with brown sugar and fresh strawberries. The same bowl I make every morning. Oatmeal is about the only breakfast food Mom and I agree is delicious. I like the feeling of the hot oats sliding down my throat, warming up my airways. We may not have won the mixer last night, but I'd managed to earn first-chair flute in last week's auditions. I plan to do the same this week as well, and snagging first-chair flute means I don't have time to veer off course. *Practice before fun!* I hear Mom's voice in my head.

"No, thanks," I say with a bright smile. "You know that water is too cold for me in the morning."

It's not exactly a lie. I love to swim, but the waterfront is shady in the morning, and my favorite thing to do there is sunning on the beach. I like to let my skin get glowy and hot, then I like to dip myself into the water and float on my back. When I've cooled off, I like to lay back out on my towel and get hot again. Morning early bird swims are more about swimming laps back and forth within the roped off area as exercise. Julie, who swims competitively at her school, loves it, but the one time I joined last year, it threw off my whole day. I was so tired afterward, I napped and then missed getting to the huts before the busy hour. By the time I was ready, they were all in use and I had to practice under a tree outside, which was super distracting. That year, I never made it past second-chair flute.

This year, I can't afford to let that happen.

"Fine," Julie says, faking a hurt look. "But promise you'll hang out later today? You're not, like, a robot, you know."

"Julie, please," I say. "You should be one to talk. You're just as obsessed with practicing as I am. Everyone at this whole camp is."

I hear laughter coming from a nearby table. I look over into the center of the dining hall and spot Andi, sitting with her friend Christopher. Christopher is new too, and given cabin one's performance at the mixer, he seems fun. He makes Andi smile, a lot. Andi's smile is hard to look away from—her angular face is all warm and open when she smiles. Exactly how she looked when she finished playing last night.

"Not everyone," Julie says, then nudges me and looks pointedly in the direction of Andi. I feel the hairs on the back of my neck stand up, and then I blurt out, "She practices. I think it's just a new experience for her. But you heard her last night; she can really play when she wants to."

"Sure," Julie says. "I just mean that not everyone has the same goals as you and I do. Not everyone is cut out to be great here, you know?"

"You don't know what her goals are." I sit up straighter at the table, making my body a wall between Julie's comment and Andi's smile. "There are lots of different ways to be great, you know." I get up and load my tray with trash. "I have to go. See you later."

I don't stick around to hear if Julie says bye. I need fresh air. Julie's comment about Andi made me feel small. I know what it's like to be underestimated. People are always underestimating me, making assumptions about who I am. I don't understand Andi, but I know she's trying. I know because every time I'm in the practice huts, she's there too, either with Christopher or alone.

I make my way toward the dining-hall exit and I inhale deeply. As I am about to push my way into the sunlight, my eyes catch on a poster on the wall near the door. On it is a photograph of a graceful Black woman leaping through the air, and at the bottom, bold black lettering reads DANCE YOUR STORY: MASTER CLASS WITH JASMINE BAKER. THIS THURSDAY, 4:00 P.M. ALL LEVELS WELCOME. REGISTER AT THE MAIN LODGE.

That's in six days! My heart joy-yells at me as I begin to plot how to convince Mom and Dad to let me take it. *But first*, I say to myself, hearing Mom's voice in my head again, *you need to focus on flute.*

I make a mental note to call Mom and Dad later, then I adjust my bag over my shoulder and make a beeline for the huts.

"You don't always have to be so perfect, Zora! We're twelve!" Kennedy's voice comes floating into my practice session as I stumble on a run. Last week, we got to audition with whatever piece we wanted to, but from now on we audition with music we'll be playing in orchestra. I'm trying to focus, but I keep thinking about the image of Jasmine Baker leaping through the air and how much my body wants to try to leap as high as her. Plus, it's so nice outside. Through the small window, I watch the tops of the nearby trees sag and sway under the weight of sparrows and wind. I close my eyes.

There's a song by Janelle Monáe that I really love. It's called "I Like That." In the song, she sings about feeling like herself and like a mystery to herself all at the same time. That's how I felt the night before I left for camp, when I let my confession slip out at Kennedy's house during our annual goodbye movie marathon—like mystery-me.

Every summer since I met her, Kennedy has gone to visit her dad in Oakland, California. Then four summers ago, I started going to camp. So, Kennedy and I always plan a movie-marathon night right before we both leave. This time around, we had planned to watch our favorite old movies from the early 2000s: *Mean Girls* and *The Princess Diaries* 1 and 2. Dad dropped me off at her house around four, so we'd have seven full hours to marathon before my weekend curfew and pickup at eleven. I'm the kind of person who likes to try to say and do all the right things. I don't like to be wrong, and I don't like to stir up trouble. But lately, whenever I hang out with Kennedy, all my planning, organized self goes away and I feel like I'm made of pollen that's blowing away in the air.

"You got the stuff?" Kennedy asked when I walked into the basement of her house, aka our clubhouse. Instead of sitting perched on the couch in her usual spot, Kennedy was seated at the desktop computer her mom set up for homework. Over her shoulder I could see she was on her Finsta, scrolling through pictures on Cole's account.

Why is she so obsessed with him? I said in my head, but on the outside, I put on a big smile, ignoring the feeling of fluttering in my belly. "You know it." I threw my backpack on the floor and pulled out handfuls of our favorite junk food: Sour Patch Kids, Pretzel M&M's, peanut-butter-chocolate fudge from the place on Main Street we love, and a bag of sweet-and-salty popcorn. "All the good stuff."

"Cool," Kennedy said, not looking away from the screen.

I got comfortable on the couch and then opened the bag of popcorn, waiting for Kennedy to join me, but she stayed where she was.

"What do you want to start with?" I asked, turning on the big TV and opening Netflix.

"Whatever you want," Kennedy said. "You know I love all these movies."

"I know, but . . ."

Kennedy let out a big sigh, and clicked on another picture. "He's low-key cute, right?" she said, her cursor hovering over a picture of Cole.

I rolled my eyes. I watched the back of Kennedy's head, her hair pulled up in a top bun, a few soft curls escaping and falling down the back of her slender neck. I didn't really get it. Cole Forrest was a scrawny, tall white boy who played the timpani (badly, if you ask me) in Youth Orchestra with us. Kennedy had been talking about him nonstop since at the reception after the final spring concert he told her she did a "good job" on her bassoon solo. He's starting high school next year, all the way across town, and might not have time to be in Youth Orchestra again, but Kennedy made sure to find all his social media accounts and had been stalking him for weeks. I thought this was supposed to be our night.

"He's whatever," I said, my throat catching. "Want to put on *Mean Girls*?"

"Fiinnnnne," Kennedy said, turning to me with her light-bulb of a smile. "Let's get this party started!"

I patted the spot next to me. "Get over here and get comfy, girl."

Kennedy grinned, sat down, and leaned her head on my shoulder like she always had. "What am I going to do without you, Zora?"

I laughed. "Same as always. Suffer."

Kennedy punched my arm playfully. "You're going to suffer. I can't believe that you *like* wearing that stupid camp uniform."

"It's easy," I said. "I don't have to think about putting together an outfit, and I can concentrate on what matters: getting first chair. You know how competitive it is, Kennedy. Your girl can't slip. I don't come from a musical family like you, remember? Some of us have to work hard just to keep up."

The first time I met Kennedy was at a state music competition in third grade. We've never gone to the same school—her parents believe in public school; my parents send me to private school—but music has always been our thing together. When we met, we were both competing in the solo junior elementary category, her on bassoon and me on flute. Most of the time, I'm one of the few Black faces in the classical music world, but on this day, there she was.

Kennedy has an amazing head of thick, dark curls that accent her light-brown face and warm hazel eyes, and her curls bounce around when she plays her bassoon. Kennedy loves every part of being a musician. "It's in my blood," she likes to say when people ask her how she got so good, since both her parents are working musicians.

"You'll be great," Kennedy said, grabbing a handful of M&M's. "You're like the queen of camp. You're going to have a great time."

"I guess. Still wish I could visit you. I've never been to California. I want to go to the beach and swim!"

"Bay Area beaches are hella cold. Nobody swims unless they have on a wet suit. The beaches are more for walking along while wearing a sweatshirt and enjoying the sights." Kennedy laughed.

"Fine. Whatever. I still want to see them."

"Maybe one day." Kennedy nodded. "Can we please focus on the movie? We already missed the beginning."

I laughed and threw popcorn in her face. "Fine."

I was going to miss her too.

Mid–*Princess Diaries 2*, Kennedy had fallen asleep. I shook her, but she just tilted her head deeper into my neck and started snoring in my ear. When the credits started to roll, I looked at the clock. Ten thirty. Dad would be here soon. I nudged Kennedy harder and said, "Wake up, sleepy. It's almost time to say goodbye."

"See you later," she'd said, eyes still closed. "We don't say goodbye; we say 'see you later.'"

"You know what I mean!" I giggled.

Kennedy sat up, and we sat there facing each other with our legs crossed, knees touching. "I'm going to miss you, Zora."

"Same . . . I . . ."

Just then, the loud ding of a notification blared out from the computer. Kennedy jumped up and ran over. "OH MY GOD!" she screamed, and then started dancing around the room.

"What? What is it?!"

"Cole. He finally just followed me back on my Finsta. What do you think it means?"

"Um, probably nothing," I said before I could stop myself, a hot, bubbling heat rising in my ears again. "Can you please focus? This is our last few minutes together. Don't be so thirsty—he probably can't even tell you apart from me or any other Black girl he knows."

Kennedy stopped dancing. "Why are you being so mean about this?" she said, all the flush gone out of her face.

"I'm not being mean. Just realistic. Since when do we care about boys anyway? They all smell, remember?"

"News flash, Zora. Everybody smells. We're in middle school, okay? It's like a constant stink-fest, and just because *you* don't care about boys doesn't mean I don't."

"Maybe I don't like boys, because maybe I like girls!" I heard myself blurt before I could stop myself.

"Cool!" Kennedy shot back. "I don't care, Zora. You're still my best friend if you like boys, girls, or unicorns. But I like Cole."

"Fine."

But it wasn't fine. My body felt like a furnace, and mystery-me blurted out: "I think I might . . . *like* you, Kennedy." I covered my mouth with my hands. I'd known for a while that maybe I liked girls, but this outburst surprised even me. Kennedy was my best friend. She was beautiful, and stupid Cole didn't deserve her attention. I hadn't realized until that moment that I wanted that kind of attention from her too. I wanted Kennedy to think I was also beautiful, worth crushing over.

Kennedy turned toward me. "Stop messing around, Zora."

I looked down at my hands and began to pick at the skin around my nails. Instead of a flutter of wings in my belly, it felt like there was a whole ocean inside me. A rough ocean with big waves slapping up against the sides of my rib cage.

"Well, I . . . ," Kennedy started, and then stopped.

Mystery-me was gone. *Why did I just say that!* "Don't worry about it," I said. "Let's just forget it."

"Zora, you're my best friend, forever, okay? But I'm not into . . . I don't like you like *that*."

Kennedy's face was all scrunched up with confusion, and

I didn't like the way her voice sounded, full of pity. I felt the waves again. They slapped harder and a roar entered my ears. I stood up and started packing up my stuff. Kennedy was saying things to me, but the roar in my head was drowning her out.

From somewhere inside the roar, I heard a car honk outside. "My dad's here," I said, throwing my backpack on. "I have to go."

"Zora!" Kennedy yelled as I headed for the stairs. "Don't be mad!"

I wasn't mad—I wanted to crawl under a rock, but instead I turned and said, "Have fun in Oakland. I'm sure you'll fall in love with all the boys there too."

And then I ran up the stairs and out to the car without looking back or giving her one last hug.

"Hey . . . ," a voice behind me says.

I whip around and see Andi standing in the doorway of my practice hut, trumpet in hand.

"Um, I just wanted to say I'm sorry. About the dance-off thing. I know you wanted to win."

I wipe a loose tear from my eye, and then shrug. "Well, I wasn't the nicest about it."

"It seemed like a big deal to you. So . . ."

"I know. I'm not good when plans change. I'm really sorry too. I don't think you're selfish. I thought your solo was amazing."

"Thanks."

Andi stands in the door awkwardly. Just as she's about to turn around and leave, I say, "How's practicing for auditions going?"

Andi steps into the hut with me. She shrugs, and picks at a loose thread in the cuff of her hoodie. "You know," she starts. "It's going okay. I'm just not . . ."

"Not a Youth Orchestra kind of player?"

"I was going to say, I'm just not good at reading music. I like to feel it, you know? Find the soul."

I laugh a sharp laugh, and Andi narrows her eyes.

"No, I'm not laughing at you. I just have the opposite problem. I mean, I'm great at reading what's on the page, but like, I don't know how to get all super passionate about the songs. Not like you did at the mixer. What's that like?"

Now Andi smiles. It's not as big of a smile as she gives Christopher, but it's one full of light. "I haven't played like that in a long time," she says quietly. "I dunno. It was the song, I think. It reminded me of someone."

Probably someone she loved. I feel my heart quicken. *What would it feel like to have someone play a song like that, as they thought of me?*

"Well," I say, shaking the thought out of my head. "If you can find a way to bring that kind of energy to orchestra, you'll be fine."

Andi shrugs again and starts to walk away. "Maybe if . . .

you know," she says, gesturing to my whole music stand, metronome setup, "you put all that stuff away and just play what you feel, you might disappear into yourself too."

"Maybe," I say.

"Cool. See you later."

And then Andi is gone.

I sit there in the room without her and take a deep breath. From a few doors down, I hear her start to play. But it's not the piece for orchestra. It's my song: "I Like That," by Janelle Monáe. I sit there and tap my foot along to the notes, then very softly I start to sing along with the lyrics, my whole body swaying. If I were a little freer, I might just get up and dance around the room. I might just leap into the singing air.

SEAT AUDITIONS #2

It's thirty minutes before my week-two seat audition, and I am in the corner stall of a bathroom in the rec hall saying my name over and over again, trying to stay focused. *Zora Zora Zora Zora Zora.* I'm sitting on the toilet lid and tapping my heels on the tile floor. I can't stop tapping. I look down at my dark knees, my thighs that look like two rich islands, and before I know it I am running my pinky nail over them, pressing down just hard enough so that I feel a dull pain. I never draw blood, but sometimes, I need a little release. Sometimes, when I am alone and all the voices of people who love me start buzzing in my head, I give myself a little pinch, slap, or scratch to remind myself that I am alive. It's not normal, but it makes me feel better. And right now, I feel like I am slipping into mystery-me, and it's not a good time for her to show up.

This morning, after breakfast, I walked over to the main lodge to call Mom and Dad. The main lodge has a section lined with little booths with old phones that attach to the wall. I shoved myself into a booth, pulled out my notebook where I'd written down Mom's and Dad's cell phone numbers, then dialed my dad.

"ZoZo, is that you?" Dad picked up. I could hear the sound of his favorite podcast, *Crime City*, on in the background. He loves anything true-crime related. It's like his version of Sunday sports. He gets up early and helps Mom meal-prep for the week, and his only requirement is that they listen to all his crime podcast episodes that have built up. They cook big batches of soup, grilled chicken or salmon, and salads for the week. It's their thing, since on Sundays they let me sleep in. I'm often awake, but I just like to stay in bed and listen to them puttering around the kitchen, commenting, giggling, and enjoying their morning. It's nice to know they can have a routine without me.

"Hi, Dad," I said. "What are you making today?"

"Oh, you know, the usual healthy stuff. Mom's got a new collard greens and apple slaw recipe that she wants to try. Don't tell her I said it, but collards are meant to be eaten one way, and one way only: boiled with ham hocks."

"Yes, I know, Douglas," Mom's voice chimed in. "You've only mentioned that five times this morning. Don't eat my slaw if you don't want to. More for me. Hello, Zora," she said. "Are you feeling good about your audition today?"

"Yes. I think so."

"You think you'll be able to keep first chair this week?" she pushes.

"Yes. That's the plan, Mom."

"Good. That's wonderful. You're right on track, honey.

We knew you would be. Johnsons are nothing if not persistent and consistent."

I started to roll my eyes but then stopped myself, as if they could see me over the phone. I should be grateful to have two parents who love me and push me to be the best, but being an only child of two Black professors who were the first in their families to finish college is a lot of pressure. Mom and Dad tried to get pregnant for many years, but couldn't. They'd all but given up, but then when they were in their early forties, I came along. They call me their "serendipitous little miracle." Hearing that used to make me feel special when I was younger, but these days it makes me feel like I can't breathe. I'm not sure I can be who they want me to be.

"So." I cleared my throat, getting to what I really wanted to ask them. "You know how the camp sometimes brings in guest artists to do elective-type master classes during the week?"

"Uh-huh," Dad answered, no doubt while he was concentrating on chopping something.

"Well, there's going to be a dance master class later this week, and I'd like to take it. It looks fun, and I thought it might help me express myself in a new way for a little bit."

"Are you sure that's a good idea, honey?" Mom again. "I mean, I know you used to love to dance, but we're paying for you to be there so you can focus on your music. I'm just not sure you need to be revisiting all of that again. Dance isn't very nice to girls like you, remember?"

"Now, Carla," Dad started, "I don't think one master class is going to set her off course. She's been working hard, and it sounds like a great opportunity."

I gulped, my throat very dry. The little phone booth all of a sudden didn't have any airflow. *I guess there's no need to tell them about the mixer and the whole dance I choreographed and performed flawlessly.*

"Well . . . ," Mom said after a beat, "why don't you see how today's audition goes. Then we'll see about the master class, which I am assuming costs extra?"

I nodded, and then realizing they couldn't see me, said, "Yes, ma'am. It's fifty dollars."

"Well, let's check in again midweek," Dad said.

"Don't get your hopes up," Mom added, which really just meant NO.

The rest of the conversation was short. Mom and Dad talked about their summer research routines, and I gave a quick update on Mr. London and orchestra. When I hung up, I sat in the silence of the booth and thought about how Mom had said "girls like you."

I pinched the flesh on my left arm until my heart stopped pounding in my ears.

I'll show them what my body can do. I yanked the door of the booth open and stomped over to the master class sign-up sheet posted in the main lodge entryway. I wrote my name neatly, and then under the payment column I checked "charge me at checkout." I'd deal with the consequences later.

But now in the bathroom stall, I am regretting that unpredictable mystery girl that had come out earlier. I should have just let the dance thing go.

"Are you okay in there?"

When did Andi come in? I inspect my thighs, but there are no visible welts or scratches. Then I stand up, flush, and open the door.

"I'm great," I say with a little too much bounce in my voice. "Just getting in the head space for my audition. Are you ready?"

"Ready as I am gonna be," Andi says, heading over to the sinks to wash her hands.

"Excellent," I say. "Well, good luck."

"You too," Andi says. "You know, if you weren't okay, that would be fine too. This camp is extra cutthroat. I don't know how you come here summer after summer and don't have a bad day sometimes."

"Well, thanks for the pep talk," I hear myself say. "But really, I'm good. Some of us are just used to the pressure, I guess."

Andi shrugs and then waves on her way out.

I wash my hands and take a deep breath. In the mirror, I smile big and bright.

The hallways are lined with my orchestra-mates sitting along the walls with their instruments out and pieces of audition music scattered all around the floor. Channing waves to me as I slide past, and I follow Andi down the hall. I watch as Andi enters the audition room with Mr. Wright, leaving the door cracked. I stand outside and start to put my flute together, but I can't help leaning in close to hear what's going on inside.

"All right, then, Andi. Let's hear what you have for me this week. Take your time," I hear Mr. Wright say.

I hold my breath and wait, but Andi must be setting herself up because the room is silent. Then, I hear Andi begin. Her playing is not at all like it was when she was playing that Janelle Monáe song. Instead, her notes are clipped and rushed, as if she's not taking in enough air before she plays. She stumbles over a few runs, and then stops to start again. I can hear Mr. Wright shuffling in his seat, and then he says, "Andi, slow down. Take your time with that part."

But Andi rushes through it again and then hobbles to the end of the piece.

It's almost as if someone else is playing for her, it's such a different sound and tone. She wasn't kidding about the whole reading music thing. I know she can play, but this is not great.

I lean in farther to hear what Mr. Wright is saying, and the door pushes open more than I mean it to.

"So sorry!" I say, jumping back and reaching to close it. "I didn't . . . I was just . . . I'm sorry."

If I were Andi, I'd be glaring at me, but instead she's looking past me, out into the hallway. Her eyes are glassy and unfocused. I turn to leave, but Mr. Wright calls me inside.

"Now, just wait a minute, Zora. I think I have an idea. You've been coming to Harmony Music Camp for years, correct?"

"Yes, sir."

"Excellent. And you and Andi must be friends, right?"

"Well, we're cabinmates," I manage. *Why do white people always assume that all Black people must automatically know each other?!*

"Great! Perfect. Andi here is having a bit of trouble with the material this week, and I think she could really benefit from your help. I'm going to ask you to mentor her, Zora. Help her learn the ropes from someone like her."

"My friend Christopher has been helping me, Mr. Wright," Andi says, her eyes coming back to life.

"Well, that's great, Andi," Mr. Wright says. "But Christopher is also new, so I still want Zora to be buddies with you this week. I know you can improve, and Zora here is an expert at reading music. So, Zora, what do you say?"

Mr. Wright is making it seem like I have a choice, but I can tell he's pretty much settled on it.

"No problem," I say, then to Andi: "We can meet up a couple of times this week to practice?"

Andi shuffles her feet side to side and doesn't make eye contact. "Sure. Whatever," she says, and then to Mr. Wright: "Can I go now?"

Mr. Wright looks the two of us over, beaming, as if he's just solved all the problems of the world. "Yes," he starts, "you're free to go, Andi. Audition results will be posted by lunch."

"I know I'm not moving up, Mr. Wright," Andi says, quickly gathering her things.

"You never know!" Mr. Wright says. "Anything can happen!"

Andi raises an eyebrow at him, and then without saying another word she flies out of the room.

"Zora, you're next, right?" Mr. Wright asks.

I nod, very aware of how bright the room is, how much I don't really want to be here.

NOISE

*H*armony Music Camp likes to go all out on the Fourth, but after a long day of auditions, keeping my seat as first-chair flute, and an afternoon rehearsal that Mr. London let run long, the last thing I want to do is celebrate this loud holiday. The truth is that I hate fireworks; they scare me. When I was little, and home for the summers, I used to hang with Ginny during the Fourth. Ginny, like most dogs, also despises fireworks, so Mom and Dad would let me and Ginny watch movies in my room with the volume on high while the booms and crackles made their way into the sky.

All I want to do is crawl into my bunk for the rest of the night, but at eight o'clock, Joanna counts us off and leads us over to the waterfront to claim a spot on the beach for the show. The lakefront is already crowded when we arrive, and I'm happy to see that we find a space father back from the water, so I don't have to shield my eyes or worry about ashes falling into them.

Beks grabs my arm and tries to pull me closer to the front of our group, but I decline and instead make my way over to Andi, who is sitting at the edge of us all. I haven't talked to her since she ran out of the audition room.

"Hi," I say.

Andi has her hoodie pulled up and ignores me.

I'm not thrilled about being her mentor-buddy either, but she doesn't have to be rude about it.

"HI!" I say again louder, tapping her on the shoulder.

Andi turns toward me and lowers her hoodie, and I see that she has her earbuds in. She takes one out. "Hey," she says, pushing pause on her MP3 player. "I didn't hear you."

"What are you listening to?"

"This album I like called *12 Little Spells*."

"Esperanza Spalding!" I almost yell. "I love her. She's a musical genius."

Andi takes out her other earbud. "I thought maybe you only listened to classical stuff?"

"I like a lot of kinds of music. Plus, I got to see her live when she came to Ann Arbor. She's, like, one of my favorite artists after Lizzo."

"You like Lizzo?"

Who does Andi think I am? "I love her. I mean, come on, she plays the flute and dances like a goddess. What is not to like?"

"That's cool. Have you ever heard of Bobbi Humphrey?"

"I don't think so."

"You need to listen to some of her tracks if you like Lizzo. I mean, she was big in, like, the 1970s, but she was all about fusion. Her stuff is, like, a combination of jazz, funk, and soul."

I don't know if Andi knows this, but her face is full of movement. She looks cute when she's like this.

"She sounds amazing," I say. "I'll have to check her out."

Just then, I hear a loud whistle and the sky explodes into a series of red, pink, and gold stars. I flinch and bring my hands up to my ears.

Andi chuckles next to me. "Not your thing, huh?" she says, pointing up.

I shake my head.

"Here. Take these." Andi hands me her earbuds. "This is a Bobbi Humphrey track. It's called 'Rainbows.' My mom loved this one. It's extra cheesy, but it's smooth."

Then Andi presses play and leans back in the sand to watch the fireworks. I close my eyes and let my ears fill with the music. And even though it is a little corny sounding, it's soothing. I start to imagine that Andi and I are riding around in a car with the windows rolled down. It's the middle of the day, and the sky is super blue. We stick our hands out the windows and let the air weave in-between our fingers. I must really get into it, because soon, sooner than I'd like, Andi is tapping me on the shoulder. I open my eyes, and the sky above is filled with ash and smoke.

"You missed the finale," she says, her grin a lighthouse in the dark.

"Oh well," I say. "That song is good."

"You should try playing it sometime," Andi says, getting up and brushing the sand off herself. "Anyway, glad you like it."

"Maybe you can help me when we have our buddy sessions this week?" I ask. "Tomorrow, maybe?"

"Yeah. Cool. Maybe," Andi says, a door closing somewhere on her face. "See you later."

I watch Andi pull her hoodie back up and join the crowd of campers heading back to their cabins. The sound of Bobbi's flute echoes in my ears, and I press my palm into the warm imprint that Andi's body has left in the sand. I close my eyes and imagine our hands in the wind again, and from inside the darkness of my mind, I feel a new melody bubbling up.

MOON DANCE

Two days after fireworks and on the second Tuesday night of camp, someone yells into a megaphone in between the junior girls' and high school girls' divisions, and all chaos breaks loose. It's past curfew and lights out, but everyone is awake and settling in. From the corner of my eye, I see Channing shed her floral nightgown; she's got underwear and a sports bra on, but nothing else. She howls loudly in the middle of the cabin, "Get out of bed, y'all! It's time to dance under the moon."

From her dark corner of the cabin, Joanna yells, "You've got twenty minutes. Then you all need to be back in here with clothes ON, ready to go to bed."

The counselors never stop the moon dance from happening, but they don't participate either. I guess it's probably frowned upon to run around half-naked with your campers.

"What the mess is happening?" I hear Andi's muffled voice from below.

I swing my torso over the side of my bed with my flashlight to peer at her, but she's scrunched down tightly in her sleeping bag. After she let me listen to that song on the beach, we started talking a little more, but when I've suggested we get a buddy practice session in, she has some excuse.

"It's the moon dance," I say. "A Harmony Music Camp tradition. You should probably see for yourself; it's hard to explain."

Andi rolls over and peeks her head out. She looks all grumpy faced and soft. Her sleeping bag may be plain, but it looks warm when she's in it, like a cocoon. *What would it feel like to be inside that cocoon with her?* Maybe she'd share an earbud with me again and we'd both fall asleep listening to Esperanza spin gold with her bass and soulful voice.

Everyone has shed their PJs and is screaming, howling, and dancing around the cabin in bras and underwear. Even Arya, who never speaks, is in rare form tonight. When Jori starts a new howl, Arya joins in so loud and so growly that for a moment the whole cabin goes silent.

"Well, all right, Arya!" Jori says. "Who knew you had that in you! Welcome to the pack, lady."

"AWOOOOOOOO!" everyone screams together.

"This is amazing!" Coop yells, flinging their shirt around their head like a fan and running around like a helicopter. "This is my kind of party!"

The lights are off, but flashlight circles dart around the room, giving it a night club effect. In her bunk corner, Joanna sits up in her sleeping bag, turns on her book light and starts reading to wait out the chaos.

"What am I even looking at?" Andi laughs. "This camp is wild."

Then, as if on cue, Beks yells, "To the streets, my friends!" and most of cabin four bursts out the front flaps of the cabin to join a collection of campers-turned-wolves howling, dancing, running, and screaming under the moonlight.

"What in the white nonsense is going on?" I hear Andi say under her breath.

I laugh. "I guess it is some white nonsense."

"You think?" Andi says then. "Shoot, my aunt would kill me if she knew I was running around in the woods without hardly anything on."

"Mine too," I say. "I mean, my mom would. I've never told her about the moon dance, and she doesn't need to know. She'd be horrified. She already thinks these cabins are full of germs and dirt; imagine if she knew everyone was just running around half-naked outside?"

"My aunt is like that too," Andi says. "She's a health freak and a neat freak, and her clothes are never even wrinkled. I bet if she saw this cabin, she'd want to sweep the mess out of it."

"My mom and your aunt sound like the same person! We should never let them meet."

Andi laughs. "For sure. Sounds like a plan."

I smile in the dark. It's a joke, but I like the idea of the two of us having a plan together.

"So have you ever participated in this sacred Harmony Music Camp ritual? I'm surprised you're not out there. I thought you were, like, the queen of everything camp related," Andi says.

I swing my torso back down over the side of our bunk again, but this time I almost smack foreheads with Andi, who is now sitting cross-legged on her mattress.

"Oh, phew," Andi says, shining her flashlight at me. "I thought you were about to be half-naked and join them. Thanks for keeping your shirt on."

Andi says it with a teasing tone, but a humming takes over my body. The thought of Andi seeing me in my bra isn't the worst thought I've had. *Get it together, Zora.*

"How long will this last?" Andi says.

"Like another fifteen minutes or so."

"Cool," Andi says. "I can deal with that." Then she pops her AirPods in and rolls back into her gray cocoon.

"Night," I say softly, pulling myself up to my bunk, which doesn't feel as cozy as I'd like it to.

I used to participate in the moon dance, until last year. It was my favorite night of camp, a time when I felt free and, for a few moments, alive in a way that was about more than rules and holding my body in a certain way. But here's the thing about growing up that I'm learning: You don't always get to be free. Sometimes, you have to hold yourself back to protect yourself. Sometimes not participating is a way to stay safe.

Last year, when we heard the howl, I was ready. I jumped out of my bed fast, and I stripped down to my underwear and bra. I twirled my flashlight around the room like a lasso so that the light from it spun in circles along the ceiling and floor of the cabin. I was unstoppable, I was Wonder Woman, I was just like every other eleven-year-old girl at camp—happy and giggly and flushed with the thrill of getting to do whatever we wanted for a glorious twenty minutes. That was until I found myself jumping up and down in a mosh pit of girls by the flagpole and someone, I don't know who, reached over and pinched the soft flesh of my butt.

Then voices, snickering and someone yelling "She got that badonkadonk!"

And another, "Looks like a stripper booty to me," and another, "It's cause she's Black. Black girls always have big butts."

When I spun around to see who had touched me, I was met with a sea of mostly white girls—some my friends, others not—nobody looking me in the eye or noticing that I'd stopped dancing. Nobody noticed that my smile had faded, and that I was covering my stomach and my full chest with my arms.

It was only a few minutes into the moon dance, but I went back to the cabin. I put my PJs back on and curled into my bunk. When I woke up the next morning, I put a smile on my face. But I'll never do the moon dance again.

"Hey . . ." Andi has pulled herself up to my bunk so that her arms rest on the side bar. "That was a joke, by the way."

"What was?"

"I mean, about you keeping your shirt on. I wasn't trying to say anything negative about you . . . I just. I was joking. If you want to go dance with all of them, I won't judge you. I know you love to dance."

"Sure," I say, my heart doing a little kick. "Thanks."

"Well, good night," Andi says, retreating back to her bed.

"Good night."

"Hey, Zora . . . ," Andi calls up to me a few moments later.

"Yes?"

"I'd be down to practice together tomorrow. I know you keep offering, and we should probably meet at least once so we can tell Mr. Wright we did the whole buddy-buddy thing."

I smile into the dark. "Okay," I say.

"Before dinner, during free time? The huts by Craft Shack?"

"Meet you there."

"Cool. Good night for real."

Thirty minutes later, all of the division is quiet again. A few campers rustle in their bunks, trying to settle down after all the excitement, but most fall asleep right away, exhausted.

I am wide awake even though I know in just a few short hours the bugle will sound, and a new day will begin. I can't stop thinking about Andi's apology. About the way she said, "I won't judge you. I know you love to dance."

POODLE

"*Z*ora, it's time to focus on other talents." I can hear my mother's voice in my head. I am seven years old, sitting in the back of Mom's RAV4, swinging my legs and eating my after-ballet-class snack: string cheese and a clementine.

Every Tuesday and Thursday, Mom sat in the waiting room of the dance studio while I pliéd, sashayed, and pirouetted my way across an oak-stained floor. I was, as usual, the only Black girl in the class, but I remember I always felt beautiful. Mom made sure my leotard was always clean and fresh, never faded, and she bought me custom tights online that actually matched my nude skin tone. She made sure my two Afro puffs were pulled up tight, my edges slicked back and held in place with hairpins and gel. But that day, that day she'd watched me through the glass windows, as two girls in my class—Suzi and Mae—grabbed onto my Afro puffs, feeling them curiously and then giggling when I swatted their hands away.

"You're like a poodle," Mae had said, and Suzi cosigned by nodding her blond pigtails vigorously.

"No I'm not," I'd said then, feeling trapped, noticing in

the mirrors how even at seven my body curved and dipped in places none of the other girls' bodies did.

"Well, your hair feels just like my aunt Jessie's poodle. So I think you must be related."

I crossed my arms. "No, no I'm not." But it didn't matter. For the rest of the time we were in class, Mae and Suzi called me "poodle girl."

I must have stepped off the dance floor with rage in my eyes, because my mom was waiting right at the door to the changing room, holding my coat, sweatpants, and boots. Before I could open my mouth, she said, "Did those girls say something to you, Zora?"

I nodded, pulling on my clothes.

"Well, do you want to tell me about it? I saw them touching your hair. Did they ask you first?"

"No."

"Did you ask them to stop?"

"Yes."

"And?"

"They called me a poodle. They told me I have poodle hair."

"I see," Mom said with a pained look on her graceful face. "I'll handle this. Please go wait for me in the car, Zora."

To this day, I'll never know what my mom said or did in the moments I was waiting in the car. All I know is that when she joined me minutes later, she slammed her door hard and sat in the front seat taking deep breaths. Then she turned on the car and started playing Vivaldi's *Four Seasons*. At this point, I was done with my cheese and was peeling my clementine. We were halfway home before she said, "Zora, I am sorry those girls called you a poodle. Are you all right?"

I nodded. "It just made me sad."

"Yes, well, what they said was mean. Sometimes people don't know how to deal with the fact that our hair is different than theirs. It's no better or worse, it's just different. People are scared of what they don't know, so sometimes they make fun of it."

"I like my hair," I said then, touching the soft curls of my Afro puffs with my hands.

"I know, baby. I love your hair. It's beautiful, and just like mine."

Then there was another pause, as Mom pulled into our driveway. She didn't turn off the car, but turned to face me.

"Zora, I think it's time to refocus your talents. I know you love dance, but you also love playing flute, don't you?"

I nodded.

"Well, let's see if we can get you more lessons, and maybe we go down to dance once a week? I think you're meant to be on the stage, my little star, but I think music is where you'll shine brightest."

I was seven, and when you're seven, you do what your

parents say. I didn't exactly quit dance; we just let it slip away. It started with going down to one class a week, and then I took a semester off, and then one year I just didn't go back. My calendar was filled with flute lessons, theory practice, orchestra, and Johnson family activities. Mom was happy to see that part of my life vanish, and Dad went along with it.

What they don't know is that in my room at home, I watch YouTube dance tutorials, and then I put in my AirPods and choreograph original dances to songs I love. What they don't know is that it comes so easy to me, thinking of different moves and piecing them together into a story. When I play flute, I feel like I'm telling someone else's story, but when I dance I'm telling my own.

BUDDY BUSINESS

*W*hen I get to the practice huts the next afternoon, I place my metronome on the windowsill, drag another music stand in from an empty room, and start warming up. Andi arrives just as I am finishing arpeggios.

"You're late," I say before I can stop myself.

"My bad." Andi shrugs and leans against the open door-way. "I didn't think we set a strict time."

"We said free time. Free time starts at four o'clock." I wish I could stop the bossy train coming from my mouth, but I can't. When I'm nervous, I just get bossier.

"Well, it's four fifteen. I'm here now. Don't be mad. I was talking with Christopher for a little bit; we normally practice together. I had to let him know what was up."

"Oh, that makes sense. Was he okay with it?"

"He was fine. I told him it was mandatory that you and I practice together, assigned by Mr. Wright. He's cool with it."

We stand in silence for a few seconds. Even though it's true that we'd been assigned to be practice buddies, I don't like the way Andi says it. As if she wouldn't want to be here if it wasn't required. I want her to want to be here.

Andi clears her throat. "So, should we do this?"

"Why don't you take out your sheet music and we can go through our parts together? I can help with any that are giving you trouble."

Andi makes a pained face. "So, all of it."

"It is a really complicated piece," I say. "I'd be lying if I said it hadn't kicked my butt too."

This week, Mr. London has us playing Tchaikovsky's *Romeo and Juliet, Fantasy-Overture*, which is, like, twenty minutes long. It's high drama, just like Mr. London, and full of moody swells and bursts of furious, frantic melodies. The overture isn't really supposed to follow the story of Romeo and Juliet, Mr. London told us at the beginning of the week, but instead to mirror the different emotional tones of the play. So lots of secret love, betrayal, heartbreak, and tragedy. The flute part is all over the place.

From the blank look on Andi's face as she stares at her part on the stand in front of her, I can tell we have a lot of work to do.

In a hut nearby, we both hear Arya begin practicing her part on the harp. Arya gets to shine in this piece too, because there are some really beautiful harp passages, especially at the beginning. She might be quiet and shy, but she's very talented. Andi and I just stand listening for a few moments.

"Well, she sounds perfect," Andi says.

"She really does. Who knew she could play like that? So expressive and loud, when most of the time you can't get a word out of her."

"Except for when she's howling like a wolf-girl," Andi reminds me.

I laugh. "I did not see that coming. She was like the loudest of them all last night."

"Maybe she has moon dances of her own over there in Seattle or wherever she's from? Maybe she's all about that Twilight werewolf pack versus vampire life."

"Wait. You like Twilight?" I pause.

"Well, I've seen the movies. They're okay. I like vampires, and stories that are dark and twisty."

I shudder. "Too much bloodsucking for me. I like old rom-coms, like, from the early 2000s."

"So, where do you stand on *Romeo and Juliet*?" Andi asks, pointing to our music.

I shrug. "I mean, I guess it's okay. My mom loves Shakespeare, but that's because she's an English professor. She'd be so excited if we play this at the final showcase. But I guess this piece has a little something for both of us. Bloody betrayal and some swoony love too."

"I guess so." Andi grins. It's a big grin, like the kind she gives Christopher. So big that I notice how straight and lovely her teeth are, how her full lips curl around her smile like soft storm clouds.

"Have you ever seen the ballet?" Andi is stalling, but I don't mind.

"Yes, my mom and dad took me once on a trip to New York. But that's when I was little and still dancing . . ."

"So you don't dance anymore?"

"No. Not really."

"Well, you should. You're good at it. I mean, from what I saw at the mixer."

"Thanks. My parents aren't really supportive of anything that isn't flute related these days."

Andi shrugs. "But it sounds like it makes you happy? My mom always said that art should make you feel alive and connected, no matter what kind of art you're into—music, dance, visual art . . . ," Andi trails off.

I wait for her to continue since I really don't know that much about her life, and the only family member I've heard her talk about is her aunt. "Well, your mom sounds cool," I say after a beat.

"Uh-huh," Andi says then, starting to flip through her music aimlessly, avoiding my eyes. "Ready? Let's get this over with."

Andi and I practice for the next hour and a half, and it is exhausting. We are opposites when it comes to how we approach the music. Andi begins by reading the music, but then gets bored and just starts playing what she feels and guesses what the next part is, and I follow the music so carefully, I don't even notice that Andi has wandered off. I put on the metronome to help us both, and that works for a little bit, but inevitably Andi starts to improvise, and even though she sounds good, it's nothing Mr. London will accept and I know it.

"Why do you do that?" I ask finally.

"Do what?" Andi says.

"You can't play whatever you want. That's not how this works."

"I guess I can't really help it. Sometimes I don't even notice I'm doing it."

I shake my head. "Let's take a break."

Andi shrugs. "Want to just jam together for a little bit?"

"Just jam? Like play a duet?"

"No, I mean have a conversation with our instruments. I play something, and then you play something back, and then we jam."

"So a battle?"

Andi laughs. "No, like a jam session. You know, let's just get free and have fun."

I blink at Andi, my whole body rooted in the spot I'm standing in, my fingers stiff and unmoving on my flute keys.

"What do you call your flute?" Andi asks then.

"Um . . . nothing. I call it a flute."

"Come on, really? This is CeCe. I named it after one of my mom's favorite singers," Andi says, holding up her

157

trumpet. "And Christopher calls his trombone Sir Barton because he thinks it sounds royal or whatever."

"I guess I never really thought that deep about naming my flute."

"It doesn't have to be deep. Just something that makes you feel like you and your instrument are a team, a squad. CeCe isn't just my trumpet; she's someone I'm in conversation with all the time."

I shake my head. It is spinning with a million little mysteries I want to solve all at once.

"I used to call my ballet slippers the Twinkle Twins," I blurt. "When I was little, obviously. Sounds really stupid now."

"No, that makes sense," Andi says, nodding at me. "I have an idea."

"Uh-oh . . ."

"No, come on. I tried your way of practicing. Now you try mine."

She has a point. "Fine."

"Cool!" Andi starts to move the music stands to the side of the hut, and then lines our bags and cases up against the far wall so that the floor is mostly clear. Then she comes over to me and holds out her hand. "May I?" she says, gesturing to my flute. I hand it to her, and she carefully places it on the windowsill. Then she picks up CeCe and motions to the center of the hut. "The floor is yours, Zora."

Before I can protest, Andi closes her eyes and starts to play whatever she is seeing in the dark of her mind. Sometimes it's part of a song I recognize, and then sometimes it's nothing I've ever heard before. I stand stiff for a few moments, until Andi opens her eyes and nods at me, then closes them again, as if letting me know she won't watch if I don't want her to.

So, I start to sway back at the notes Andi plays, and then I move one foot and the next, I spread my arms up to the sky and then do a little twirl, and before I know it, Andi and I are jamming, except it's the Twinkle Twins and CeCe helping us understand one another.

"Wow!" Andi stops after I don't know how long, and I leap to a stop. "That was nice." Andi holds her hand up for a high five, and I bring mine to meet hers with a loud *slap*, and for a few seconds we keep our hands together, feeling the heat of one another's palms.

"Thanks," I say, pulling away. "I guess I don't do that in front of people often."

"Well, you should. You're good at it. Are you going to take the dance master class they posted about all over the main lodge and dining hall? Christopher was talking about it. He'd be there if it didn't cost too much."

"I'm thinking about it," I say. "I heard Jasmine Baker, the instructor, is really amazing. I put my name on the list. I just don't want to get distracted from the real goal."

"What's that?"

"Flute. Flute is the goal. Staying ahead of the game for orchestra."

"Well, why can't there be two goals?" Andi says, shrugging. "Seems like you should be able to do both."

"Maybe. Like I said, I'm thinking about it. Is it just me or is it super hot in here?" I change the subject, waving my hand in my face like a fan. What I don't say is that some of the heat is my own, my body bonfire flushed and tingly with sparks.

"Yeah, it is."

"I guess we should pack up for the day. It's almost dinnertime."

Andi nods. "Thanks for helping me. That wasn't so bad after all. I know I still have work to do, but it helped."

"Good. And thanks for that jam session."

"No problem."

We pack up, and I move slowly, not wanting our time together to end.

"Hey," Andi says as if reading my mind, "want to go get ice cream? I haven't been to the Cavity Cave at all since I've been here. I heard it's good."

The Cavity Cave is a makeshift window on the side of the rec hall that sells snacks, fries, and soft serve. I haven't been yet this year either, but last summer Beks, Julie, Jori, and I would meet there every Saturday to get a snack.

"But it's almost dinner," my bossy-train mouth says ahead of my heart.

"So? You've never had dessert before dinner?"

"I don't think I have."

"It's the best. Let's go. My treat since you got stuck with me as a buddy."

"Oh, I don't feel stuck with you . . . ," I start to say, but Andi is already halfway out the door.

So, I follow her.

When we get to the Cavity Cave, there is a line wrapped around the rec hall. I guess Andi's dessert-before-dinner idea is popular, because tons of campers are also sitting around the building in clusters eating cones. We get in line. Andi shuffles her feet, and without thinking I stand a little taller, my feet in ballet first position.

"Chocolate or vanilla?" It's the only thing I can think of to say.

"Vanilla," Andi says. "In a cup."

"In a cup?!"

This makes Andi look at me again. She raises an eyebrow. "In a cup with sprinkles and chocolate syrup."

"But you could get all that on a cone too."

Andi shrugs. "I know. I just like eating ice cream with a spoon, and sometimes sugar cones taste papery to me. I like waffle cones or a waffle bowl sometimes."

I shake my head. "Well, I like chocolate everything. On

a cone, preferably dipped in chocolate. The cone is what makes it."

"Well, I guess we both like what we like," Andi says. She doesn't say it like it bothers her or she's judging me, but just like it's a fact. I wonder what else Andi likes or dislikes. Who she hangs out with when she's not at camp, what her room at home looks like, what her favorite movie is, but instead of any of these questions, I say, "So, is your mom some kind of artist?"

Andy's face turns cloudy, and I watch her ball her hands into fists at her side.

"I mean . . . you said back there that she—"

"She was an artist. But she's gone now," Andi cuts me off.

Gone like lives somewhere else or gone like not on this earth anymore?

"Oh, okay," I say then, feeling like I hit a nerve. "Sorry, I didn't mean to be nosy."

"It's whatever. I just don't like to talk about her with people that much. She died last year."

"I'm really sorry, Andi. That's awful."

Andi nods, and turns away from me to look up into the nearby trees.

We order our ice cream next, and Andi pays for me like she promised.

"Thank you," I say, raising my cone like a glass.

162

"No problem," Andi says, raising her cup and spoon and clinking my cone.

We look around for a place to sit. I point to a bench under a nearby tree, but before we can make our way over, I hear someone calling my name.

Beks is waving at me from where she sits in a circle with Julie, Cooper, and Jori. It takes me two seconds to notice that they're also right next to a group of high school boys, including Davy Edwards.

"You can go over there, if you want," Andi says.

"No. I need a break from all the boy crazy."

Andi laughs. "I get that."

"Plus, I'll see them at dinner."

"Sure."

We make our way to the bench, and just as we're about to sit down, a trombone case comes running up to us with Christopher attached.

"Good evening!" he says, dropping his things and sitting in the middle of us.

"Hey," Andi says, concentrating on her ice cream cup.

"Hi!" I say, reaching out a hand. "I'm Zora. I don't think we've officially met. I've seen you in orchestra, though."

"Oh, I'm acquainted with you," Christopher says, in a way that sounds super snotty. He shakes my hand lightly and then pulls away. "I'm Christopher. Andi's *best* friend."

Andi chokes on her ice cream when he says this, but doesn't say anything.

"Well, nice to meet you, I . . ." But before I can finish, Christopher turns his back to me and starts to talk Andi's ear off about something Craft Shack related. While he talks, he pulls out a half-started lanyard from his bag, attaches it to a clasp on Andi's backpack on the ground, and begins to weave as he talks.

I lean in and catch Andi's eye for a second, and she gives me a small, apologetic smile between bites.

"Anyway"—Christopher leans back, remembering I'm there—"how was your buddy-buddy practice?"

"It was fun," I say.

Christopher raises an eyebrow at Andi. "Is this true?"

"Yup," Andi confirms. "Zora really helped me today. It was cool."

"Wonderful," Christopher says, but by the way he says it, I can tell he feels the opposite. "Well, I guess we can pick up where you all left off tomorrow. Since you fulfilled your buddy assignment."

Andi nods.

I take a big bite from my cone to keep from showing the messiness on my face. *What if I want to practice with Andi again? And what if she wants to practice with me too?*

"Well," I say, getting up, "I guess I'll see you later, Andi. Let me know if you need any more help."

"I think we've got it covered," Christopher answers for her.

"I'll let you know," Andi says.

"Okay, bye. Thanks for the ice cream."

"Hey, Zora!" Andi calls after me.

I turn back.

"You should definitely do that dance class tomorrow. You'll crush it."

Christopher looks suspiciously between us, but I don't care.

This is between me and Andi.

I smile so big my cheeks hurt. "I will." And then I walk away with a little skip.

NEGATIVE SPACE

*T*he next day is a perfect Harmony Music Camp Thursday. From the moment Davy sounds the morning call, the sky is a calm hazy purple that slowly turns into a cartoon blue with not a cloud in sight. The sun shines through the trees, dotting the inside of the cabin with intricate patterns of shadows and light. When Beks comes running over to my bunk to catch a glance of Davy, I jump down and decide to head outside to flag early.

"Hey, where are you going?" Beks asks. "Don't you want to stare at his dreaminess with me?"

"Not today," I call over my shoulder. "I've got bigger things on my mind. Plus, like I said, what's the point? You can't date him."

"I know that," Beks huffs, "but it's not a crime to look."

"Look all you want! I don't care," I say.

"Ohhh burrrrnnn!" I hear Jori say to Beks.

"Shut up, Jori!" Beks yells.

At flag, Aubrey goes over the general announcements, and I tune them out until I hear her start to talk about this afternoon's master classes.

"All right, today we have two guest instructors teaching

master classes during free time. The "Dance Your Story" contemporary dance class will be held in the rec hall with Jasmine Baker, and "Paint Your World" with Logan Falls will be held in the band shed. If you've signed up for either of these, please make sure you're on time. We don't want to keep our guest instructors waiting or waste your parents' money. Now go forth and have a magnificent day!"

"You're still going, right?" Andi says, sliding next to me as everyone starts to head back to the cabins to get dressed.

I nod, and pat my canvas tote, which today is not just full of music and my metronome, but also my sports bra, a black leotard, footless tights, a pair of loose jogger sweats, and a scarf to tie my locs back with. "Yes. I'm still going."

"Good," Andi says as we head toward the dining hall. "I kind of wish I'd signed up for the painting one, but it's all good. I should probably head to the practice huts during that time. *Romeo and Juliet* calls."

"You paint too?" I ask.

Andi laughs. "I'm not good at it. It just makes me feel closer to . . ."

"Your mom?" I say quietly.

We walk in silence for a few seconds, just listening to the crunch of our feet along a pine-needle-strewn dirt path. I bite my tongue to keep from saying more.

"Yeah. Painting is cool, but I like working with charcoal best," Andi starts again. "Before I came here, I was working on this piece in my art class that was all about drawing negative space."

"Negative space?"

"Stop here for a second." Andi tugs on my arm and we stand in the sunlit path. "Look up at that tree. See where the light is peeking through the leaves and branches and you can see the sky?"

"Yes."

"That's negative space. It's what's in between or surrounding an object. So instead of drawing the tree, you draw everything else, and by drawing everything else, you also end up drawing the tree."

Andi is looking up into the canopy, and I follow her gaze. For a moment, it feels like the two of us are inside of our own painting. I want to be frozen here forever.

"That's really cool," I say after a beat. "I'd like to try that sometime, even though I can't draw to save my life."

Andi shrugs, and we keep walking toward the dining hall. "I didn't think I could draw either. But this exercise really helps get you out of your head. All you are doing is drawing shapes. Takes all the pressure off."

I nod.

"Hey, I'm sorry about Christopher," Andi says. "I think he was just in a mood yesterday."

"Is he your boyfriend or something?" I don't know why I say this; I know he's not.

Andi stands rock-still on the path. "You're kidding, right? No. I'm not interested in him like that."

I shrug. "He just seemed jealous. That we were hanging out."

"I think he just . . . Well, he knows how things went down at the mixer, after I played for too long, and I think he was just trying to protect me."

"Right. That makes sense. Sorry again about all of that."

"It's all good. I'm over it, and I told Christopher that you and me are cool now. Plus, next time I'll know what to expect with the intro dances and know to *never* mess with that time limit."

"So, you think you'll come next year?" I smile.

"I didn't say all that."

We've reached the dining hall. I scan the tables for Christopher, but he's not here yet. "So, do you want to sit with—?"

"I'm gonna take my breakfast to go. I have some practicing to do this morning. But I'll see you at rehearsal. Good luck with that dance class later if I don't get to say it again."

"Thanks." I wave, watching her walk away, wishing she'd invited me to join.

DANCE YOUR STORY

*B*efore I know it, it's free time, and I'm racing over to the rec hall. When I get inside, I shove all my things into a small bathroom stall and change into my dance gear. When I emerge, I stand in front of an old mirror and wrap my locs up into a thick bun, then I take out my bright teal-and-purple scarf and wrap it around my head a few times until it ties into a small bow above my forehead. I smile at my reflection, feeling the soft stretch of my leotard against my skin and rising up and down on my toes to warm my feet up. I don't need ballet shoes for this class, just bare feet, but I look down at my toes and wiggle them anyway. "Let's do this, Twinkle Twins!" I whisper.

When I leave the bathroom, there are already ten or so other campers stretching and warming up in the main room. The room doubles as a dance studio–performance space, and, like on the night of the mixer, all the chairs and tables where campers can normally play board games are pushed to one end of the room. I drop my things on one of the tables and then pick a sunlit spot and sit in the center of the floor. I look around for a familiar face and spot Angie from my cabin a few feet away. I wave, and she nods quickly back at me but is predictably deep in conversation with one of the only two boys in the class. Like Beks, Angie is boy obsessed, but instead of having her eye on just one guy, Angie has already been on Cavity Cave dates with two of the three boys in her French horn section. I shake my head and pull my legs up into a butterfly stretch, then I lift my arms up and fall over my legs until my shoulders and back relax into the movement.

One thing people always assume about me is that I'm not flexible, but I love proving them wrong. You don't have to be skinny to do the splits or reach your toes. You just have to practice deep breathing and focus little by little on strengthening your hamstrings, glutes, shoulders, abs, and neck. I love the way I can feel my body getting stronger each time I stretch, each time I push myself to perfect a new pose, to fill the space of a room up with the alternating shapes of my limbs and arms. It's one of the only times I can quiet my mind and just listen to the breath entering and leaving my lungs.

"Good afternoon, everyone!"

I pull my head up and adjust my gaze on the voice. I lock eyes with a petite Black woman wearing a navy jumper made out of flowing fabric. Her shaved head is smooth like an almond and glistens in the afternoon light. Her feet are bare, but her toenails are painted a neon orange, and on her left bicep she wears a gold arm cuff in the shape of a snake.

I should recognize her from the master class flyers, but she looks so much smaller and even more beautiful than in her pictures. This is Jasmine Baker—the famous contemporary dancer and choreographer from Detroit—and her presence fills the whole room so that everyone falls into a hushed, attentive silence.

"Please, everyone, let's make a semicircle." Then she points at me. "This young person here, what is your name?"

I gulp. "Zora."

"Great. Everyone please make a semicircle around Zora here, who is at the center. And, while we're sitting and getting to know one another, we'll warm up. Zora has a great stretch going, so let's all do the same, by putting our feet together at the soles, and sitting up tall and straight as we push our arms down onto the top of our butterflied legs to get a nice deep stretch in our inner thighs."

I try not to look pleased as everyone scrambles to meet me on the floor.

As we sit, Ms. Jasmine starts to pace gracefully in front of us, placing her hands behind her back and lacing them together to get a stretch in her shoulders.

"Good. My name is Jasmine Baker, but you can just call me Ms. J. This class is called *Dance Your Story*, and I'm going to ask that you all open your minds and let your understanding of what dance can be expand. How many of you have taken a ballet class before?"

Everyone's hand shoots up.

"And how many of you have taken a contemporary dance class or another form of dance?"

Most of the hands go down, including mine. Angie and the boy from cabin one she was flirting with keep theirs up, and Angie says, "I take hip-hop and tap back home."

"My parents made me take swing dance," the boy—Ethan, I think is his name—says bashfully.

Ms. J. nods. "Wonderful. So, it sounds like many of you have the fundamental techniques that ballet provides, which is a good place to start. But today, I'm going to ask you to forget about some of that. Contemporary dance— the kind of dance that I practice—is all about finding freedom and relaxation within your movement. What do you think I mean by that?"

The room is quiet. I press down harder on my butterflied legs and lean in to hear what Ms. J. will say next.

"Anyone? Take an educated guess. I'll wait," Ms. J. continues. "And while we wait for someone to answer, let's transition into a new stretch. Everyone extend your legs out in front of you. Let's flex our feet and roll our ankles around to warm them up."

We shuffle our bodies and extend our legs out, but still nobody says anything. I feel a tangle of mystery words fall out of my mouth. "Maybe it means, try not to be so perfect? Get a little weird with your movements?"

Ms. J. is on the floor with us now. "Yes, and . . . ?" she asks as she twists her ankles around like slow, powerful wind-mills. "That's a great start, Zora. What else? And please say your name when you talk, so I can start to learn them."

"Uh. I'm Sam," the other boy in the class pipes up. "Is it less about learning the steps, but more about creating inter-esting shapes with your body?"

Ms. J. nods and motions with her hands for us to keep going.

"I think you also probably have to be really in tune with your breath," Angie says.

"Indeed," Ms. J. says. "Everybody stand up now. Let's roll our shoulders and neck out. There's one more thing I'm looking for. You all are right on track."

I stand up. I'm definitely one of the tallest people here, but I stand strong and firm in my spot, my mind search-ing for the last piece. Then I remember being in the practice huts with Andi. How she'd closed her eyes and just felt her way through a melody while I responded back with my movements.

"A conversation!" I yell out, then, quieter, "it's the free-dom to be in conversation with your body, the music, and another dancer's body."

Ms. J. leaps off her feet and does a little joy-filled move-ment in the air. "Yes! Exactly. Today, I want you to be curi-ous, get messy—and ugly, even—with your poses; think about how your breath is shaping your movements, and I want you to express yourself, your feelings, your emotions in a way that tells a story and invites conversation."

My heart sings with anticipation when she says this. I, too, want to do a little joy-leap into the air. I look around to see if everyone is with me, as excited for what's next as I am, but most of the other participants have nervous looks on their faces.

"Excellent. Now that we've cleared that up, it's time to begin." Ms. J. walks over to where her phone is plugged into the sound system. "I'm going to play a series of songs— about two minutes from each—and I want all of you to just listen, absorb the mood of the music, and then tell me a story with your movements. Any questions?"

"But what are the steps?" a girl with pigtail buns says, standing in a neat ballet first position.

I shake my head. *There are no steps*, I say to myself. I can't believe I'm so excited for this, but this is what I do all the time, in my room. Listen to a song I like, then start to move. There are no rules, no expectations—other than to just be true to yourself in the moment.

"Well," Ms. J. answers, "if it makes you feel more comfortable, you can start with some steps or moves you already know, but the point of this is that I'm not going to tell you how to do it. You have the freedom to make it yours. Everyone ready?"

Nobody says a word, but I nod furiously, my legs aching to start.

"Good! First song is called 'My Girls,' by Animal Collective. Here we go."

Ms. J. hits play, and the room fills with a song I've never heard before, a synthesizer and faraway echoing voices bubbling through the chaos. It's both joyful and full of longing. As if Ms. J. knows we're going to need a little encouragement, she starts to roll her shoulders and then creep-slink-crawl her way across the floor. She moves as if none of us are here, as if this is her own private dance studio. I've never had a teacher who dances with us. It is awesome. "Don't forget your breath!" she yells as she twists on the ground and then leaps up onto her feet in one big, blooming movement.

We all exhale together, and then start to move. I close my eyes so I can just focus on myself. The music makes me feel like I'm spinning, like when my dad used to whirl me around the yard by my arms. How I'd watch our backyard turn into a blur of rosebushes, oak trees, and green grass. I start to turn my body around and around, pulling my arms in and out, slowly standing up until I'm so dizzy I fall to the ground and lie flat like a leaf pinned by gravity. I giggle and open an eye, but nobody is watching. I lie still and breathe in and out until I feel my way to the next movement, which is more of a stretch as I curl my body into itself and uncurl myself as if I am being pulled back by the earth. Right as I am getting really into this, the music ends.

I open my eyes and scramble to my feet.

Ms. J. is at the sound system again. "That was a good start. Try not to compare yourself to others around you. If you need to, close your eyes. I saw some of you doing that. Okay, this next song is called 'Rise,' by Andra Day. Go!"

This song I know. This song I love. Andra's gravel-silky voice fills the room, and I don't hesitate this time. I fly across the floor in a series of leaps. When I get to the other end of the room, I stop. I plant myself firmly in the space I'm in. Stand tall. I hold my arms up and start to sway and move them around in different shapes. I think about the light shining through the trees. About how Andi said, *When you draw the negative space of the branches and leaves, you end up drawing the tree.* So, I stop tree-swaying. Instead I try to turn my body, my breath into some of the light-filled shapes I'd seen this morning; instead I paint a picture of two girls who belong to the woods, to the sky, to everything that's unseen and unspoken. I'm so focused that I don't even realize the music has ended until Ms. J. claps her hands.

"Brava!" she says as I come to a halt. "That's what I'm talking about. What Zora just did there was a whole story. Let's keep going."

After a few more songs of free dance, Ms. J. teaches us a

short routine, but it still has areas where we insert our own interpretations. Too soon, it's time to cool down and do some recovery stretches. The sun melts into the lake in the windows behind us, and Ms. J. makes sure to thank us all for taking the time to dance with her. We end class with three deep, cleansing breaths and then a round of applause, and then it's over. I am drenched in sweat and everything in my body hurts, but it is a good hurt—the kind of hurt that means I've worked hard. I've grown stronger.

As I pack up my things, Ms. J. comes over to me with an eyebrow raised.

"So, Zora. Do you dance back home?"

"I used to, but only ballet. Flute takes priority in my life now."

"Well, you have a musicality when you dance that can't be taught. You should be dancing more. I can tell it brings you joy."

"It does . . . I guess. Well, I like to make up dances on my own. Kind of like what we did today."

Ms. J.'s eyes twinkle knowingly. "I thought so. The great thing about dance is that you can do it anywhere. Where's home for you, Zora?"

"Ann Arbor."

"Ah-ha! Perfect. I have something for you then." Ms. J. runs over to her things and then glide-skips back across the room and hands me a flyer. "This is a special dance troupe I run specifically for Black youth in the Detroit-Metro area. I think you'd really enjoy it, and we've had a few dancers join us from Ann Arbor and Ypsilanti before. We are audition based, but we don't require prior training—just a passion for dance and storytelling. We hold auditions the first week in September. I'd love to see you there."

I stare at the flyer and feel my body turn heavy. *Mom and Dad will never drive me the forty-five minutes to Detroit for this.* "I don't think my—" I start.

"Just consider it. No pressure," Ms. J. says. "I can just tell you're a storyteller, Zora. You were one of the most expressive people today in class."

I was! I feel a thousand little feet dancing lightly around my rib cage, but all I say is a shy "Thank you."

"You're welcome. Keep doing what you're doing. I really hope I see you this fall." I nod, not quite believing what I am hearing, and then Ms. J. floats away to talk to another student.

I shove the flyer into my bag. *Maybe there is room for dance and flute. Maybe.* My body hums.

PADDLE, PADDLE

Thwack thwack thwack. I roll over onto my stomach on my towel and watch as Andi and Christopher hit a volleyball back and forth with some other campers. It's Friday afternoon, and the lakeshore mixer is in full swing. After a long morning rehearsal, where Mr. London lectured us on making it through week two of camp and the importance of keeping focused for the remainder of our time together, it's finally the weekend. Time for some fun.

Unlike last week's dance mixer, the lakeshore mixer is one large beach party. In midafternoon, the lifeguards get out all the kayaks and inner tubes, the counselors set up the sound system and blast loud, upbeat music, and the sand fills with towels and bags as campers from the boys' and girls' junior division join the fun. Delicious, woody-smelling hickory smoke floats through the air as the dining-hall staff stand over a large grill flipping burgers and hot dogs.

My towel is laid out in a cluster with Beks's and Jori's, but they are out on the lake floating and tanning in donut-shaped inner tubes. Julie's towel is also here, but she's swimming furious lap races in the water against Coop. Turns out

Coop is an even more competitive swimmer than Julie, and they keep beating her, so Julie keeps asking for do-overs. It looks exhausting, if you ask me. I took a quick dip earlier, but I am happy in my spot in the sun. It feels good to rest my tired muscles against the warm sand, my body still aching with joy from yesterday's dance class. Plus, I can see Andi from here, and I'm trying to get up the nerve to ask her to go kayaking with me.

Last night before bed, she'd popped her head up to my bunk. "How was it? Your dance class?"

I grinned, and leaned closer to her. "Amazing! The best. Totally worth it."

"Nice! I bet you killed it."

I nodded. "What you taught me about negative space really helped. I mean, I thought about it as I was dancing, and I—"

"Lights out!" Joanna yelled, interrupting us. "Everyone needs to be in their own bunk in the next ten seconds."

"I'm glad it helped," Andi whispered quickly. "Maybe you can tell me more about it tomorrow? At the lakeshore mixer?"

I nodded. "Sounds good!"

"Cool. Night," Andi said, disappearing below me into her own bed.

"Night," I said into the dark, my mouth full of stories I wanted to tell her, and only her.

Now is my chance, but Andi has been playing volleyball since she got to the beach, laughing and joking with Christopher, and I have yet to catch her eye. I'm not sure she remembers her offer to hang out. I sigh and sit up, turning my back to Andi. *Stop being so obvious.* I rummage through my bag and pull out an unopened letter from Kennedy, her neat handwriting scrawled across the front of a long envelope. To be honest, I've been avoiding it since it got delivered a few days ago. I take a deep breath now and tear it open.

Wednesday, June 30

Dear Zora,

I can't believe it's almost been a whole week since you left for camp. I just got to my dad's in Oakland a few days ago, and it's pretty good. My dad has a new girlfriend, a woman who sings in his band, so I guess we're meeting her for dinner in San Francisco tomorrow.

Anyway, I hope it's ok I'm writing to you. I've been thinking a lot about movie night and how I acted. You said some pretty mean things, but I also don't think I reacted very well. I was surprised.

Zora—I love you. I love you so much, but I guess the way you know in your gut that you like girls, well I just know in my gut that I like guys. So, maybe when we get back this summer we can start over? I'll be better at listening, I promise. I want you to have a crush too, then you'll be the one acting all stupid and mushy over someone who shares your feelings. I know that we like to watch all those rom-coms where only white girls get the guy, but I think we both deserve our own rom-coms—where we are the stars. Where we get asked to the prom, where we get to dance, feel breathless and beautiful. Gah! I hope this makes sense. I hope we are still best friends. I miss you.

Your (straight but very supportive)
best friend for life,
Kennedy

I laugh at her sign-off and carefully fold her letter back up. I sniff the envelope, and for a slight moment I imagine I get a whiff of ocean and eucalyptus. How strange that just last week, I was sure I'd ruined everything, but today feels like the beginning of something bigger than just me and Kennedy. There are so many things I want to tell her. I take out a blank sheet of stationery and pen a reply:

Friday, July 9

Dear Kennedy,
I can't lie, I was really nervous when your letter came. I didn't open it for a few days, because I was sure you were mad at me. I've been thinking about what happened at movie night, and really just hating myself for how it all went down. I'm sorry. I'd really like to start over too, and I am sorry that I said nasty things about you and Cole, and boys in general. I was just hurt when you laughed at me, and I guess, you're the first person I've admitted that out loud to—that I like girls more than boys. It's just kind of new, like I'm still a mystery to myself in some ways. And you're the girl I spend the most time with, so, you know, I guess...well. I just want, like you said, to feel like someone sees me too, thinks I'm beautiful. This probably makes no sense, but I just feel like I have all this energy inside of me, and I'm not sure where to put it. I thought it was enough just to put it all into my music, but I think this summer I'm learning that

that's not enough. Anyways, write to me again and
let me know how meeting your dad's new GF goes.
See you soon.

Your (questioning but probably gay)
BFF,

Zora

"Who's that to?"

Andi plops down next to my towel, out of breath, her
knees dusted with sand.

I stuff the letter into an envelope and quickly put everything back into my bag. I'll swing by the main lodge and
send it out after the mixer.

"My best friend back home," I say, trying to ignore the
way I can feel heat and sweat radiating off Andi's body,
how it makes me sit up taller and lean slightly toward the
sweet smell of her, my legs stretched out long in front
of me.

"Cool," Andi says, wiping her brow. "She's not a camp person like you?"

"No, not really," I say. "Do you want some of my water?
You look . . . thirsty." I change the subject, not sure I'm ready
for my Kennedy and Andi worlds to collide.

"Sure. Thanks. It's hotter than I thought out here."

I try not to stare as Andi takes a few big gulps. *Ask her.
Ask her now.* My heart beats faster and faster.

"Do you want to go out in a kayak with me?" I say, at the same time she says, "Want to go on an adventure?"

We smile.

"*You* like kayaking?" Andi teases, handing me back my water. "I thought for sure you were a stay-on-land kind of Black person. Thought I'd have to force you to do something fun."

I stick my tongue out. "For your information, I go kayaking with my parents all the time. They're big on exercise and getting outside on the weekends, and I love the water and water sports. I'm a Michigan girl, after all."

"Well, okay then. Let's go. Show me." Andi stands, and holds out her hand to me.

I take it and she pulls me to my feet. "Sure, but I'm steering."

"Fine by me. I like sitting up front."

A few minutes later, Andi and I are strapped into our life vests, me in the back seat of the tandem kayak, her up front ready to push out gently into the water.

"Hey! Andi. Where are you going?" Christopher appears next to us, his shadow looming. "I thought we were going to swim?" he says, side-eyeing me.

"We can swim when I get back," Andi says.

"Well, how long will you be?" Christopher says, tapping his foot on the sand.

"I dunno, not long."

"Hi, Christopher," I say. "Do you want to come with us? There's still a free single kayak." *Say no, say no, say no*, I think to myself, but I keep a welcoming grin on my face.

Christopher looks at me, a glint of something wounded in his eyes. "Yes, I think I will."

"Really?" Andi says. "You told me earlier you hated boats!"

"I said no such thing. I said I hated being on big boats. But how hard can it be to steer your own small one?" With that we watch as Christopher runs over to the lifeguard managing the kayak gear, gets a life vest and a paddle, and drags a single-seater red kayak over to us. Very tentatively, he steps into it and teeters as he sits, finding his balance. Andi turns back to look at me as if to say, *Sorry about this*, and I raise an eyebrow.

"You ready?" Andi says to me, and then to Christopher.

"Most certainly," Christopher says.

"Ready," I say. "Let's go."

As soon as we start out, I can tell Andi and I have a natural rhythm. We dip our paddles into the silver-blue water and glide effortlessly toward the center of the lake. Behind us, Christopher teeters and grunts, trying to keep up, and then we hear a yelp and a *splash!* When we turn around, Christopher is standing shoulder-deep in the water, his kayak flipped over not far from him.

"Are you okay?" Andi yells.

Christopher sputters, then sweeps a mop of black hair from his face. "Fine. I'm fine!" he yells, but then, assessing the overturned kayak, he says, "I think I'll stay on the beach after all."

"You sure?" Andi says. "Need help?"

Christopher nods. "I'm fine. I don't need your assistance." And then he wades his way back to land, dragging his kayak with him like a sad fish. When he gets to shore, he attempts to march away from us, head held higher than necessary. But it's not really a march, more of a shaky-knee jerking hobble.

I stifle a laugh. "Is he going to be all right?"

Andi shrugs and shakes her head, turning back around to face the front of our kayak. "I knew that was going to happen. I'll check on him later. Let's keep going."

"You got it."

As we paddle, I talk to Andi about Ms. J.'s class and how I really felt like I was telling a story when I danced. She listens, nods, asks a bunch of questions, and before I know it we stop in the middle of the lake and just float. Above us a pair of hawks circle in the air, locked in a graceful duet. I go quiet as Andi looks up, shielding her eyes from the sun, following the birds' movement across the sky. I can't see her face, but her shoulders start to climb toward her ears, and her back goes tense as if the sun has finally gotten to her and maybe she is tired of our adventure already. Or maybe

I've talked too much, and she's regretting agreeing to spend time with me.

"Do you want to go back?" I ask.

Andi shakes her head, and then, still looking up at the hawks, says, "Do you believe in ghosts?"

"I think so. I mean, I've never seen one. But I guess anything is possible. Why?"

"So, you think it's possible that a person or place could be haunted?"

"Well, maybe. I don't like to think about revenge hauntings, like some of the scary stories counselors like to tell at campouts. But my dad says that sometimes he feels like his grandpa, my great-grandpa Earl, is close by whenever he does activities they used to do together when he was a kid, like fishing or hiking. Like, he feels a presence."

Andi nods. "I get that. But . . . do you think ghosts, even when they are family ghosts, can be mad at you?"

I stare at the back of Andi's head. I wish she would turn around and look at me so I could see the expression on her face. *Was she thinking about her mom? Why would her mom be mad at her?*

"I—"

"Never mind," Andi says then, looking away from the birds and turning to face me in the kayak. "It's stupid."

"No, it's not. You can tell me more if you want."

"Thanks, but I'm good. And you," she says, motioning

around us, "are letting us drift a little too far away from camp."

"Me!" I splash Andi with my paddle. "I thought we were in this together?"

"Yeah, but you wanted to steer, Captain." Andi grins wide, her face and shoulders relaxed again.

I splash her some more, and she retaliates, until we are both soaked. We hear a whistle, and look over to the beach where the lifeguards are waving campers back in from the water.

"Is the mixer over already? I guess we've been out here for longer than I thought," Andi says.

"I guess so. That went fast. Sorry, I know you were supposed to swim with Christopher."

Andi shrugs. "This mixer is much more my speed. Plus, I had fun with you. I haven't been on a kayak with anyone since—my mom."

I smile, and nod. "I had fun too," I say, trying to ignore the fluttering in my chest.

To think that last week I'd been fuming at Andi for messing up our dance, and now we are paddling back to shore, our arms pumping in rhythm, our skin sparkling with sun and water.

I almost wish we could stay out on the lake forever.

Harmony Music Camp

I learn new things too
Like the other afternoon, a passing conversation
Two cousins, floating in inner tubes
Toes hovering, but not touching Lake Harmony's
Calm, blue-silver surface

Did you know   says the girl with skull earrings
And Sharpie doodles all over her legs
          That Lake Harmony is a tributary? It flows
          Into the Cherry River, and then the Cherry River
          Flows into Lake Michigan
Did you know all this water is connected?

I don't hear the other camper's response
Because I am watching the girl with the black hair
Hold her arms out wide, as if she is trying
To gather all the water she speaks of into her heart

I've never known any other water
If I wasn't nestled here, against Lake Harmony
Waiting for the cannonball splash of kids
Jumping off my dock
          I don't know what I'd do
I've never seen any other kind of blue
Or imagined what other lakeshores might be out there

But that's the thing about being a place
People return to again and again
Sometimes you stay where you are
So someone else can grow up and fly away
Sometimes you only get a glimpse of the world
Through someone else's eyes

I don't wish to be anywhere else
I'm happy here, on my land
But, long after the two girls are gone
After the loud music from the beach has quieted
I can still feel the spark of their words
Dancing in my wooden mind
> *All this water is connected*
> *A tributary is a river that flows*
> *Into a larger river or lake*
> > *Did you know?*

I learn that even when I can't see
Past the tree line of my own woods
I am a part of something
Bigger than myself
Many rivers
Many songs
Coming together as one

WEEK THREE

Andi

HAUNTED

I am old enough to know that ghosts don't appear the way they do in movies—all white-sheet-like and spooky. They don't yell *boo!* or have empty, hollow holes for eyes. Ghosts are more like memories—memories you can't shake, memories that appear in dreams or daydreams.

And I can't dream without Mama showing up. After the lakeshore mixer, I don't sleep well, even though at curfew I collapse, exhausted, into my sleeping bag, thinking about being on the water with Zora, the sun glittering on our skin, my muscles tight and sore from paddling. No matter how hard I try to be normal, to let go of the past, I keep dreaming the same dream and then waking up all sweaty and windblown in my bunk.

In the dream, Mama and I are standing at the bottom of a dune climb. It's early morning, so no one else is around. We take off our shoes and roll the hems of our jeans up. "I'll race you!" Mama says, a hungry wind weaving through her Afro. She starts running before I can answer.

Mama is a bold black paint stroke against the tan sand. She smears joy all over the morning with her laughter. I scramble after her until we get to the top and collapse, and then we roll over on our backs to inspect the sky.

Mama puts up her hands and laces her thumbs together. Then she flaps her fingers like wings, moving them in circles. When I squint my eyes, her hands look like the real thing—a hawk maybe, soaring through the air. I put my hands up too. I interlace my thumbs and I start to follow her. Then we are flying together as the sun rises.

"Andi?" Mama says. "Life is what you make it. Don't forget to paint your own reality."

"I won't," I say, even though I'd say just about anything to stay like this forever. I just know I don't want to land.

I close my eyes and disappear into the coconut scent of her hair. When I open them moments later, Mama is gone. I put my hands down and try to sit up, but my whole body is pinned to the sand. I lie on my back, frozen, for what feels like hours. I wait and wait and wait for her to return. Then I wake up.

I am old enough to know that Mama and I have more to say to one another. That this dream, and the ones before, mean we are unfinished. I sit up in the early-morning dark of the cabin, feeling all the air gone out of my chest. That familiar panic setting in. *Not now, not now.* I start to inhale *1, 2, 3, 4,* exhale *1, 2, 3, 4 . . .*

Above me, I hear Zora shift into a new position. When

Zora isn't bossing people around, she isn't so bad. I like talking to her, kayaking with her.

I think about shaking her awake so I can tell her what I couldn't say out on the water: *I did it. I'm the reason why my mom can't rest easy. I ruined everything she loved.*

But this, this is between me and Mama. Mama and I are an unfinished painting. A sky with nothing in it. We need an ending that makes sense. I take a deep, long breath in and out. I snuggle down into my sleeping bag. Soon it will be morning, a new week. Maybe, if I can get my soul-sound back, if I work harder on my parts, Mama will understand: I never meant to hurt her. I loved her. More than anyone.

SEAT AUDITIONS #3

On Sunday, when I audition for Mr. Wright, I manage to stay above water. I don't float away from myself, and I keep a steady focus on the notes in front of me. It's not my most heartfelt performance, and I still get tripped up on some of the more technical runs, but I read the music, and it is my best seat audition since I arrived at Harmony Music Camp.

"That was such an improvement, Andi!" Mr. Wright claps when I'm finished. "Really good work this week."

I nod and shrug. "Thanks."

"It seems like being paired with Zora helped you. I knew it would. Sometimes it's just nice to have someone from the same background to help translate."

I cross my arms. "I don't need translation, Mr. Wright. I understand just as well as anybody here what's going on. I just learned to play music a little differently than some of the kids here."

"Oh, of course, Andi," Mr. Wright says quickly. "I just meant, well, there are studies that having a role model or peer of the same race is important to . . ."

"It's cool. I get it. Am I done now?" I can't stand listening to any more of this.

Mr. Wright laughs and stacks and restacks the pile of music in front of him. "Yes, great work again, Andi. Go ahead and send the next person in."

I pack up my things and head out of the room so fast, I run right into Channing in the doorway.

"Oh my word—slow down, Andi."

"My bad," I say. "He's ready for you."

"I know. That's why I was standing here. How did you do?"

"I did fine."

Channing furrows her brow just a little but then puts on a big fake smile. "Well, I'm glad you managed to keep up. I better go in. First-chair duties call."

I want to smack Channing in her smug face, but I don't. For once, I just wish Channing could admit she's working just as hard as everyone else. That she's not the only one who has talent. That even though she's been able to hold on to first-chair trumpet so far, that doesn't make her a better person than me. But I keep my mouth shut. I don't need to get into any more fights. Especially not after what happened at the end of school this year.

If there's one way I'm like Mama, it's that I'm not really a "school is cool" person. I'm smart; I just don't care as much about grades and doing things the way everyone else does them. Music has always been my thing. When I put my lips to my trumpet and blow, the world fades away. I become one with my breath, the notes and the rhythms. I guess I play trumpet the way Mama painted—wild, dreaming, and free. Even though school isn't my favorite, I hadn't meant to get suspended in the last week of seventh grade. In fact, everything was finally going okay in my new life with Aunt Janine and Uncle Mark. Instead of sitting in the back of the class with my AirPods in like I did all through September when I'd first arrived at East Hills, I'd really been trying. Sure, I didn't have many friends at East Hills, and most kids ignored me, but I had some dudes I was cool with in band, and at home Aunt Janine, Uncle Mark, and I were getting along. The only other class I had an A in at East Hills, besides band, was art. I'm not good at art—I paint like a toddler—but taking the class made me feel closer to Mama, helped me understand what she loved so much about throwing colors onto a canvas. It was the one class where I could just sit in front of the big art-room windows and escape from my reality for a while.

I liked working with the charcoal best. I liked how messy it felt in my hands, how you could smear and rub and blend it into different shades of gray and black. That day, the day of the incident, I'd been in a foul mood by the time the fifth period rolled around after lunch. Earlier, in first-period math, Amy Vanden-Vampire had been giggling with a group of boys a few rows over from me when she passed me a note. When I opened the note, there was a T-chart drawn. One column said *Chicks* and the other said *Dudes*, and then under it said *How many of each have you kissed?* I crumpled the note up, and then as the bell rang I hissed in her ear, "I kissed your mom last night!" before heading out to my next class. As I was leaving, I heard her turn to the group of guys and say, "See, told you she was a lez."

I spent all of lunch that day sitting with fellow brass-heads Tommy and Will from band as they flicked fries across the table at each other. I glared at Amy as she waltzed into the cafeteria and winked at me. Amy was very pale—the kind of white person who is almost see-through—with white-blond hair, accented with teal tips, which is the only color besides black I'd ever seen her wear (we have that in common). Like she did most days, Amy was wearing a black jean jacket, torn-up black jeans, and combat boots, and she was carrying a filthy canvas tote that read FEMINIST WITCH. I looked away and grimaced. Tommy, who plays tuba, caught my grimace and followed where my gaze had been.

"Ew," he said. "Forget Amy Vanden-Vampire, Andi. Everyone knows she's a pasty mess. Want me to push her out into the sunlight so she melts?"

"Would you?" I said, and then laughed hard and long until the urge to punch someone vanished.

I'd almost forgotten about her little note trick when I got to art, but as I walked in, there she was, glowering at me from behind her easel. By some sick luck, I had almost every afternoon class with the witch. As I tied on my smock, Amy blew an exaggerated kiss my way.

I grabbed my easel and a fresh piece of charcoal, ignoring Amy. Then I set myself up a couple of rows in front of her, facing the window so I could get a good view of my subject—the oak tree. I was working on my final showcase piece that day. It was all about negative space. I'd been working on the piece for a couple of weeks, and it was starting to take shape nicely. I probably could have worked on it forever, but Ms. Dunbar always said, "A piece of art is never really done. You just have to get to a point where you let go and let it be what it's going to be." I understood where she was coming from, but I also wanted it to be the best I could make it. I wanted to have at least one positive thing to show Aunt Janine and Uncle Mark at the end of the year. When I'd worn my piece of charcoal down to a tiny nub, I headed to the supply shelves for more. But the noise of the room faded in slowly, and I became aware of the hushed voices behind me.

"What even is that charcoal mess?" Amy Vanden-Vampire's evil giggle snaked its way into my ears. I knew she was talking about me. My piece. "It's so dark, so scary. Like, she might be clinically insane."

Another girl, Bella, giggled nervously. "Right? What's her damage anyway?"

"Well, you didn't hear it from me, but I heard her mom was a crackhead from the D."

"What?! Really? I heard that her mom died in a car crash. Was she on drugs when it happened?"

"Probably. So, you know what that means . . ."

I whipped around to face Amy, who knew I could hear her and smirked at me. I watched as she scrunched her arms up to her chest, and mimicked a twisted, disfigured infant. "Andi is a crack baby."

I got up then, without saying a word, and walked over to where Amy was sitting in front of her easel. She'd been working on a mixed-media collage with paint and scraps of magazines. I actually liked her piece. It was full of color and texture. Unlike her bland, bullying, translucent face.

"You need to QUIT talking about my mom, RIGHT NOW," I said.

"Andi. Will you please get out of my personal space?" Amy said, leaning away from me like I smelled. Her eyes were wide.

"I will get out of your space, when you stop talking about things you don't know anything about."

"I have no idea why you're so angry, but you're making me uncomfortable," Amy said, even louder this time. "Ms. Dunbar! Ms. Dunbar!"

Before Ms. Dunbar could make her way over to us, I was already moving with the same hot-headed power I'd felt the day Mama died. I picked up a tub of green paint from a nearby table and I threw it directly onto Amy's piece. It splattered everywhere and dripped down onto the floor.

The room went still. Amy blinked in disbelief, and then like a baby she scrunched up her face and started to cry. I didn't wait for Ms. Dunbar to tell me anything. I just gathered all my things, took off my smock, and stormed right out of that stupid class. Ms. Dunbar yelled for me to come back, but I was having a hard time breathing.

It's one thing to be the new kid, but it's a whole other thing to be the new kid whose mom died. People either ignore you or act jealous and mean because of the attention they think you're getting. Amy Vanden-Vampire had been torturing me since the first week I arrived at East Hills, and I'd never, not once, done anything to her. Not until the paint-throwing incident.

"We have zero tolerance for violence here at East Hills," Principal McBride explained to me and Aunt Janine in his office an hour later. After running out of art class, I'd sat in a bathroom stall for twenty minutes or so, deep breathing and cooling off. I'd felt an anxiety attack coming on, and the last thing I needed was to have it in the hallway or anywhere other kids could see me. When I'd calmed down, I splashed some cold, rusty-smelling water onto my face and then took myself to the main office. There was no use in hiding.

"I'm sorry, but I have no choice but to suspend Andi for the rest of the year," Mr. McBride continued. "We will be happy to have you back in the fall, Andi, and hopefully by then you will have learned a lesson. I have to keep the safety of students in mind, and what you did today violated that. Do I make myself clear?"

I sank down into the hard wooden chair I was in and nodded. "Yes, sir." I was afraid to turn my head to see the expression on Aunt Janine's face, but I could feel the anger radiating off her body as she straightened her back and leaned forward.

When Aunt Janine finally spoke, her voice was even and strong. "Mr. McBride, I understand that Andi's actions were not the right ones, and that she needs to face consequences; however, what is being done about the young lady who was bullying her? What actions will be taken to ensure the safety of Andi if she returns next fall? It was my understanding, from reading the parent handbook, that East Hills also has a zero-tolerance policy for bullying?"

Wait a minute. Did Aunt Janine say "if" I return next fall?

"Well, yes. We did get both sides of the story, and talk with some other students who witnessed the incident, and the other party involved is facing consequences."

"So, she is also getting suspended for the rest of the year?" Aunt Janine pushed.

"Well, uh, seeing as Amy did not deface another student's

property, she has not been suspended, but has received three days of detention."

"But she used a classist and, quite frankly, racist term, which I believe is just as violent as, if not more violent and harmful than, defacing property. And not only today, but, as Andi has revealed, most of this year she's been calling Andi names. If I'm hearing correctly, you don't see the connection?"

A stuffy stillness entered the cramped office. I snuck a glance at Aunt Janine, who, to my surprise, was smiling, but it wasn't a friendly smile—it was more of a gritted-teeth I-will-kill-you-with-my-kindness smile.

"Well, no, now you're twisting my words. Everyone has received an equitable punishment."

"I don't think you know what *equitable* means, Mr. McBride."

"Yes, well, Ms. Byrd-Rogers, like I said, we are happy to have Andi back in the fall, and both girls will be expected to reach out to one another with apologies."

"But Andi is suspended, while the other girl gets three days of detention? I don't see how that's fair," Aunt Janine pointed out again.

"That's technically what is happening, but again it's only because—"

"I see." Aunt Janine cut him off. "This is very disappointing to hear, Mr. McBride. I'd hoped East Hills was a little more inclusive than this, but I guess I was wrong. Andi, get your things. We're leaving, and I doubt we'll be coming back."

I jumped up from that chair so fast to follow Aunt Janine out, you would have thought I was a shooting star.

"Are you for real about me not coming back?" I managed to ask as we made our way down the shiny-floored hallways and out the big double front doors.

Aunt Janine didn't respond; she just marched over to the car and unlocked the doors. Once we were inside, I put on my seat belt and leaned back. Aunt Janine was extra quiet. She was never this quiet. Before we drove away, she turned to me with sparks in her eyes.

"I don't want you to think what you did was all right, because it wasn't. But, Andi, what just happened in there, *that* is the reason I told Uncle Mark I was hesitant to raise our kids in this neighborhood. I'm sorry that happened to you. That white girl should have been suspended too, but unfortunately that's not how the world works."

"I know," I said, surprised to see Aunt Janine so emotional. Even more surprised to find out she and Uncle Mark disagreed about something. I always thought it was Aunt Janine who wanted to live in this bougie area.

"You know," Aunt Janine said as she started to drive away, "I might have handled that differently than your mom would have, but lord did I want to lay my hands on that man."

"Aunt Janine, you fight?" I said, my mouth actually hanging open.

"Andi, even though your mom and I took different paths in life, don't forget we grew up together. We didn't have a mother around when we were your age, and even though your grandpa worked hard to keep us fed and housed, he wasn't present much. I had to learn to fight and stand up for myself, and so did your mom. These days, I just know that some fights are not worth losing your dignity over. I fight with my intellect and my ambition. But today it took everything in me not to throw something at that man's balding, sunburned head."

I stifled a laugh. I'd never seen Aunt Janine so heated.

We drove through the manicured and tree-lined streets of East Hills in silence. Mama wouldn't have laid hands on Mr. McBride, but she would have called him some choice words and then stormed out. But then, when we'd gotten home, Mama would have gone into her studio, closed the door, and thrown paint around until she got all her rage out, even though it was something that happened to me. Art was how Mama dealt with her anger, her hurt, and her joy. And it was beautiful but lonely to watch her create, because when she was creating, she'd forget anyone else was there. She'd forget what was my hurt and what was her hurt, what was my fight and what was hers. She'd forget me.

"Aunt Janine?" I said as we turned into the driveway.

"Yes, Andi?"

"You did it right."

"What?"

"Standing up for me."

Aunt Janine parked the car and studied my face.

"I'm sorry I let you down," I said.

"Hush now, Andi. You did no such thing. And that's what I'm here for. To protect you. Now, let's get inside."

Mama protected me too, but sometimes her way felt more like being pushed out of a nest and encouraged to fly on my own.

Aunt Janine's way felt like being tucked under a cozy wing during a storm, and I liked it.

PROFESSIONAL ONE-OF-A-KIND CREATORS

*O*n Monday, Mr. London stops us in the middle of our first full run-through of Suite I of Leonard Bernstein's *On the Waterfront.* We're only learning the first two suites— Suite I: Andante (which means "played at a walking pace") and Suite II: Adagio (which means "played slowly"). If I'm being real, both are complicated and heavy for the brass section. To my surprise, my audition landed me third chair this week. So, now there's even more pressure to keep up.

"Stop, STOP!" Mr. London shouts, and we all put down our instruments as a sound like a balloon deflating rings through the band shed. "This is week three and you all are giving me week-one focus. In fact, I'd like to hear just the brass and woodwinds now."

I gulp, and get into position. Of all the pieces we've learned this is by far my favorite, with some jazz and blues elements, and I actually want to get things right. The flutes, French horns, trombones, and timpani are also heavily featured, so sometimes in the middle of playing, I imagine Zora, Jori, Angie, Christopher and I are having a conversation, and that helps me stay on course.

We start again, and this time the strings don't join in. I focus on the notes in front of me, and also try to let the mood of the piece sink into my body. I bob my head and keep my eyes on the music.

"STOP!" Mr. London barks again.

We all stifle a collective groan.

"I want to hear JUST the French horns, trumpets, flutes, and trombones in the opening section, please. You all set the tone of this piece, and it needs to be perfect. You have to listen to one another, and right now something is off."

I relax. The third and fourth trumpets don't take part in the opening section, and I'm fine letting Channing and Jacob be in the hot seat for their duet. I need a break. Angie is also in the hot seat. She sits taller in her chair, for once not flirting with anyone and· zoned in on her music. Angie opens the whole piece with a difficult French horn solo. She's followed by flutes one and two, then the trombones, and then Channing and Jacob come in with their trumpets, then later still the rest of us join in.

Mr. London raises his baton, and Angie starts. Her playing is clear and full of emotion. Mr. London nods and tilts his head in anticipation for Zora and Ella to come in on flute, and then Christopher and his first-chair partner start to play as well. Mr. London nods them on, and then it's time for the trumpets. Channing and Jacob sit taller in their seats and take deep breaths before they begin their duet, Channing bulldozing ahead and Jacob trying to catch up.

"STOP!" Mr. London yells. "This is what needs work. Channing, your phrasing is sounding mechanical and it feels like you're rushing, which means Jacob is getting lost. I need you both to imagine your breath is a thick fog drifting off a dark dockside in the early morning, and that your instruments are calling out across that fog to the others. Can you do that? Let's hear just the two of you."

Channing's face is a little red, but she nods. "Yes, sir," she says, getting into position again. Jacob furrows his brow and sends Channing an annoyed glare, but nods.

Mr. London raises his baton, and Channing and Jacob begin again. This time, they barely make it halfway through their part.

"No, no, no!" Mr. London shouts. "Channing, you're rushing again."

"Jacob, you need to keep up! You're making me look bad," Channing hisses down our section.

Jacob opens his mouth to reply, and then closes it again.

Anna and I shift, uneasy in our seats.

Mr. London lifts an eyebrow. "Channing, I think you're missing the point. You're playing all the notes correctly, but you're forgetting that this is team effort, not a race. You need to listen a little more to Jacob, and the rest of your section, for that matter."

A dark cloud falls over Channing's face. She lifts her chin a little higher and stares straight ahead.

Mr. London continues. "Now, I've heard really beautiful phrasing coming from the rest of the trumpet section as we get further into this piece. In fact, let's try something now. Andi and Anna—I'd like each of you to try playing this duet with Jacob. Maybe one of you can help Channing hear what is missing.

"Anna, we'll start with you."

Anna, now sitting fourth chair, inhales a big gulp of air next to me. "Mr. London—I didn't prepare . . . this isn't my part . . . I . . ."

"Anna, it doesn't have to be perfect, just try your best. I know I'm putting you on the spot."

Anna nods and gets into position, and Jacob leans across me and whispers, "You got this."

After a beat, they both begin, and even though Anna is timid and plays much too quietly to be heard clearly over Jacob's more confident sound, she makes her way through the part until the end.

"Pretty good, Anna," Mr. London says. "Great breath control, but you could play louder next time. All right, Andi, you're next. Let's hear how you sound with Jacob."

I feel like I am going to sweat out of my knee socks. My

sight reading has gotten so much better since I got here, but with everyone's eyes on me, I feel like I might hurl. Jacob gives me a smile and a thumbs-up. I nod at him and hold my trumpet to my lips. *Thick fog, Andi*, I say to myself. *Just imagine a thick fog rising off water.* I take a breath alongside Jacob, and we start to play. As I begin, I keep my eyes on the notes. Then, I start to remember what Lake Michigan looks like early in the morning, the way water can be still one moment and then full of swells and waves the next. I think about how Mama and I loved to show up to that kind of stillness on our camping trips, how we'd hike in the early-morning dark just to be the first ones on the beach, the first ones to dip our toes into the lake and watch the ripples expand like hearts into the water. "It's never really still," Mama would say. "It was just waiting for us to wake it up." Mama's voice is so loud in my ears that I hardly notice the silence in the band shed when I stop playing, my mind full of ghost-memories.

"Brava!" Mr. London claps, and soon a few other members of the orchestra join him in some soft applause. Zora is turned in her seat and gives me a smile.

"That was beautiful, Andi. Very moving. And you and Jacob were great collaborators," Mr. London continues. "If you keep playing like that, you might take second chair next week. And, Channing, you could stand to learn a few things from Andi's phrasing, especially on this piece."

It's hard to focus on what Mr. London is saying, because I'm trying to get Mama's voice out of my head and also avoid the death stare I feel coming from my left, where Channing sits. My hands shake, so I shove them under my butt to calm them down. I want to return Zora's smile, I want to catch Christopher's eye, but more than anything I want the bluster of song I feel racing around my body to stay. For just a moment, playing had felt like flying again. For just a moment, I'd found my way back to my soul-sound.

"You were *amazing*!" Christopher says after rehearsal ends.

I shrug. "Thanks. That felt good."

"You killed it," Jacob says, giving me a fist bump from his seat next to mine. "I mean, I'm still going to beat you in seat auditions next week, but that was fire. We make a good team."

Channing doesn't say anything, but she's putting her things away very slowly, so I know she's listening.

"I wouldn't be sure," Christopher says, giving Jacob a friendly head shake. "Anything can happen in the last weeks of camp, and Andi's really talented. I knew it from the very beginning."

"I mean, it's clear that this camp has been good for her," Channing pipes in, "but that's to be expected with a little world-class training."

"Channing, don't be rude." Zora is by my side now. "Andi

is just as talented as any of us, and she has experience. You don't know anything about her training or life before coming here."

"And you do?!" Channing is outnumbered. "What are you, her girlfriend or something?" she snorts.

It's a joke, but nobody laughs.

So what if she were! I think to myself, my heart beating loud. But I bite my tongue instead of speaking.

Jacob gives us all an awkward peace sign and then dips out.

Next to me, I feel Zora's whole body go stiff. "Um, no," Zora stammers. "Why would you say that? We're not— We're just—"

"Friends," I say, finally. "We're just friends, just like me and Christopher are friends."

"Right," Zora adds.

Christopher is quiet. He looks back and forth between me and Zora and then clears his throat. Ever since the kayaking day, he's been a little nicer around Zora, although still weird whenever I bring her up in conversation. "Anyway," Christopher says, turning his back to Channing and blocking her from our view, "this is so not the point. Andi—you were outstanding. That's all that matters. I hope you get second chair next week, so you get to play that part."

"I agree," Zora says, letting out a sigh of relief.

"Whatever," Channing says, getting up. "I was just trying

to be nice. Clearly, y'all have formed some little P-O-C squad, and I don't feel welcome anymore."

"A what squad?" I say, winking at Zora and Christopher. "You mean a Prodigal, Outstanding, and Cool squad?"

"Yeah," Christopher says, catching on, "or maybe you mean our squad full of Perfectly Orchestral Comrades?"

"No, no," Zora says then. "She means that we're a squad of Professional One-of-a-Kind Creators."

Channing gives us a confused look as she walks out the door, but we're all laughing so hard we barely notice. Sometimes it's just easier to laugh when someone is being an ignorant fool.

LETTER FROM HOME

*Z*ora invites me to hang out at the Cavity Cave after rehearsal, but I am too tired and need some quiet. All I want to do is lie down and listen to some tunes. When I get to cabin four it's empty, and I am grateful for the privacy. I'm just pulling off my second knee sock when I notice a medium-size package at the foot of my bed. I tear it open and find an envelope with Aunt Janine's handwriting across the front, a blue rain poncho, a few boxes of Annie's strawberry toaster pastries, some extra knee socks (no, thank you!), a container of vanilla-yogurt-covered pretzels, and a bag of sour worms. At least Aunt Janine tried to send me versions of my favorite foods, even if they are the off-brand healthy ones she's always trying to get me to eat. I tear into a toaster pastry, sit back on my bunk, and open the letter.

Thursday, July 8

Dear Andi,
We hope camp is going well! Uncle Mark
is painting the baby's room, and I've been
supervising from the couch where I've been
napping and resting a lot. This pregnancy is

really kicking my butt, and I'm not feeling very well these days. That means I've had a lot of time to sit and think up fun things to send you. I hope you're not just eating junk up there, Andi. Here are some snacks that are just as delicious as the name-brand ones you love. Give them a try for me, will you? What are you playing in orchestra? Are you making some new friends? Uncle Mark and I can't wait to come see you in your final performance. I know this camp wasn't 100 percent your idea, but if you like it, maybe it can become a summer tradition for you? Anyway, we are thinking of you and will see you soon. Stay strong and bright.

Love,

Aunt Janine and Uncle Mark

PS If the baby is a girl, we want to name her after your mom, Augusta—Star for short. Would that be all right with you? I hope so. That way, your mom lives on in all of us.

I'm mid-bite when I read these last lines. (A) the Annie's pastry is okay, but it's nothing like a regular one and (B) I want to throw it across the room when I read the final part of the letter. *No. No it's not okay to give the baby Mama's name. It belongs to Mama, and no one else!* I want to yell. But instead, I shove everything back into the box and put it on my shelf. The good feeling I'd left rehearsal with is gone. Before I know it, I am running out of the cabin, out of division, past the rec hall, until I'm on the dock, which is now quiet and closed since most people are headed to dinner. I put my AirPods in and lie down on the dock, then I hit play on a Wynton Marsalis track called "Bona and Paul." I close my eyes and listen.

Mama surprised me with tickets to a Wynton Marsalis concert downtown at Orchestra Hall when I was eight. It was a crisp fall Saturday, and Mama had taken the whole day off from work just to spend time with me. We sat in the balcony that night, Mama holding my hand and squeezing it tight as the music began, and I swear I barely took a breath the whole time he was playing. My favorite part of "Bona and Paul" is when Wynton uses his mute to change the color of his trumpet's sound. He puts the mute against the bell of the horn and then flaps it open and closed as he plays so that his horn makes a *wah wah wah wah wah* kind of sound. The *wah wah wah* sound sneaks into my very bones and my whole body fills with a sad, sweet ringing. Mama knew how much I loved the trumpet, and after that concert I was even more determined to play for the rest of my life. When we left Orchestra Hall a couple of hours later, Mama and I were so full of wonder that we walked all the way to the West Riverfront Park. We stared across the Detroit River, which glittered under a bright moon.

"I'm going to play trumpet just like that one day!" I said.

"I don't doubt it, my little bird," Mama said as she wrapped me in her arms. "You're going to create beautiful things in this world, just like your mama. Now let's get our butts home. I'm cold."

As the sun nods into the horizon, I feel the lake water moving by my side, and for a moment, just a moment, I feel like Mama is holding me tight, telling me I'm going to be great. But then another memory seeps in, and I grow cold.

"Andi, stop sulking. You don't ignore inspiration when it strikes you; you have to stop everything and pay attention to it."

It's that same Saturday, the morning of the concert. I am dressed and sitting on our couch, glaring at Mama. Mama is still in her PJs, washing her brushes in the sink. She'd promised me we'd have the whole day to ourselves, that we were going to drive out to Wiard's Orchard to pick pumpkins, get lost in the corn maze, and drink cider and eat cake donuts. But Mama was barefoot and showed no signs of making any moves to head out.

"Listen, I just need a couple of hours in my studio, and then I'm all yours. We should still have time to get our pumpkins and donuts and drive back before the concert."

She breezed over to me then, hands still damp with water, and kissed me on the head.

"You're an independent girl, Andi. I raised you that way. Find something to do with that sulk, okay? Get inspired! Make something great; the day is young."

Before I could respond, Mama ran into her studio and shut the door.

I threw my body against the couch pillows, trying to hold back the tears I felt pooling. My throat was tight with heat and bad words I wanted to hurl at her. I didn't want to be independent. I wanted the day she promised. The whole day. I was eight.

How did I forget this part? How two hours had turned into five, and when Mama finally emerged from her studio it was too late to drive out to the orchard. I'd been watching TV all day, and Mama ordered pizza and brownies as a peace offering for dinner. We ate in silence, and it was only when we finally sat down in our seats at Orchestra Hall and felt the magic of the lights dimming and the musicians sitting ready that she reached over to hold my hand in apology. Mr. Marsalis played his first notes, and all the badness of the day melted away.

I sit up and take out my AirPods as my cheeks dampen with tears. I look out at the lake beginning to darken as the sun goes down. Everything is so mixed up. I forget how sometimes loving Mama meant feeling left behind. I want her back but also I want to tell her about how sometimes I needed to stay tucked under her wing, safe, and not be left out in the cold. All I have now is her name, and a few paintings stored away in Aunt Janine and Uncle Mark's garage. Paintings they offered to put up in the house when I moved in, but I couldn't look at them. I still can't. Her paintings remind me of all the ways Mama didn't belong to me at all. And of what I did the day she died.

PINKY PROMISE

"Now, hold your hook like this and then make a loop, like this," Christopher says to me the next afternoon, demonstrating with his own hands and ball of hot-pink yarn. We are in the Craft Shack, and as promised, he's teaching me to crochet. Holding my own black ball of yarn and hook, I try to make a loop like his and create a neat beginning stitch, but I immediately lose my grip and everything falls apart.

"Watch me again," Christopher says. "You'll learn with a little practice."

I try again, and fail. I throw my ball of yarn and hook down on the ground. "I'm never going to get this," I say. "It's just not my thing."

"You're not even trying, Andi."

"Yes, I am."

Christopher raises an eyebrow at me and shakes his head. "I tried kayaking for you," he mutters. "It was a disaster, but at least I tried."

Neither of us is in the best mood. At this morning's rehearsal, Mr. London had singled out the brass section to work on another tricky part of the *On the Waterfront*

Suites. Christopher is barely holding on to second-chair trombone, and I've been distracted ever since that letter from Aunt Janine.

I was starting to feel like I belonged here, at Harmony Music Camp, but now I'm not so sure.

"I didn't ask you to kayak," I say before I can stop myself. "You just decided to tag along."

Christopher inhales sharply and puts down his project. He gets up and starts to pace around the room. "I see," he says. "What's up with you and Zora anyway? I thought you were just hanging out because Mr. Wright made you be buddies, but all of a sudden, you're best friends or something? I thought I was your best friend."

"You are," I say slowly as I try to put together words for how I feel about Zora. "Zora and I are bunkmates, and so, I think we got close because of that." It's the truth, but not the whole truth. What I don't say to Christopher is this: *Zora helps me feel free. You help me feel brave.*

"Look, can we just forget about all this?" I say. "I don't want to fight with you."

"We are not fighting, Andi. We are simply having a tiff."

I laugh. "A tiff?"

"Yes," Christopher says, cracking a smile. "It means that we are slightly annoyed with one another. But all can be remedied if you promise me one thing."

"What?"

"Don't abandon me during the camping trip this week. Promise me you'll be by my side as much as possible? I'm not looking forward to sleeping in the woods."

I laugh and nod. "Deal. I'm looking forward to the trip. Especially since it's taking the place of a mixer this week. I cannot handle another stupid dance."

"Well, there's still the final mixer, but yes, I see your point. Sleeping under the stars sounds romantic, but also, buggy."

"Don't worry. You'll survive, I promise."

"I'd better. My family did not send me to this fancy camp only to be eaten by a bear."

"You won't get eaten by a bear. They want as little to do with us as we do with them. As long as we keep all our food sealed up, we should be fine."

"And how do you know all this? Am I in the presence of a real live Girl Scout?"

"Ew, no. I just went camping a lot with my mom. She taught me things."

"Oh," Christopher says then, quieter.

"Just, trust me. Everything will be good, I promise. It's only two nights anyway."

Christopher sits back down next to me and holds out his hand. "Pinky promise?"

I lock my pinky with his pinky and smile. "For sure. I'll be by your side, no matter what. Except for when they separate us at night."

"Excellent," Christopher says. "Now, do you want to try this one more time?"

I sigh and pick up my ball of yarn and hook. "Sure. But go slower this time."

Christopher claps his hands and starts to show me again, and this time I manage to make a stitch.

ORB WEAVERS

"*D*on't take more than you can carry!" Joanna yells at us on Thursday morning as we all scramble to our cubbies. Instead of our before-breakfast daily chores, we're preparing for the camping trip. We're set to leave in the evening after rehearsals, around 6:30 p.m. "We will be hiking about a mile and a half this afternoon to get to the campsite," Joanna continues. "And I will not be carrying your things if you get tired. You don't need to be in uniform, but please wear your name lanyards and sensible shoes."

Packing light is not an issue. I stuff some extra clothes, the rain poncho Aunt Janine sent, my flashlight, a water bottle, my MP3 player, and my AirPods into my backpack and zip it closed. Then I roll my sleeping bag into its case, take my pillow, and tie it to the sleeping bag with some extra knee socks so that I have a neat bundle. A change of scenery will be nice after the week I've had, and camping always makes me feel better.

"Wow," Zora says, eyeing my things. She's staring at her own bunk, which is piled with clothes, bug spray, books, and other random items she can't seem to decide between. "That was quick. Where did you learn to pack like that?"

I shrug. "It's just always what I've done. And for once these knee socks came in handy."

Zora leans over and grabs my sleeping bundle, lifting it up and then putting it down by the knee-socks straps I've tied around it all.

"Do you think you can help me do that to mine?" Zora says, handing the bundle back to me and extracting her flower comforter and pillow from her bed.

"That's what you're bringing to sleep in?" I try to keep my face together. "You don't want to borrow an actual sleeping bag?"

Zora shakes her head. "No way. Do you know how many people have slept in those? Some of them smell like pee. I'd rather just bring this and then use a foam camping mat."

"I can try. It might not work as well since you don't have a case or anything, but I can try."

We lay out her blanket and then fold and roll it tight. Then Zora adds her pillow on top of the roll, and hands me a pair of her knee socks. We manage to tie one around each end of the pillow-blanket roll, but only because Zora sits on it to keep it from unfurling.

"Voila!" I say, when we're done. "I think that should hold."

Zora beams at me. "Thanks, Andi."

"No problem."

"Hey," Zora says. "We should be buddies again. I mean, for the hike later. They make us walk in pairs. It's stupid, it's not like we're even going that far. The campground is just across the highway."

I swallow hard, remembering my promise to Christopher. "Thanks, but I told Christopher I'd stick with him this trip."

"No problem," Zora says quickly. "That makes sense."

"But hey—"

"Really no big deal. I'll just ask Jori."

I nod. "Cool."

"Cool," Zora echoes, getting busy again packing her own bags.

Hours later, all campers from the junior division march two by two across the highway and into the Red Pine National Forest. Christopher is at my side, huffing and puffing as he carries a duffle bag that looks like it's been filled with rocks.

"What on earth did you bring?" I ask, lifting it off his shoulder for a moment to feel its weight.

"Just a couple of my eighth-grade textbooks. I've been trying to get a head start for the school year. I read a little from them each night before bed."

"Textbooks?! Christopher, you're going to get heatstroke carrying those. It's, like, eighty-five degrees out here."

"I will not," he protests. "Because I also brought three refillable water bottles. I heard it's very important to stay hydrated in the woods."

I can't help rolling my eyes. "You know some of the

dining-hall staff is driving over all our food supplies, which I'm pretty sure includes water?"

"I do," Christopher says. "But this is my own survival stash. Just in case I get lost or something happens to us out there."

"You won't get lost," I say. "I promise."

"Well, I don't plan to, but I always like to be prepared for anything."

I shake my head. "You are something else, Christopher."

We have crossed fully into the woods now, the sound of the highway is growing quiet behind us. I focus on my feet and the shuffle of my shoes on dry leaves, and with each step I shed something heavy. Hiking always makes me feel alive. Mama taught me everything I need to know about the woods. The first time she took me camping was when I was in first grade. "Your legs are long and strong enough now, Andi," she'd said, loading our small car up with gear one July morning. "Michigan is beautiful in the summer. Just wait. You're going to love it."

We drove to Saugatuck and spent two weeks camping in the woods by the beach. Mama taught me how to collect small sticks for our fires and how to twist pieces of old newspaper into strong ropes to help start the flames. When we went on hikes, she'd point out all kinds of wildlife and trees and edible plants. She taught me how to read a compass, but also how to determine which way is north without one. "If you ever get lost, Andi, always remember that the sun rises in the east and sets in the west, so you can follow the light. If you're looking for north, check the trees. Moss will gather on the north side of the tree, where it's less sunny. Look, here," she'd said then, crouching low by a small tree hollow. I leaned down with her and saw a spider with bright yellow and green patterns that kind of looked like a colorful African mask. It sat in the middle of a complicated web, like a queen. "This," Mama said, "is an orchard orb weaver spider. It's too small to be poisonous to us, but look at that web. Isn't it beautiful?" I nodded. "If you want to know which way is south, look for spiderwebs, Andi. Most spiders will build their webs on the south side of trees."

"How do you know so much stuff?" I'd asked her.

She'd laughed and stood up to adjust her pack. "I just like being outdoors. People think Black folks don't like the woods or nature, but that's just a stereotype. Plenty of us like the outdoors; we just don't like being hunted."

I was too little then to understand what she meant, but at the time I understood that my mom, the artist, found some kind of freedom outdoors with the woods or at the lake. We loved to dive into the warm Lake Michigan waters, kick our legs hard, do handstands, and float on our backs to watch the clouds. At night, when we'd fall asleep in our tent, there was always sand in our sleeping bags. "Good for the skin." Mama laughed. "A little sand won't kill us, Andi."

It was true—sand and dirt were harmless. Something else would bring our reality to an end.

"You won't get lost," I say again, more to myself than to Christopher. Then, I look back on the trail and find Zora. She's walking arm in arm with Jori, holding her sleeping pack in her free arm. I'd like to be walking arm and arm with Zora right now. To say to her, *Don't you feel like a spider? Small but also full of purpose?* But I don't say anything. I just keep walking. We are deep in the forest now and I can smell fire smoke and sap. I can smell wind and water, earth and moss. And I can feel the memory-ghost of Mama all around me.

STEW PROBLEMS

We arrive at the campsite just in time to settle in and eat dinner before it gets dark. There's already a huge, roaring fire in the middle of the site, and Christopher waves goodbye to me as the boys' division splits off to set up in a clearing to one side of the fire pit, while the girls head to a clearing on the opposite side.

"We'll be sleeping under the stars for the next two nights!" Joanna yells as she gathers us into a circle and instructs us to lay out our things. "Al fresco! Won't that be fun?"

It's not a question, but Coop grumbles: "Not really. Why can't we sleep in a tent? I'm a city kid. This is a lot more nature than I signed up for."

"It's just two nights, Coop," Joanna says. "I think we'll survive."

"What if a bear comes?" Julie says then, rolling out a dusty loaner sleeping bag next to Coop. I wrinkle my nose, remembering Zora's pee comment.

I walk away and find a spot at the edge of our group as Joanna explains why a bear attack is highly unlikely. I'm smoothing out my sleeping bag when I feel a shadow standing over me. *Zora.* "Hi," I say, looking up.

"Can I stay next to you?" Zora asks as she sets down her things and starts unrolling her comforter and pillow.

"Sure," I say, a quick burst of heat rising in my cheeks. "You don't want to sleep next to Jori and Beks?"

"Not really," she says. "I guess I'm just used to sleeping with you—I mean, close to you, since we share a bunk and all."

I nod, trying not to make eye contact with Zora, or else I might smile at her like a big fool. I've gotten used to sleeping close to her too, listening to her faint snore above me and the *creak, creak, creak* of bed springs when she fidgets in her sleep, as if she is dancing in her dreams.

"So are you ready to try your first Harmony Music Camp stew?" Zora says.

"Is that what's for dinner?" I say, unable to stop the look of disgust making its way onto my face. "I don't like soup."

Zora laughs. "It's not, like, soup-soup; it's hamburger meat, potatoes, veggies, and cheese all thrown together in a packet of foil and then cooked in the fire.

"What kind of veggies?"

"Oh em gee, you're so picky," Zora teases, standing up and holding out her hand to me as we hear a loud bell clang. "That's the dinner bell. Looks like everything's ready. Come on, I'll show you how it works."

My stomach grumbles as if on cue. "I am extra hungry."

"Me too," Zora says.

The dining-hall staff has set up a big table with trays full of uncooked sliced potatoes, veggies, beef and Beyond burger meat, and cheese. I follow Zora's lead and grab a piece of foil, then watch as she expertly folds it into a little boat-shaped bowl and begins to add her stew ingredients.

"Start with the potatoes," she commands, "and then add your meat, veggies, and cheese on top. There's also a few spices if you want."

I nod and add my ingredients, skipping the broccoli, corn, and mushrooms, and instead adding extra, extra cheese and some salt and pepper. Then we fold down the excess foil over everything until we each have a neat, tight packet. Zora grabs a pen and scrawls her name across hers and then hands it to me to do the same. Then we hand our stews to a counselor who throws them over the fire.

"Now we wait!" Zora says, as we step aside. "They'll call our names when it's done. Let's find a place to sit, maybe over there." Zora is in full boss mode, but I don't mind. She finds us a spot under a trio of pine trees. Beks and Jori wave to us from the stew line, and Zora motions for them to join us when they get through it. I settle into a comfortable seat next to Zora, and when our shoulders bump by accident we both giggle for some stupid reason. "My bad," we say at the same time, and she leans into whisper, "Jinx!" which makes us both smile, and I feel my face flush with warmth. I like Zora's smile. I like when she leans close and I can feel her body heat and smell the coconutty lotion on her skin. I'm just about to get totally lost in Zora's smile when I catch Christopher in the corner of my eye. He's marching toward me, his arms crossed and his face a mess of rage. My mouth goes dry. I'd completely forgotten about my promise.

"I've been waiting for you for fifteen minutes, Andi!" Christopher says, not even bothering to say hi to Zora. "Like we agreed upon during the hike? Did you forget? You were supposed to wait for me at the end of the buffet line when we heard the bell?"

"I'm so sorry, Christopher," I begin. "Zora wanted to show me how it works, and I just—I didn't mean to forget. We haven't eaten yet; we're still waiting to hear our names called. You can go get your stew packet made and then come sit with us?"

"I will not," Christopher says, his voice shaky. "I asked you to do one thing for me on this trip, and you've already messed it up and you're over here whispering about me with her. I think I'll eat with some of *my* other friends, Andi. Enjoy your evening."

I open my mouth to reply, but Christopher turns on his heel and stomps away. *What on earth?* "Christopher," I finally yell out, "we weren't whispering about you at all—" But Christopher is too far away to hear me.

"Um, you can go sit with him if you want? He seems mad," Zora says, breaking the awkward silence. "I don't mind."

"No, I'm going to let him cool off. I don't know what's up with him. He could still sit with us—everyone is sitting in groups!" I say this last part a little louder than intended, but it's true. Everyone is eating in big huddles, in community. *I don't understand why he can't just hang out with me and Zora.*

"Think I heard our names," Zora says, scrambling from her seat before I can have any more outbursts. "I'll grab yours. You keep our spot safe."

I try to enjoy dinner, but my fight with Christopher stays on my mind. I thought he trusted me, but now I'm not sure it matters. I sit quietly while Beks, Jori, and Zora chat about some epic capture the flag game they'd played last year on this same trip. Every so often, Zora tries to bring me into the conversation by saying "Right, Andi?" and I just nod and take another bite of stew, which turns out to be extra good. I'm so hungry that I eat all of it, and it's not until the counselors put out the s'more makings and ring the bell again for dessert that I snap out of my haze. I jump up. "See you guys later," I say to the group. "I'm gonna get dessert." I don't stick around to see if they are following. I need a little space.

LEGENDS

I love a s'more. When Mama and I would camp, she'd get the really big marshmallows from the store. After building a fire, we'd hunt for the perfect roasting sticks. I like my marshmallow burnt, almost too burnt. I always have to find a thick stick that can stand to be held in the fire longer. Mama liked hers just barely browned. I used to make fun of her for that. "Oh hush, Andi. Just because I don't want to eat a charred piece of nastiness. You let me enjoy my process and I'll let you enjoy yours. We don't have to be the same."

My marshmallow has started to blacken and bubble. I push it into the flames a little more, until it catches fire. Then I take it out, blow out the flames, and expertly slide it between two graham crackers and a thick bar of chocolate. Before it cools I take a big, gooey bite. Chocolate drips out of the corners of my mouth, but I don't care. It tastes like heaven. Chocolaty marshmallow heaven.

"So, you like them burnt too." Zora has appeared at my side again, with her own stick and a marshmallow smoking at the end. I know I said I needed space, but I didn't mean Zora. Zora is the one person who gets me lately, or at least is trying to. I wish Christopher could see how nice she is, how when she's not being all perfect and competitive, Zora can be really funny—like that day at rehearsal when we'd all laughed about Channing's little POC comment.

"The only way to eat it." I nod back at Zora, trying to wipe the goo from around my mouth before she sees me looking a mess.

"I agree. Who wants a lukewarm, barely roasted marshmallow? I want to be able to taste the fire, you know?"

I laugh. "I guess I do too. Never thought of it that way. You get a better melt the longer you leave it in, and it makes the whole s'more just stick together better."

"Preaching to the choir!" Zora says. "My mom doesn't even let hers get golden. She leaves it in for, like, two seconds and then takes it out. She barely even eats it, but just nibbles at the crackers. Waste of a s'more, if you ask me."

"My mom was like that too. Well, she'd eat the whole thing, but the marshmallow would basically be raw."

Zora nods as she puts together her s'more, and doesn't ask me any more questions. I watch her take a bite equally as big as mine, her mouth also covered in sweet goo, and then she does a little happy dance as if to say *This is so good, so, so, so good!*

I laugh and then take another messy bite of mine, doing a little happy dance back.

"Are you making fun of me?" she says, putting a hand on her hip.

"No! I just thought that's what we were doing. Dancing because it tastes so good!"

"There's just nothing like it." She sighs then, her hand relaxing at her side. "And you know what goes well with s'mores?"

I shake my head.

"Ghost stories! Looks like we're getting ready to start," she says, motioning to a counselor who has started to hush the crowd. Most campers stop talking and silently chew on dessert as they take seats on big logs that surround the fire pit.

Zora and I make our way to a log occupied by Angie and some boy I vaguely recognize from the cello section. Angie is running her hand through his greasy hair and giggling.

"Gross," Zora whispers to me, as she slides in close on the log. "Get a tent."

I snort-laugh, but I stop when Aubrey starts to speak in a creepy, whispery tone into a small microphone attached to a portable speaker. All conversation around the fire stops. I lean in. I can get into a ghost story. Hopefully it's a good one. The light of fire dances into the gold of Aubrey's hair as she begins the tale.

"Many years ago, back when Harmony Music Camp was

founded and these woods were much less populated, there was a small, hidden lake. This lake wasn't much to look at during the day, but at night when the stars and moon came out, its waters shimmered so black and bright under the moon and stars, it looked like it was covered in diamonds."

"I love this one!" Zora whispers. "They like to tell us this story so we know never to go in the water unsupervised."

I nod. "Ssshhh," I say. "No spoilers."

"Well, the third summer Harmony Music Camp was open, in 1956, tragedy struck. Twin junior campers, age eleven, Cora and Elaine, wandered off campus during the lunchtime rush into these very woods of the Red Pine National Forest.

"When the twins were discovered to be missing, the whole camp went on alert and a search began. They searched all day and into the evening, and just after the sun set, the camp director found two sets of abandoned shoes by the shore of the small hidden lake. When he looked out over the water, he saw a boat, but only one of the twins, Cora, was in it. He called for help, and jumped in to swim to the boat and bring Cora back to shore. When asked about her sister, Elaine, Cora just shook her head and pointed to the middle of the lake.

"So, all the adults from the camp began to comb the water and water's edge for her sister. But nobody could find her. Elaine was lost, assumed drowned. It was a huge tragedy. The twins' parents lived all the way in Montana, and it would take them a few days to make it back to pick up their surviving daughter. So, Cora was taken to stay in the first-aid cabin with two counselors until her parents arrived. But the next night, Cora went missing again, except this time she left a note.

"'*She's not lost. She's just in the sparkling water,*' it said. '*Gone to see Elaine.*'

"There was a full moon, but a few clouds were covering it. The counselor who discovered her missing rushed back to the lake and arrived just as the clouds cleared. Cora was back on the water, in the boat, the black surface glittering like diamonds under the revealed moon. And she was talking to someone.

"The counselor called out to Cora from the shore. But Cora just turned and waved. She smiled. 'I see her. She's still here, in the sparkling water. She's not gone,' she yelled.

"The counselor started to swim out into the water as Cora giggled and sang and talked.

"When the counselor reached her, a dark cloud covered the moon again, and the water turned still and dull.

"Cora screamed, 'No! Don't go, Elaine. Come back!' as the counselor pulled her and the boat back to shore."

Aubrey takes a dramatic pause here to swig water from a nearby bottle.

"So, the story goes, for those three nights Cora was still

at camp, she tried to sneak out to the lake to wait for her sister to appear. She claimed that when the moon was out, when it shone bright and clear on the water, and if she called out, Elaine would appear. When her parents finally made it back, she tried to show them, but nobody else ever saw Elaine but Cora. So, the lake was named the Lost Lake, and it's maybe half a mile or so from our campsite. Rumor has it if you've lost someone you love, they might appear to you on the lake. But only when the moon is out and the water sparkles like diamonds."

A few campers who have heard the story before start to clap. But Aubrey isn't done.

"So, we tell you this tale to remind you of two things: (1) Never swim or go out onto any lake alone. It is for your safety, and (2) Always respect any ghosts you may encounter in the woods. I really thought it was just a story, but when I was your age, I was a camper here. One night, during this very annual campout, I heard through the trees a girl's voice calling out: '*Cora, Cora, it's Elaine, I'm here in the sparkling water. Come see me.*'"

"You did not!" a chorus of campers erupt, shifting in their seats with fear.

"I did. Clear as day. I think Elaine is still haunting the lake and this wood. So, when you get into your sleeping bags tonight, and when we have our Glow Hike tomorrow night, watch out. You might just hear her."

Zora does a dramatic shiver next to me like a spider is on her. "Can you imagine? I better not hear any creepy girl ghost voices tonight."

"Yeah, me either . . . ," I say, and then: "So, wait, what's the Glow Hike all about?"

"Oh, it's chill. Tomorrow night after dinner, the counselors make a path in the woods lined with glow sticks and lamps that we all have to follow. It's supposed to be a whole bonding, team-building thing. We get to hike through the mostly dark woods in pairs, and then end at a big bonfire."

"Sounds fun . . ."

"It is," Zora says. "I've never heard a ghost on that walk, but some girls last year claimed they did—but, you know, it's not like it's even that late when we do the walk, and . . ."

I'm nodding at Zora, but my mind is full of rushing thoughts. A plan so thick and twisty has popped into my head it might as well be a root.

What if Mama is waiting for me at the Lost Lake? I might get the chance to say goodbye, to talk to her one last time. To say sorry.

Even if it is just a stupid story, what do I have to lose by trying?

And the Glow Hike sounds like the perfect time to sneak away.

UNDER THE STARS

Sometime in the middle of the night I sit up in my sleeping bag. No, I lift off from my sleeping bag. My black Miles sleep shirt is torn into feathers, feathers that snap and flap and become wings. I rise into the crisp summer air, and then aim my body at the dark sky. The dark becomes a tunnel. I twirl myself into it and spin and spin and spin my way back to Detroit. Back to last August, the first week of school. Back to that Friday, the last day I saw Mama alive.

"Have a good day, baby," Mama said, pulling me into a quick hug before I could protest. "You have what you need?"

I nodded and pointed to my black backpack stuffed with new folders, notebooks, and some pens. "All good." I looked out the window, watched kids stream into the building. "Do I have to go?"

Mama laughed. "Uh, yes. Yes, you have to go. You'll be fine. And I have to get to work or else I'll be late."

With that, Mama leaned over me and opened the door. Then to be funny, she picked up her foot and reached it over the seat to kick me lightly on the knee. "Go on, learn yourself some things today and get out of my car. I'll be back for you later."

"You promise?" I yelled, jumping out of the car quick.

"Yes, I promise. I'll be back at three to get you. But don't get too used to it. You know, after this first week, you need to take the bus home. My work schedule changes after Labor Day."

I nodded. I knew.

"Bye, Andi Byrd." And with that Mama sped away. I stood at the curb and watched the top of her Afro disappear into a halo of gold light.

The thing I don't tell people is that Mama was also my best friend, and the summer was our time. The summer was when she took off work so we could have adventures of our own. So we could get lost together in the woods up north or meditate by the lake or search for the different kinds of green moss coating trees and rocks on a hike. Summer was when she put down her brushes, closed the door to her studio, and shook off whatever winter had laid heavy on her mind. Summer was when she let me be close.

I always hated the first week of school, watching her speed away, a reminder that fall was coming, that soon she'd be holed back up in her studio with her paintings, and not me.

"Mama!" I dream-yell after the image of her speeding away that final day, again and again.

"Who do you love more? Me or your art?"

I wake up with this question on my tongue. My sleeping bag is a sweaty black hole.

"Are you okay? You were talking in your sleep," Zora whispers from her spot next to me.

It's very dark, the campsite still and quiet.

"Yes," I whisper. "Just a weird dream. I'm good." But my voice cracks and I start to cough lightly.

Zora hands me her water bottle. "Here," she says. "I always keep one close by."

I nod and take it from her. The water rushes down my throat and cools me off. Zora is sitting up now. I can't see the expression on her face, but the dark shape of her stands out from the darkness around us.

"Thanks," I say.

"Andi—I know—I know you must miss your mom. And I just wanted to say, I'm sorry she's not around anymore. I realize that the ghost story earlier might have been hard for you to hear."

"I don't really want to talk about her," I say softly. *Can Zora tell what I'm planning? This is one thing I don't need her to be in my business about. I have to do this. Alone.*

"I just thought maybe the dream was about—and you were saying—"

"Zora, I'm really tired. Thank you for the water, but I'm good. Can we just go to sleep now?"

"Okay," Zora says, lying back down.

I wait for her to start snoring again, but she never does. The next thing I know, Joanna is shaking us all awake.

THE GLOW HIKE

The next morning it feels like there are hundreds of birds flapping their wings hard in my chest. *Who do you love more? Me or your art?* The thought that I might get to ask Mama this question from my dream, to explain to her why I did what I did, and to maybe, just maybe, see her again has me extra distracted. So distracted that I end up in line for a breakfast of cereal, granola bars, and fruit right behind Christopher and his cabinmate Ethan.

I was going to avoid Christopher, but oh well, here we go. I tap him on the shoulder. "Good morning," I manage to get out. "I'm sorry again about yesterday. Are we good? And I promise we weren't talking about you. I'd never do that. Okay?"

Christopher turns on his heel, and even though he's shorter than me, he angles his chin up as if he's trying to look down on me.

"Good morning," he says cooly. "I think it's best if we just keep our distance for the rest of this trip. Ethan has asked me to be his partner for the Glow Hike, and I've accepted. So, now you're free to be partners with Zora."

"But I didn't ask Zora—"

"I don't need any more fake best friends stabbing me in the back. I have enough of those at my school back home. Good day," Christopher says then, turning back on his heel, whispering something to Ethan that makes them both laugh loudly.

"You're being really mean," I say to Christopher before I can stop myself. "And selfish. You know you're allowed to have more than one best friend, right? I don't belong to you, and you know I'm not fake. I'd never do what your friend Samantha did. Never."

Christopher's shoulders stiffen, but he ignores me.

"Fine. Be that way. I don't need you, or anyone else. I'm better at being on my own anyway. This is stupid," I say, leaving my spot in line and stomping away. I've lost my appetite.

The rest of the day is pretty boring, or maybe it feels that way because I've checked out. We play a big game of capture the flag after breakfast, make leaf-imprint art after lunch, and then get some much-needed free time, which I use to pack my backpack for the Glow Hike, adding some extra items while no one is looking: a couple chocolate-chip granola bars I took from lunch, a water bottle, my poncho, some extra socks, and my flashlight. Before I know it, it's time for a late dinner. At eight p.m. the bell clangs and we all rush to get into the buffet line. *Almost time to fly*, I think, stuffing my face with three hot dogs and some chips. I chew hard and fast, my heart thundering in my chest.

Finally, an hour later, Joanna's voice booms out over the mic-speaker set: "Campers, it's about time for the annual Glow Hike. Find a partner. The sun is mostly down, the path is lit, and one final adventure awaits you."

I scan the area, looking for Coop, whom I have decided will be an ideal partner, since they're from a big city and probably won't follow me into the woods when I sneak away. But then I feel a tap on my shoulder.

"Need a partner?" Zora says.

I do. But not Zora. Zora will never stop talking long enough to let me slip away. "Um, I was going to ask—" But I cut myself off when I spot Coop linking arms with Arya and getting in line. "Fine. We can be partners."

Zora beams at me.

"But I'm not really in the mood for a ton of talking. So, I might want to just walk a little ahead of you and just enjoy the woods, you know?"

"Sure, no worries," Zora nods. "I promise to be quiet, so you can enjoy the full experience. I can give you your space, but just don't walk too fast. It gets really dark, and the whole point of having a partner is so you don't end up lost in the woods alone."

I nod. "Got it." But I fully intend to ignore her and walk as fast as I can. I've got to get to that lake, and she is not coming with me. It will be better for both of us if I lose her.

Joanna stands up on a log at the tree line and gets

everyone's attention on the mic. She is wearing a ridiculous-looking hat that she's made out of a bunch of glow sticks stuck together. This must be her favorite thing ever, because she's practically screaming at us with excitement as we all line up in pairs in front of her.

"Tonight," she begins in a dramatic singsong voice, "you have come here to journey into the unknown. You've come here from all walks of life, from near and far, not only to engage in the fellowship of music, but to build lasting connections with people from all across the country. As we head into the final week of our time together, let's take this time to be present, to appreciate one another and the bonds we've formed. While you walk through the woods tonight, remember that you have already been brave, you have already grown, and that you are more than your fear. Let the glow sticks along the path guide you and your partner through the dark, let the stars comfort you, and when you reach the end of this journey, let your hearts be more open in the knowledge that you can do anything you set your mind to. Now go into the woods, and be bold."

I roll my eyes so hard at all of this, but also, in some ways, Joanna's words are exactly what I need to hear. Around me, campers giggle and make fun of the journey they are about to take, but none of them are looking for what I am. I tighten the straps on my backpack.

"Let's go!" I say to Zora, heading down the path, which,

so far, is very well lit. Zora follows, and as we get farther and farther into the woods, I start to pick up my pace.

"Wait up!" I hear Zora call, but I walk even faster. The pair ahead of us has disappeared, and soon it's just me, almost running, and Zora's pitter-patter of feet behind me.

"Andi, slow down. I can barely see you!" Zora yells.

I take one last look behind me, and then I veer into a thicket of trees to the right of the glowing path. I don't stop to check if anyone has seen me. I just start to run, my feet picking up speed until it feels as if I am soaring.

LOST GIRLS

I should be scared, but I'm not. I don't know how I am seeing so well without my flashlight, but each step I take, I feel a weight off my shoulders and feel more in tune with the night surrounding me. I look up, and the stars blink down at me, and the trees seem to part and lower their roots into the earth so that my path is smooth and easy. As my legs pump forward, I can't help thinking of Mama's back tattoos. She got them before I was born. On her right shoulder blade, a quote from the painter Frida Kahlo: *Feet, what do I need them for, if I have wings to fly.*

On her left shoulder another quote, this time from a novelist named Toni Morrison: *You your own best thing.*

Then, surrounding each quote, delicate feathers in the shape of wings.

When I was little and I used to fall asleep in Mama's bed, I liked to imagine I was nestled in between the feathers of her shoulder blades. Then I would fall asleep and dream about exploring the dark sky, the two of us almost invisible, speeding into the heart of the night.

Mama is not here, but I can feel her ghost-memory close by. I run and I run, all my questions and anger and grief propelling me on. When there is no air left in me, I stop and let the soft hush of the woods rush into my ears.

But I am not alone. A minute later, Zora comes crashing through the trees after me. I know it's Zora because I smell the coconut oil she uses on her locs. Coconut oil mixed with the damp earth smell of the woods.

I gasp. "Why did you follow me?"

"I know what you're doing, Andi," she says, just as out of breath as I am. "I know what you're looking for."

I turn on my flashlight and shine it into Zora's face. She puts her hand up and walks closer to me.

"You shouldn't have followed me," I say, not wanting to let her closer to me. "This is none of your business. Go back."

"Andi, I know you're looking for the lake. So you can see your mom again. Last night, in your sleep, you were yelling out to her."

"You don't know anything about me, Zora!" My wings are gone, and in their place, I feel that heavy blob-girl feeling creeping back into my body. "Why do you have to stick your nose in everybody's business? Why don't you just focus on yourself?"

"I'm trying to," she says softly, "but I'm not really sure what that feels like. To focus on myself."

I lower the flashlight and try to steady my breathing. I feel my chest tighten. I'm losing time.

"Do you even know where you're going?" Zora asks then, glancing around us with her flashlight. "It's really dark out here."

"Sort of," I say, looking up at the sky. "I studied the trail map by the campsite entrance during my free time today. The lake should be just to the north of here, so I'm following Polaris."

"What if it's just a story? The Lost Lake?" Zora continues.

"I know it's probably just a story, but I need to at least try . . . I didn't get to say goodbye."

I wait for Zora to convince me to go back, but she is quiet.

"Fine," she says. "I'm coming with you, then."

"You could get in big trouble."

"I know."

I sigh and shrug my shoulders. "We need to hurry."

I point my flashlight ahead of us. With the light on, I see how thick these woods really are. I take a deep breath and steady my backpack on my shoulders. Zora opens her backpack, pulls out a bottle of water, and takes a big swig.

"I always come prepared when I hike," she says.

I shake my head. *Of course she does.* I start walking again, and this time we go on together.

WOUNDS

In the woods time passes like there is no time at all. When I used to hike with Mama, the only way we knew how long we'd been at it was by the slide of the sun in the sky. Neither of us liked to wear a watch. But now, in the darkness, it's even harder to tell how much time has gone by. All I know is that by now I am sure they've realized we're missing, and if they find us before I find the lake, everything will have been for nothing. To Zora's credit, she is extra quiet as we walk on. She doesn't complain, not even when she trips and falls over a rotted log and scrapes her knee on a sharp rock.

"Are you okay?" I pause.

"I'm fine. Just a scrape. I think I have Band-Aids in my backpack. I get blisters on the back of my heels a lot."

"Let me see," I say, working fast to open her bag and fish a Band-Aid out.

Before she can say no, I shine my flashlight on her right knee and kneel down to roll up the yoga pants she's wearing.

"Wait . . . ," Zora says.

Her legs are covered in a series of fine scratches and welts. They are in perfectly even rows, and you wouldn't really notice them unless you looked hard at them, her perfectly smooth Black skin masking them—mostly.

"Did you do those?" I ask, already knowing the answer.

Zora nods. I can feel her leg shaking against my hand. In fact, her whole body is trembling. When I look up at her face, there are tears. She wipes them away violently.

I lower her pant leg. "There's no blood on your knee; you'll probably just get a bruise. You might need to ice it later." I stand and hold out my hand to help her get up. She takes it and wipes off the leaves and dirt from her backside. "Why do you do it?" I hear myself ask before I can stop.

"It makes me feel better."

"But it hurts, right?"

"Yes. I don't know how to explain it. The pain, well it helps me remember to breathe."

I am quiet as we start to walk again. "I have a hard time breathing sometimes too," I offer. "Ever since my mom."

Zora is quiet. "Andi?"

"Yeah."

"I'm scared."

"Of the dark?"

"No. Of not being perfect."

"Me too," I say. "I don't want to be this sad all the time."

Maybe it's the blinking stars or the fact that in that moment, wrapped in the bubble of our confessions, Zora reaches out and laces her fingers with mine, but whatever it is, we both hear it at the same time: a soft lapping of water. And then, still hand in hand, we run through a patch of thick trees and find it. The Lost Lake: glossy with shine like the night sky itself, just as beautiful as the legend tells.

"It's beautiful," Zora whispers.

"I knew it would be," I almost yell.

"So, what now? The legend says you have to go out on the lake. How're you going to do that?"

"I thought I might just wade into the water as far as I can stand instead?"

Zora squeezes my hand tighter as if she's trying to tether me to the sand next to her. "That's dangerous, Andi. We don't know how deep it gets. I don't want you to—"

"I'm a good swimmer. Plus, what choice do I have?" I say, turning on my flashlight and scanning the surrounding area. "I don't see a dock around he—" I stop talking when my flashlight hits the shape of an overturned ancient-looking canoe hidden poorly in a thicket of brush by the tree line. I break free from Zora's grip and run over to it. I drag it to the water's edge. "Help me turn it over!" I say, my voice shaking.

"You can't be serious. That thing looks so old—and busted. That's probably why it's still here."

"Maybe, but it might still float. I only need it to work for a little bit."

Zora helps me turn it over, and then we push it into the shallow water. It leans a little to the left but looks pretty solid. I look up at the sky and notice a collection of dark clouds rolling in toward the moon. *I have to go now.*

"Wait for me here," I tell Zora as I climb into the shaky canoe and grab hold of the rough oars.

"Andi, do you even know how to row that thing? Let's think this through. We're not supposed to even touch water without a lifeguard—"

"I think we've already broken the rules by running away, Zora. A canoe can't be that different from a kayak."

"I guess," Zora squeaks. "Please just be careful. I'll be watching and waiting for you."

"Thanks . . . ," I start. "I know this is wild and might seem stupid to you, but I have to try something."

"It's not stupid. I understand," Zora says, giving the canoe a little push.

The moon is a milky eyeball above, and a symphony of crickets crescendo from the nearby reeds. I begin to row out into the middle of the lake. I watch Zora get smaller and smaller on the shore. She waves as if to say *Don't get lost out there.*

But I already lost my mother, so what does it matter if I get lost? Maybe I am the kind of girl who belongs to the songs of the dark and the movement of the trees and the blue of a lake that swallows everything I love. Maybe I don't belong on shore. Maybe I belong in the middle of the water, in the middle of the night, with the stars blinking down on me like magic.

THE LOST LAKE

*W*hen the moon is clear of clouds, go to the center of
the lake and call out.

I stop paddling when I get to what feels like the middle of
it all. The ancient canoe seems to be holding strong except
for a tiny bit of water pooling around my feet. As long as I
don't move around too much, I should be fine. The moon
is brilliant. My skin under its light is a flash of metallic, and
the lake water's shine is so fierce I can't look at it directly.

You made it, I say to myself. *You can do it. It's time to say
goodbye.*

But no tears come. No tears ever come, just the panic and
all my breath escaping my body.

I know you miss your mom, Zora had said. *I am so sorry.*

She was addicted to drugs, that means Andi is a crack baby.
Amy Vanden-Vampire's voice sneaks in next.

I don't know what I would do if I lost my mom. Christopher's
now.

*If the baby is a girl, we want to name her after your mom,
Augusta—Star for short.* Aunt Janine is here too.

*Andi, what happened to your mom is not your fault. What
happened was a horrible tragedy, an accident. People die all*

the time, and sometimes there's no reason for it. It just happens, and those of us who are left behind have to learn how to heal. It's okay if you were mad at her the day she died, that you lashed out. If she were here, she'd forgive you, Dr. Raynor reminded me at almost every one of our sessions.

Here on the lake, all their voices crowd my head. Here on the lake, the water lapping stronger now at the side of the canoe, the events of last August come rushing back to me.

Black is Mama wrapping me in her arms before school. Black is the smell of her strong coffee wafting out of the travel mug she held between her legs. Black is the sound of her voice singing Aretha at the top of her lungs in the car as she drove me to school. Black is Mama's paint-splattered hand waving to me as I headed into the front doors. Black is the last time I saw her smiling. The last time I saw her whole.

"Mama, are you here?" I squeeze my eyes shut and whisper into the dark. But all I see behind my eyes is red.

Red seeping into the beautiful, moonlit black. Red is my phone case as I picked at its edges, watching the time change from 3:00 to 3:25 to 4:00 p.m. as I waited for Mama to pick me up that first Friday of the year. No sign of Mama, no text saying she'd be late even though she promised to be here. Red is the angry face emoji text I sent letting her know I took the bus home even though my pass was expired and I had to dig into my bag for change. Red is the personal pepperoni pizza I made for myself that night for dinner when she still wasn't home, the splattered tomato sauce all over the microwave. Red is the soft glow of the sunset traveling around our apartment as I checked my phone, waiting for a reply. Red is the cloth she collaged onto her latest paintings in her studio, a series of self-portraits leaning every which way, all the faces of Mama—the good and the ugly—distorted and broken and made whole again without any trace of me. Red is my baby face, my toddler face, my eleven-year-old face peering into that studio, waiting for her to invite me in. Red is her mouth yelling "NO. This space is just for me, Andi. A woman has to have some things that are just hers. Go entertain yourself. I'm busy." Red is the scream running out of my throat that night as I grabbed a pair of scissors and slashed a neat hole through each one of her pieces. Red is the flash of police lights in the apartment-building parking lot. Red is the sound of a heavy hand banging on our apartment door. Red is riding through the streets in a police car toward the hospital. Red is the flickering exit light in the hospital waiting room. Red is watching the digital clock above the receptionist desk change minute by minute, hour by hour, as Mama underwent surgery. Red is the color on Aunt Janine's polished nails when she wraps me in a hug as the doctor delivers the news. Red is Mama's car, wrapped around a guardrail on the highway. Red is the doctor's thin, serious lips telling Aunt Janine that Mama was hit by a drunk driver on her way to get me at school.

Red is that blinking exit sign and my soul and every song I'd ever played running out of my body toward it. Red is the pile of her canvases I'd destroyed, heaped on her studio floor. Red is the last art she'd ever make, gone, gone, gone, and all because of me. Red is all the heat and blood and missing, and knowing that she died because she was rushing to get home to me, after all. Red is my whole life twisted into metal, shattered glass, and pieces of her on the side of the highway. Red. Red. Red.

Now on the lake, all I see is red, and Mama is not here, no sign even of her ghost-voice in my head. I shift in the canoe and notice that the water at my feet is now up to my ankles. I need a little more time. I cup my hands and start to throw some of the water out over the side. From the shore, I hear a muffled yell, but I'm not going to give up now. Summer is our time. Lakes are our place. I need Mama to know that I loved her, even when she was kicking me out of the nest of her studio.

I don't have tears, but my hands are fists, and they begin to pound at the rising water all around me in the canoe. The water is coming in faster now. The glimmer of the lake flashes sharp in my eyes every time I make contact.

"Mama! I need to see you."

Nothing. The canoe tips dangerously to the side. I hear Zora yelling at me from the shore, but I am not ready. She has to appear. She's here, I know she is. She needs to give me a sign. I cup my hands again and throw more handfuls of water out of the boat. I look up and notice two black clouds, two black mouths ready to swallow the moon. The light will be gone soon; the lake will turn dull and plain again.

Black is Mama's smile thrown across a fresh canvas. Black is Mama, turning her wings to me and letting me sleep between her shoulder blades. Black is the waffle iron she fired up that one snowy day. Black is the wooden spoon in her hand as she sings and dances her way around the apartment. I cast a tear and then a whole net of tears into the water, my whole body letting go, the water soaking every part of me now. The black mouth clouds are almost touching the moon, but the water still glitters.

"Where are you? I'm sorry. I need you," I croak.

But nothing. Mama is not coming. I am not a baby bird anymore.

I hear a shout from the shore as the canoe tips, and sinks. I jump into the water, and go under for just a second. I know how to swim, but for a moment when I pop back up, I float on my back and watch the clouds eat the moon. I am part of the lake—floating and crying and trying to swim away from the heaviness of me without her. Swimming, sinking, swimming, sinking, until I feel arms around my waist and a rising, a pulling, as Zora meets me in the shallow water and helps me to the waiting shore.

NOSES

I don't know how long we sit on the beach. We must have been out here for hours, and I can't even guess how much trouble we'll be in when they find us. But I can't move just yet. I can't leave the lake. Instead, I let go of all the tears I've been holding in all year, and Zora doesn't leave me. Zora springs into action, rummages through our backpacks and hands me a dry shirt from hers, then she towels herself off with what I think is a hoodie before sitting down next to me and wrapping us both in the blue rain poncho Aunt Janine sent. It's not cold, just cool out, and I am grateful for the cozy warmth of our bodies. With the moon behind clouds now, it's hard to see, so Zora flips on her flashlight and we stare out onto the dim path of light it makes on the water.

Zora is so close to me, I can feel the goose bumps dotting her bare arms, which are wrapped around me. I lean my head on her shoulder, still sobbing, and a twig scratches my cheek. I feel around her hair, and she doesn't stop me. There are pieces of tree and dirt tangled in her locs, her beautiful locs that spread out and over her shoulders like strong, brown roots. I begin to pick the debris out with my wrinkled fingertips. I make a little pile between us. As much as I was annoyed that Zora followed me into the woods, I am glad she is here now. I scoot closer to her and close my eyes again.

"Just breathe, Andi," she says with a voice so gentle and tender it surprises me. Zora exhales deeply as a reminder, and so I imagine I am inhaling her breath into my mouth, then I give her back her breath and focus on the music of us. The racing in my chest slows, and my sobbing stops.

Maybe we can stay like this forever. Maybe if we sit here long enough under the sky and the leaves, we'll turn into the forest. Maybe we can run around eating berries from the bushes, pulling fish from the lake. Maybe we don't have to be girls anymore, but part of something bigger, something more like the energy of wind and water and sky. Maybe we can decide who we want to be here, maybe we don't have to be weighed down by the dreams or memories of our mothers. Maybe we can just be. I'd like to just be.

"What are you thinking?" Zora's voice hums into my half dream like a subtle key change. When I open my eyes again, she is looking directly at me, her nose so close to mine, they are almost touching. I stay very still.

"What if we don't go back?" I say, finally.

"We have to," Zora says in her matter-of-fact way. "But not this second. We're already going to be in big trouble. We might get sent home, so we may as well stay out here a little longer." She softens again, and clears her throat: "I'm sorry about the shirt. I know it's not your favorite, but I . . . well, you were really shivering when you came out of the water. I just thought it was better for you to wear something dry."

Zora shines the flashlight at me, and I look down and see that I am wearing her "Stay Magical" unicorn PJ top. I snort, and then my snort turns into uncontrollable laughter. Zora loosens her grip from around my body.

"No. No," I say, pulling her back. "It's all good, thanks. Why did you even bring this?"

"I didn't mean to. It was stuck to the inside of the hoodie I brought just in case I got cold. I used the hoodie as a towel, but you were soaked, so I just thought it was better than nothing . . . You hate it, I know," Zora says.

I don't know why, but I lean over the pile of sticks and dirt between us, and touch our noses together again.

"What are you—?" Zora asks, her body falling toward mine.

"Can I—?"

Zora nods, and so I lean in closer until our lips touch too. Zora freezes for a moment, and then I feel the pressure of her kissing me back. It's only a short kiss, but it feels like it lasts as long as a Miles Davis track. My ears ring with a chorus of crickets that have decided to accompany the moment, and then it feels like there are a thousand wings flying around the sky of my torso.

"What was that for?" Zora recovers, a half smile pulling at the corner of her mouth.

"I . . . I'm sorry."

"Don't worry," Zora says. "I didn't mind."

Then the wings fly out of my torso and into my throat, my skull, until I am sure there is an explosion of birds from the top of my head.

"Let's stay here," I say.

Zora's face lights into a full smile, and I feel her arms tighten again around me. She closes her eyes and then wiggles her body closer to mine on the sand. "Okay," she says. "Just for a little while. But no more canoes, Andi. That was scary."

"I know."

"Watching you try to get back. I know you can swim, but you were so upset, I thought you wouldn't make it."

"I just needed more time. To wait for her. I'm all alone without her."

We are quiet. The crickets serenade us. Then after a beat, Zora hugs me tight. "You are not alone. I'm here."

FOUND

We sit in the quiet afterglow of our kiss until we hear someone run out of the woods behind us.

"I found the last two!" Joanna yells into a walkie-talkie. "False alarm. They just wandered off the path a bit farther than the rest."

Zora and I jump up. A mess of mismatched damp clothes and sandy skin.

"Girls!" Joanna runs up, giving us both huge hugs. "I'm so glad to see you. I was really worried."

"I can explain . . . ," I start. "It was my—"

But Zora steps on my toe, silencing me.

"We just got a little turned around, Joanna. It was hard to see the path once we got deeper into the woods. You really need to fix that for next year!"

"Yes, yes. We know. You're not the only two we've had to come looking for tonight. It seems that the fork in the path was a little confusing for everyone. Now, let's get you back."

Joanna stops talking and runs her flashlight over the two of us again as if just understanding something. "Did you go in the water? You know that it's against camp policy. I'll have to report this if so."

My tongue swells in my mouth. I'm all out of words.

"Well, technically, yes," Zora says. "But it's not what you think."

"Well, what do I think?" Joanna says.

"We were trying to help."

Where is she going with this?

"There was this old canoe, and when we got here, it was drifting out into the lake. So we tried to bring it back in with a long stick, but it kept going out farther and farther, so we waded into the shallow end a little to try to get closer, but it was too late. And then I tripped on a rock and fell—see, my knee is all scraped," Zora continues, lifting up her damp pant leg. "Anyway, Andi helped me get out, and so we got our clothes wet . . . so that's it. We got out as soon as we realized it was hopeless. We've been sitting on the beach most of the time."

Joanna looks out into the dark water and shivers.

I grab Zora's hand and squeeze it hard. If Joanna believes this, it will be a miracle.

"And the canoe is gone now?" Joanna says, still looking out at the lake.

"It sank." I find my voice again.

"Interesting. Perhaps a ghost needed it? Did you see any

ghosts while you were sitting here? This is the haunted lake, after all. The one from the legend."

"We know," Zora says. "That's why we're glad you found us."

"We didn't see any ghosts, though," I add.

"Well, there's still time," Joanna says, turning back to us now. "Who knows what you'll hear or see after bed tonight? Let's just keep the canoe incident to ourselves, shall we? I'll need to make a report that we found you by the water, but technically I didn't see you touch the water. So, let's leave it at that."

"Yes, ma'am," Zora says, stepping on my toe again. "Our lips are sealed."

"Oh, please don't call me ma'am, girls. That makes me feel super old. Now, let's get a move on. There are s'mores waiting by the fire."

"Everyone is still up?" Zora says.

"Of course. It's ten fifteen. You girls have only been out here for an hour or so. We went searching for the Glow Walk stragglers after most campers made it back in forty minutes. That's on us. We have to light the way better next time."

I just nod. It feels like we've been gone for days.

I gear up for a long hike back to camp, but Joanna leads us around a few bends, and less than fifteen minutes later we see the familiar glow of our campsite and hear everyone's voices.

"Here we are!" Joanna sighs. "Why don't you both take a moment and meet us by the fire in five?" Then she leaves Zora and me standing at the edge of the group.

"It felt like we were miles away," I manage to get out. "But we were just around the corner all along?"

Zora nods, and in the faint light of the far-off fire, she steps close, takes my hands, and looks at me with the same softness she'd held me with by the lake. "I'm glad you came to camp this year," she says.

"Me too," I say.

I hope, tomorrow, when the sun comes up, we'll still be these same girls. Lost girls, found again. There's so much I want to say to her still, to know about her. "I'm glad—" I start to say, but then I feel the force of someone run into me from behind and catch me in a big hug.

Zora lets go of my hands and steps back as I find my balance.

"I'd thought we'd lost you forever, Andi," a familiar voice says. "I was so scared. I knew something bad would hap-pen—I just knew it. Who does a hike IN THE DARK? Not us, we cannot be out here Black and brown as we are all up in these creeptastic, nighttime woods."

Christopher. Christopher is hugging me.

"I'm good," I say, as Christopher releases me from his grip and steps back with a sheepish grin. "We're both okay. Zora made sure I didn't get lost."

Christopher looks at Zora then. "Thank you," he says, and then he gives her a quick hug too.

I try not to gawk.

"Anyway, Andi," Christopher continues, "I'm so deeply sorry. I acted horribly. This would have never happened if we hadn't fought, and I was being stubborn this morning at breakfast holding a grudge. I got insecure because of what I went through in sixth grade with all the bullying about my parents, but you're not those kids, Andi. I know that in my heart. You're a magnificent friend, and when I found out you were missing in the woods, I just—"

"Christopher." I cut him off.

"Yes."

"You're really important to me, and I'm sorry I let you down. I want to tell you everything that happened in the woods because you're also a magnificent friend, but can you give me a minute?"

Christopher wraps me in another hug, and then pulls away. "Of course, m'lady."

"Thank you, good sir," I say, bowing.

"But may I just ask this last thing now: What on earth are you wearing? You're all . . . sparkly."

Zora laughs then. "Oh, I gave her that to borrow. You probably want to change, right?"

I look down at the glittery unicorn party on my chest. The shirt smells like Zora, and now the lake. I don't want to take it off yet, but I feel shy about rolling up to the whole campfire wearing her clothes. It's bad enough that Christopher has seen it.

"Uh, yeah, I'm going to throw on a dry sweatshirt on top," I say, "if that's okay?"

Zora's grin is full of beautiful flame flickers. "Sure. You can give it back to me later." She turns to Christopher then. "Want to go make a s'more? We can make one for Andi too, while she changes. I know just how she likes them cooked."

"Yes, that sounds divine. My s'more-making skills are a disaster. Maybe you can give me some tips?" Christopher says.

"I know all the tips," Zora says with just a hint of her bossy edge.

"See you shortly, Andi?" Christopher says then, taking Zora by the arm. "We'll be waiting for you."

"I'll be there," I say, grinning. "I promise."

Then I watch Zora and Christopher walk away, their shadows dancing behind them.

Harmony Music Camp

If I wasn't a camp
I'd want to be
     A campfire
A warm center of sparks
Dancing up into the black mane
Of a summer night

A campfire is a gathering place
Is a circle of friendly shadows
That hide-and-seek around the edges
Sending laughter or questions in the blazing dark

It's always a shock when
For two whole nights
Half of my cabins are empty
The young ones, hidden deep
In the forest across the highway
Learning the shape of another land

But just when I begin to miss them the most
To miss their voices laughing through their divisons
The sun goes down and turns the lake
The color of a freshly bitten plum
And up from the trees across the way

A faint wisp of smoke
Curls through the air like a wave

A campfire is a signal of the existence of life
        What humans can make and build together
        A reminder that nobody is ever really left behind
As long as there is light to follow

WEEK FOUR

Zora

CONCH SHELL

I should be practicing, but I'm not. My hands are still as I sit holding my flute in my lap, staring at a jumble of notes on the stand in front of me. It is late afternoon on Saturday, and I am in a practice hut with the metronome ticking on a windowsill, waiting for me to get in sync with it.

This morning, we arrived back from our camping trip sun-soaked and reeking of bonfire smoke and Joanna had made us all take showers.

"I love you all, but you stink," she said as we dropped our things all over the floor of our cabin. "I know tomorrow is your final seat audition, but before you head out to practice today, I strongly suggest rinsing off."

Nobody protested at her request, and except for Ivy (whom I hadn't seen bathe since arriving), we all took shifts carting our shower caddies back and forth from the bathrooms.

"You go ahead. I'll get the next one," Andi had offered when Jori came back and tagged one of us in. "Plus, I know you hate feeling grimy, and I'm the one that made you go in that lake water."

I shuddered. *Who knows what was in that Lost Lake water.* "Thanks. It's true, I feel like a swamp witch right now," I said, standing up from where I had been sitting next to Andi on her bunk. We'd been listening to Lizzo on her AirPods, our bodies just close enough that I could feel the small hairs on her bare arms standing at attention and tickling my skin. After being found the night before and stuffing our faces with s'mores with Christopher, we'd both fallen asleep instantly when we hit our sleeping spots. I'd hoped we'd stay up talking or that we'd maybe hold hands again, but we just slept hard. When the sun came up this morning, everything felt different—not bad, just new—and we both fumbled getting our things together. I felt shy and unsure if what had happened the night before was real. But we hadn't left each other's side since leaving the campsite. That is, until now.

In the practice hut, I hear music all around me. Campers running scales or their parts, hoping to move up a seat one final time in the last week of camp—back to the normal, competitive routine. I am trying to drown out all the noise so I can daydream about how less than twenty-four hours ago, I had had my first kiss. Today, mystery-Zora is in full effect, and mystery-Zora can't stop thinking about the ocean.

When I was seven, Mom and Dad took me on vacation to North Carolina. Well, it wasn't totally a vacation for them— they had to attend one of their academic conferences and we stayed a few extra days to explore. Because my parents are who they are, they planned every minute of that trip with something touristy. We visited museums and bookstores, but my favorite part was the day we just spent on the beach. Mom and Dad read under a big umbrella, and I wandered around collecting treasure. I'd grown up at the lake, but the ocean was different. The ocean was louder, and I felt how big it was, standing at its edge, the waves slapping at my feet with more urgency. How when I dipped my hand into the water and then put my fingers into my mouth I tasted salt. How nets of seaweed would catch on my toes and little sand crabs would scramble, and bubble into the wet sand like a million little blinking eyes. And the sound, the ocean roar and suck and swell—well, that was like hearing a newly composed symphony every time I closed my eyes and inhaled. I could listen to that sound forever. I found a conch shell and placed it between my feet in the shallow water. Each time a wave made it to my toes, I imagined the shell filling up with that sound. I imagined that I was bottling every ounce of the ocean's magic to take home with me. And I didn't let that shell out of my sight. I carried it with me for the rest of the trip, held it on my lap in the airplane, and tucked it next to me in bed when we got back to Ann Arbor in the middle of the night. I remember, falling asleep with it pressed against my ear, the lullaby of the Atlantic singing into my dreams, my pillow melting into a pool of kelp and foam and deep-sea notes. Eventually, the shell ended up on a shelf in my room full of other trinkets and souvenirs.

I'd forgotten about that shell, until now. Until Andi kissed me. Being close to Andi made me feel like I was inside that seashell. Andi kissed me and when I kissed her back, I became the sound of the ocean, I became a swell of waves, I became salt and seaweed and a girl bubbling into the cool, wet sand. And even though neither of us had our instruments near us, a whole chorus of chords and notes and songs roared in my head, as if we'd both written and composed a new song together, something in the key of us.

"What if we stay here?" Andi had asked me. The rushing roar barely gone from my head, I almost didn't hear her. Before my head could respond, I heard my heart say, "Okay. Just for a little bit."

And here I was, unable to read music anymore, unable to think about anything else, except that kiss. I'm pretty sure the old Zora Lee Johnson is gone. Instead, here I am: Zora Lee Johnson, totally crushing on Andi Byrd.

I put my flute down and take out a sheet of folded stationery and a pen from my bag.

Saturday, July 17

Dear Kennedy,
You're not going to believe what happened to me.

First of all, I miss you! Second of all, I broke camp rules to search for a haunted lake in the woods. Third of all, the reason all of this happened is that I met a girl named Andi. She's my bunkmate, and my friend, and well, WE KISSED, so now I think we might be soul mates. Is this how you feel about Cole, totally obsessed? I've never felt this way about anybody. Not even you (no offense, you know I love you). Halp. I think I'm losing it. So, so, so much has happened this month. I can't wait to tell you all about it. Till then.

      Love,
        Zora

PS This will be random to you, but when I get back to Ann Arbor, can I show you some of my dance routines? I'm thinking of auditioning for a youth dance troupe in Detroit, and I think I could make it with some practice. I promise to tell you the whole story when I get back, but for now, just know I think dance might be just as important to me as music is to you.

I fold up the letter and unzip the front pocket in my backpack to place it inside, but another envelope stares back at me. *I forgot to send the last letter I wrote.* I must have gotten distracted after kayaking with Andi. I need Kennedy to be my friend just as much as I need Andi to like me back as much as I like her. I pack up my things and head to the main lodge to send them both out. *I hope I haven't waited too long.*

PRESSURE

"*Z*ora, wait up!"

Fifteen minutes later, I turn around on the path on my way back from the main lodge and watch as Beks, Jori, and Julie approach. Jori is holding her timpani mallets and air-playing as she walks, Beks has her viola case strapped to her back, and Julie carries her violin case at her side. Without thinking, I pinch the skin hard on my left wrist as they approach. *I shouldn't have left the practice huts early. Stupid.*

"We miss yoooouuuu!" Beks throws her arm around my shoulder to give me a side hug. The charms on her bracelet brush my shoulder.

I force a laugh. "Um, I'm right here."

"Well, I know that. I mean you haven't been hanging out with us much this week."

"Yes I have."

"Not really." Julie pipes up then, "You've been distracted, to be honest. And what even happened with you and Andi last night? How did you get so lost? You were out there longer than anybody else."

Jori just nods in agreement and keeps air-playing.

"Well, I—We took a wrong turn on the path, and then

we ended up talking until Joanna found us. Nothing major. It was nice . . ."

"I mean, I know none of us are Black like Andi, but we're still your friends," Beks says, picking at her nails with her teeth. "You can still talk to us too."

Who said anything about this being a Black thing? I feel my cheeks flush, but I try to keep my voice calm: "Beks, that's not what this is about. It's low-key rude to assume I like hanging out with Andi just because she's Black."

Beks's cheeks turn red. "Okay, fine, sorry. I just—never mind. Can we drop this? You're here now. Let's go to the Cavity Cave? This might be the last time we all get to go together before camp ends."

"You just want to see if you-know-who is there." Jori speaks, finally. "You need to give it up. He's dating that high school girl we keep seeing him with. He's not interested in you."

"Shut up, Jori," Beks says. "We don't know that for sure. That could just be his friend. So what if I want to see him? I also happen to want ice cream, and to hang out with my girls."

Jori rolls her eyes. "Whatever you say, but that's for sure his girlfriend."

Beks sticks out her tongue at Jori, a little furrow of worry above her eyes, but she smiles then and loops her arm with mine. "So, are you coming, Zora?" Beks says. "My treat."

The last thing I feel like is ice cream, but I follow along and swallow the knot building in my throat. Beks's ignorant comment is still bothering me.

It is true that because Andi is Black, there are just some things that we both understand—like how people automatically group us all together, assuming that we all like the same things and feel the same way. But what they don't see or understand is that Andi and I are also unique, and that's what makes me want to hang out with her. Andi is her own person, with a history and life that looks nothing like mine. I like her because for those few moments by the lake, I could be me—without fake smiling or pretending. And right now, eating ice cream with Beks, Jori, and Julie, I am not myself. In fact, I am not really here at all. Sure, my body is sitting in the shade as Beks pouts and Jori gloats about the fact that Davy is clearly under a nearby tree making out with a high school girl wearing a flower crown, but really I'm floating above the scene, watching. I look like I fit in, but I don't. The entire time we sit, I am thinking, *What would they think if they knew about the kiss? If I told them about the part of me that's Black like the inside of a wave crashing on the wet sand? Black like the burst of color I saw behind my closed eyes when Andi's lips met mine? Black like me!*

But I don't say anything. I just smile and laugh and pretend, and I feel the new, brave parts of myself I'd discovered at the lake slip away.

When I get back from the Cavity Cave and dinner later that night, there's a letter waiting for me on my bunk. Kennedy's bubble handwriting greets me as I tear it open.

Friday, July 9

Zora,

I'm really hurt you haven't written me back. I never thought you'd be like this. Not that you care, but I met my dad's girlfriend and found out that they're not just dating, they're engaged. Her name is Karen, she's a yoga teacher—and yes, she is white and basic just like her name. She tried to put her hands all in my hair when we met and called me adorable. Adorable is what you call a toddler. She talks to me like I'm a baby. Everything here sucks. I got into a huge fight with my dad about how even when I come to visit him, he always puts his gigs and now his fiancée first. I really needed to hear from you. Not everything is about you, you know? I thought you were my best friend, but now I'm not sure. Hope camp is more fun than here.

Kennedy

I slump back into my pillows and reread her letter. She wrote it over a week ago, and that means she won't get the letters I just sent until I'm home from camp. If I had my cell phone, I'd text her right now, and it's too late to use the phones in the main lodge. I roll over and press my face into my pillows until I can't breathe. If I were alone, I'd scream.

This morning, everything had been wonderful, and now my head is spinning with everyone's expectations.

"Are you good?" Andi is standing up, peering at me on my bunk. "I mean . . . I saved a spot for you with me and Christopher at dinner. Didn't you see us waving?"

"Not everything is about you!" I snap, sitting up and jumping down from my bunk. "I have things going on in my life too, you know."

"My bad," Andi says. "I know that. I just wanted to give you your shirt back."

Andi hands me my unicorn PJ top folded neatly and smelling like fresh laundry. "I washed it for you. Thanks for letting me borrow it."

"You're welcome," I mumble. "I just need some alone time."

"Did I do something?" Andi says then, taking a step back with a hurt look.

"Everything is wrong today," I say, holding back tears. "I just can't deal with everyone needing something from me. It's too much."

"Zora—I'm not trying to pressure you, I—"

"Never mind. Forget it, I'm just stressed. Sorry for yelling," I say, and I jump down from the bed and run to the bathrooms. Locked safely in a stall, I run my pinky nail over the top of my left thigh and press down hard until it stings and throbs. *Zora, you have to get it together.*

SEAT AUDITIONS #4

*T*he moment Davy's horn sounds on the last Sunday of camp, I open my eyes, already in a bad mood when I realize I've slept through my early alarm. Beks does not come over to drool out the window, and instead shuffles across the room to whine to Angie about her broken heart. For once, I roll out to flag looking like Jori's burrito twin, wrapped in all my blankets.

In line, Andi leans around Jori to catch my eye. "Good morning. Are you feeling better today?" she asks.

I shake my head yes, but she knows it's a lie, because she mouths, "You sure?"

I look away and ignore her. I don't have time to talk—I have to get myself together and out of this funky mood. First order of business: a trip to the main lodge to call Kennedy. When announcements are done, I run back to the cabin, throw on my uniform, grab my bag and flute, and race across campus. I arrive at the main lodge just as a sleepy-eyed counselor is opening the front doors with a key.

"Can I help you?" she asks.

"I need to use the phones. Really quickly to call—uh, my mom," I lie. "It's important."

"Okay, keep it quick. You don't want to miss breakfast."

"I will," I say, running into a booth and rummaging around in my bag until I find the little notebook I wrote Kennedy's phone number and address in before camp.

I dial fast, my hands shaking. *Pick up, pick up, pick up.* I say to myself as it rings and rings and rings. Then I realize, if it's seven thirty a.m. here, it's four thirty a.m. in California. *There's no way she's awake.* I get Kennedy's voice mail, which I know for a fact she never checks.

"Why bother with voice mail when you could just text instead?" she always says.

But I can't text her, so when I hear the beep, I take a deep breath and speak into the receiver:

"Hi, Kennedy. It's me, Zora. I really hope you get this, because I don't have my cell. But I got your second letter, and did write you back, but I forgot to send the first letter. It's in the mail now—in fact I sent you two letters, but I'm worried you won't get them until I'm home from camp. I'm so sorry. That's big news about your dad. You're still my best friend. Please don't be mad. My letters will explain everything. I have to go, but know I am thinking about you. I can't wait to see you soon. Okay, bye."

I wish I felt better, but as I hang up the phone, my gut churns at the thought of Kennedy being upset with me. *Gurgle gurgle gloop.* My stomach growls, reminding me that I still have a couple of items of business before my audition:

breakfast and a quick practice; but looking at the time, I realize I'll need to make it a grab-and-go meal.

An hour later, after eating only a granola bar and trying to perfect my piece, I slide into the rec hall room with Mr. Wright.

"Zora!" he says, looking at his watch. "Cutting it close today for your final audition?"

I put together my flute and try to stand tall and confident, even though I feel horrible.

"Are you warmed up?" he asks, shifting in his chair.

I nod, and then I notice Andi standing outside the door. She waves at me and smiles before disappearing from the window frame, presumably to sit on the floor outside.

"Zora?"

"Yes. I think so," I say. My tongue feels like cardboard in my mouth and I'm out of breath, but now is not the time to make excuses.

"All right," Mr. Wright says, tapping a pencil on the music stand in front of him. "Let's get started."

I try not to think about Andi outside, but when I look down at my sheet music, all I see are funny shapes. I shake my head and close my eyes to center myself. I begin, and after a few notes, my shaky breath evens out.

It's not my best audition, but I autopilot through it.

"Very good. Thank you, Zora" is all Mr. Wright says, scribbling down a few notes. "Results will be posted by lunch, as always. You've had an excellent summer; I hope you're proud of your growth."

"Thank you," I say, and then I open the door and stumble right into Andi.

"Sorry!" I say in a higher-pitched voice than I want to.

"No worries," Andi says, holding her trumpet in her hands, a folder of sheet music under her arm.

We stand there, in each other's way. There's so much I want to say to her.

"Um, I should go in," Andi says after a beat. "Maybe I'll see you after? At lunch?"

"Of course. Sorry. Good luck in there." And then for some stupid reason, I set my things down on the floor and give her a double thumbs-up, which I've never done in my life. Andi steps inside and closes the door. It takes everything in me not to press my ear against it and listen to her play. I stand there long enough to hear the first blare of her horn, and then I run out into the morning light.

When I find my name posted on the audition results list at lunch, it takes me a minute to process what I am seeing. I look closer, and there it is in plain letters:

Zora Johnson—2nd chair.

Oh no. Oh no no no no! The worker bee in me starts to buzz. The fried chicken sandwich I have on my plate suddenly smells full of grease, making my stomach lurch. *Mom and Dad are going to be so disappointed. How could I let this happen?*

"YES!!!" Ella from my flute section shouts, standing next to me now with her tray. When she sees my face, her smile fades. "I mean, sorry Zora. I really thought it was going to be you again. I didn't expect to get first chair in the last week, but at least we still get to play the solo together. We just swapped seats."

I make myself smile even though I am gritting my teeth. "Congratulations, Ella. You'll be great. Really, you deserve this."

But I don't know how convincing I sound. I'm definitely not hungry anymore. I dump my food in the trash and turn in my tray. Then I escape into one of the private bathrooms in the dining hall. Once inside, I lean my back against the closed door and slam my fists against my upper thighs, harder and harder and harder until they are numb and I am out of breath. When I'm too tired to hit myself any more, I slide down till I am seated on the cool concrete floor and put my head between my knees. *You're so stupid, Zora. You let everything distract you: Ms. J.'s dance class, the stupid Lost Lake legend and most of all, Andi.*

"Zora?"

Someone is knocking.

"Zora, are you good? It's Andi."

No. She cannot see me like this.

"Yes. I'm fine. I'll be out soon." I mean it to sound clear, but my voice sounds like tree branches scraping against a closed window—scratchy and dry.

"Are you sure? I saw the list. . . . and I know that you . . ."

"I'M FINE! YOU DON'T KNOW EVERYTHING ABOUT ME, ANDI. JUST BECAUSE WE FOUND THE LAKE AND I TOLD YOU SOME THINGS ABOUT MYSELF DOESN'T MEAN I NEED YOU ALL IN MY BUSINESS RIGHT NOW!"

The words come like thorns. My mouth prickles full of sorry, but I let the sting hang in the air between us.

Andi shuffles outside the door. "I was just trying to let you know I am here if you want to talk, but never mind. I'm not here for this. Peace."

After thirty minutes of hiding in the bathroom, I stand up and check my reflection. A hot-mess express stares back at me. Rehearsal will be starting soon. I splash some water on my face and smooth out my uniform shirt. Then I retwist my locs up into a tight bun and leave the bathroom. My thighs are tingling now; there will probably be bruises.

I make it to the band shed and into my chair—second chair—just as Mr. London steps on the podium.

"Good afternoon, everyone. As you know, this is our final week together, which means we'll be revisiting many of the pieces we've learned over the past month so we can play them for your families at the final showcase on Friday."

I stare down at my lap. Mom and Dad always come up early in the last week of camp. They like to rent a little cabin so they can visit nearby shops and restaurants. Just like we agreed before I left, they'll be here this Wednesday to take me out to lunch, and I'll have to tell them I failed.

"So, let's start today by rehearsing the first two suites of *On the Waterfront*. Angie will start us off with her solo, and congratulations to Andi Byrd. She'll be playing the opening-section trumpet duet with Channing now. It's not often someone moves from fourth chair to second chair in one summer. Channing is lucky to be playing this duet with you. Brava!"

I sneak a glance behind me at the trumpets. Andi is indeed second-chair trumpet! Channing has a pained look on her face as if a thousand horses are stampeding over her feet. *Serves her right.* Andi shrugs her shoulders but sits tall and proud in her seat. Before she raises her trumpet, she catches my eye. I am about to get the nerve to mouth "sorry" to her when she looks away. Then rehearsal begins.

GIFTS

I don't know how I make it through, but when Mr. London dismisses us two hours later, I get my things together fast so I can catch Andi, but when I turn around she's gone.

"Are you looking for Andi?" Christopher says, eyeing me from the trombone section, where he is still sitting.

"Um . . . well . . . it's no big deal . . . I'll find her later."

Christopher stands up and comes over to me so I can hear his whisper. "Andi told me what you did for her at the lake, helping her get back to the beach after the whole canoe fiasco."

I gulp and nod. I wonder if she also told him about our kiss. She said she was going to tell him everything, but that—our kiss—felt private.

"I get it now, Zora. I'm Andi's best friend, but you're also important to her, in a different way."

I was important to her, until I yelled at her. "Do you know where she went?" I ask.

"She had to run back to her cabin, but we're going to meet at the Craft Shack for free time in fifteen minutes. Want to join?"

"I don't want to mess up your time with her . . ."

"You won't," Christopher says, strapping his trombone to his back. "I was worried about that at first, but not now. Not anymore."

"Okay, maybe," I say.

"Well, then maybe see you there," Christopher says with a wave.

Twenty minutes later, I'm outside the Craft Shack. Inside it's mostly empty, so I wander around, looking at all the supplies and materials. I used to come here a lot my first years of camp, but I guess I just haven't had the time. I'm running my hand over the basket-weaving supplies when I hear laughter coming from the back room. I peek my head around the corner, and Andi is there, sitting on top of a table, making a lanyard while Christopher is doing some sort of impression, a piece of shaggy yellow fabric thrown over his head like a wig.

"Well, Andi," he says, "Mr. Wright and Mr. London must have felt some kind of sorry for you, because lord knows nobody moves up that many chairs on their own. Plus, none of y'all can play as well as I can—that's just facts. I just pray you don't mess up our solo."

Andi is laughing so hard that her slim shoulders shake. "Christopher, stop. You sound just like her. I thought she was going to murder me all rehearsal. I was just as surprised as she was."

"Well, you earned that spot, Andi," Christopher says, snapping out of character. "Don't let her bully you into feeling like you didn't. I heard you rehearsing for the audition; that's the best I've ever heard you play. You were on fire, as they say."

"Thanks," Andi says. "I think that camping trip really helped me get out of my head . . ."

Channing. Christopher was doing an impression of Channing, and it was low-key funny. His accent is perfect. Before I can stop myself, I laugh out loud.

Andi jumps off the table then, and Christopher pulls the fabric off his head. They both turn to look at me as I stand in the doorway, frozen.

"You came," Christopher says. "I'm going to go get more . . . yarn." Then he slides past me and leaves me alone with Andi.

"Congratulations," I manage to get out. "On getting second-chair trumpet, I mean. That's really amazing."

"You don't have to say that. I know you're mad you didn't get first-chair flute again—"

"No," I interrupt. "I'm really happy for you. You deserve it. I . . . um . . . I didn't mean what I said earlier. I just kind of went off. You know, I'm not used to . . ."

"Messing up?"

"Yes. I guess so."

"But isn't that what we're supposed to do right now? I

mean, we're still growing. We get to mess up sometimes, and adults, they're a mess too."

I wish I could brave-talk like Andi.

"I guess I had this whole perfect idea of my mom in my head since she died," Andi continues, "and it's been hard to remember the times that she wasn't perfect. The times she let me down and I let her down. But then I came here, and I don't know, this camp is cutthroat, Zora. There's so much pressure, and I don't need any more of that. I was just having fun with my audition today. I stopped worrying and just played, just let go of it all. It felt extra good. Like it used to. You helped me with that."

I look up to meet Andi's gaze now.

"What do you mean?"

"I mean, even though you don't seem to think it meant anything, or that we're not friends, that time at the lake, it meant something to me. But now, we're back and you seem like you're not about us, or yourself even. I like the Zora I met in the woods better, the one who likes to dance and get free."

A swarm of words get lost in my belly. *It meant something to me too. I am free.*

"You don't know everything about me," is what I repeat instead. A broken record, a robot girl.

"Yeah." Andi shrugs. "I guess you're right, but I don't know everything about me either. That's the whole point.

We still have time to grow." She holds out the lanyard she's been working on. It's made of teal and sparkly gold floss. My favorite combo. "This is for you," she says. "I'm going to go find Christopher. I'll see you later."

I watch her leave, holding the lanyard in my hand, and it's still warm from her touch.

BFFS

"Zora, what are you going to wear for the final mixer?" Beks asks from across the cabin. It's Tuesday during free time and Beks is rifling through a pile of non-uniform clothes on her bunk.

There are only three full days left of camp, and these are supposed to be the fun ones—a celebration of the summer. Tomorrow, Mom and Dad are coming to take me off campus for lunch, then we have our dress rehearsal and final mixer on Thursday, followed by our showcase on Friday night. Unlike the opening mixer, the final mixer of the summer is almost as important as prom. The counselors decorate the rec hall, and the dining hall caters, so there's always cookies, cupcakes, popcorn, and other fun snacks. Sometimes there's even a cotton-candy machine that they pull out, and a big bowl of punch. It's a whole deal, and anyone who's had any kind of crush knows it's the very last time to make it known. I wish I were more excited about it all, but I can't seem to shake my mood. Ever since Sunday's blowup, Andi and I have gone back to the way we were when we first met, barely talking, and faking being fine has been harder than normal. I still don't know where I stand with Kennedy, and on top of everything, I'm dreading lunch tomorrow. I can already see the disappointed looks on Mom's and Dad's faces when I tell them about my chair in orchestra.

"What do you think about this?" Beks asks, posing with her hand on her hip to show off her outfit: a short jean skirt, black-and-white-striped tank top, accessorized with dangly R2-D2 earrings.

"Cute," I say absentmindedly. "That's the one."

"Totally," says Julie from her bunk, where she and Jori are sifting through an equally large stack of outfits.

Beks smiles. "Now, what about you? You have such good style, Zora."

I had my final-mixer outfit picked out before I even arrived at camp—a red romper with gold and teal flowers all over it and gold sandals. I pull out the romper now and lay it on my bed for Beks, Julie, and Jori to inspect.

"So cute," Beks says.

"You always have the best clothes," Julie adds, fingering the soft romper fabric. "And your skin looks so good in bright colors. Plus, it fits your bubbly personality."

"Thanks," I say, not feeling very bubbly or happy at all. I glance at Andi's empty bunk. She's made herself scarce, and to be honest I'm not sure how to make things right again.

"Are there any boys you want to ask you to dance?" Julie continues. "Because I heard that Sam has a crush on you."

"Who is Sam?" I ask, folding up my outfit and putting it back on my shelves.

"Sam! You know, he plays cello in our orchestra, and sits next to Coop? He's from boys' cabin two—remember how they were all trying to dance with us at the opening mixer?"

I furrow my brow and think back over the summer. "You mean Sam from Ohio, the one who wears that same *Black Panther* sweatshirt over his uniform every day?"

"Yeah! He's adorable. You'd be the perfect couple. You could be his Nakia."

I've never even seen the movie *Black Panther*, but people always assume I have. I'm not into superhero movies at all. I bet Julie thinks I should date Sam because he's one of the few Black boys here. I shake my head. "Sounds like *you* should ask him to dance," I say to Julie.

"Oh no no," she says, her cheeks flushing. "I would never. Plus, he likes you, I think."

"Well, I don't really want to dance with him . . . or any guys," I say, glancing at Andi's Nike slides neatly placed under her bed.

"Amen to that," Jori says, sitting in the middle of the cabin floor, eating handfuls of Goldfish from a huge carton her parents sent. "We don't need no boys to be great. We're fierce on our own."

Not exactly what I meant, but I smile in agreement.

"Well, I hope someone asks me to dance," Julie says quietly. "It will be so embarrassing if not."

The longing in Julie's voice matches the pang in my heart: *The only person I want to dance with is Andi, but I bet she'll never ask me now.*

Joanna peeks her head into the cabin entrance. "Goodness! It's a mess in here. You know the mixer is still a couple days away, right?" she asks us, surveying the piles of clothes everywhere.

"We know!" Beks calls. "But you can never be too prepared."

"Right," Joanna says, stepping over Jori's Goldfish carton in the middle of the room. "Well, I know you all are going to look great. Now, Zora, I came to here to let you know you have a phone call from your Mom in the main lodge. So, hop to it."

"She's probably just confirming our lunch. As if I could forget." I roll my eyes at Julie and Beks. "Be back in a minute."

"Yes, I know, you'll be here at twelve p.m. sharp," I sigh into the phone propped on the front desk in the main lodge a few moments later.

"Uh, hi to you too. This is Kennedy. I had to pretend I was your mom so they'd let me talk to you. Security at your camp is really extra; it's stupid they don't let anyone but family members call."

"Kennedy! I— Hiiiiiiiii. Oh em gee."

"How are you?"

"How am I? I'm horrible. I'm really sorry, Kennedy. I never meant to hurt you . . . and I—"

Hearing Kennedy's voice is so overwhelming that I fumble my words for a few moments.

"Sorry, let me start again," I say, taking a deep inhale. "I'm really glad you got my message and I'm sorry that you didn't get my letters yet. I did write to you, and I do care about your life, and I'm sorry I've been such a jerk to you this summer. Are you still mad at me?"

"No," Kennedy says softly. "I just really miss you, Zora. I miss us. This summer has been trash."

"I know," I say, feeling my eyes fill with tears. "I'm sorry about your dad's fiancée. She sounds . . ."

"Like a witch?"

I laugh. "You said it, not me."

Kennedy laughs then too, a deep, familiar cackle, and the sound reminds me of home.

"Zora. I can't talk for long, but I just wanted to say, I'm sorry too. I should have reacted better when you told me about . . . you know . . . your crush on me. I hope we can still be friends, even if I don't feel the same way."

"I know," I say. "I get it. Listen, let's make a plan to start over when I get home? By then you'll have my letters, and I promise I'll tell you everything about my summer if you promise to tell me everything about yours?"

"Deal," Kennedy says.

"I can't believe you found a way to call me at camp!" I squeal.

"Me either," Kennedy says, "but that's just what BFFs do."

If I could reach through the phone and hug her, I would, but instead I do a little joy dance from where I stand, not caring how I look or who is watching.

OFF CAMPUS

"ZoZo! ZoZo! Over here."

The next day I'm walking back from morning rehearsal when I see them: my parents. They are standing in the middle of division by the flagpole, talking with Joanna. My dad is waving his big hand at me and smiling with all his white teeth. "ZoZo!" he yells again, and I rush over to say hello before the whole of camp learns my nickname.

"I thought I was meeting you at the main lodge?" I say, giving dad a little hug, which he then turns into a bear hug, motioning for my mom to join.

"We missed you so much!" Mom says now, pulling away. "Your dad wanted to see where you've been living, since you didn't let us help you get set up this year. I tried to tell him no, but, well, here we are. We brought Ginny too, but she's in the car, waiting for you, and, yes, we left the windows open and parked in the shade. She'll be fine for a few moments."

I wish dogs were allowed in division, because I could really use some Ginny snuggles right now. Mom knows how protective I get of her, and I never think anyone can take care of Ginny as well as me. We're bonded; that's just how dachshunds are. Ginny tolerates Mom and Dad, but I'm her person.

"You ready to get some eats, ZoZo?" Dad booms. "Joanna seems really great, and she's a Wolverine! You didn't tell us that."

"Dad, please don't call me that here," I say, looking around.

"Oh, eh, sorry, baby girl, I . . ."

"And don't call me baby girl either!" I say, my teeth gritted. I know they are happy to see me, but I'm already dreading telling them about my seat in orchestra, and I don't know why they couldn't just wait for me in the parking lot.

"Don't talk to your father like that," Mom snaps, adjusting the collar of her button-down. "We're just excited to see you, but it appears maybe we've caught you at a bad time?"

"Sorry," I mumble. "I'm glad you're here. I'm just stressed out about the showcase on Friday. We're playing some hard pieces, and I need to practice."

"Well, we can keep our lunch short, and then we promise we'll get out of your hair, Zo . . . I mean, Zora," Dad says.

"Thank you. That sounds good."

Mom and Dad sign me out in the main lodge, and then we're free to head off campus. When I climb into the back seat, Ginny licks every inch of my face as she makes her happy grunts and squeals. Mom steers the car out of the main gates, and Harmony Music Camp disappears into the trees behind us.

Dad rolls down the windows and I lean my head out to smell the fresh air.

"It's good to see you, Zora," he says again, catching my eye in the passenger side mirror. "We missed our talented girl."

"Good to see you too, Dad," I say, feeling a drop in my gut. *I'm not as talented as you think.*

When we get to town, we walk around until we decide on a local brewery for lunch. They have a dog-friendly patio, so we can bring Ginny. My mom and dad love sampling local beers, and Michigan has some of the best. I think beer tastes like actual garbage (my dad let me have a tiny sip once last New Year's Eve), so I don't get it. I follow my parents to a table on the patio, which overlooks the main street lined with cherry trees. Michigan really is beautiful in the summer—you just have to be ready to outlast the winters.

"So," Mom starts as soon as she and Dad have put in their drink orders, "what pieces can we look forward to hearing on Friday?"

I take a long swig of my water. I have to tell them at some point, but does it have to be right now? Once I tell them, this lunch is going to be ruined.

"Mom, you'll be happy to hear that we're starting off with Tchaikovsky's *Romeo and Juliet, Fantasy-Overture*."

Mom claps her hands together. "Oh, I just love that piece."

I nod. "Yes, and we're ending with the first two suites from Leonard Bernstein's *On the Waterfront*, which is the one I'm most worried about, since it has a really challenging flute part—well, it's challenging for all the brass and woodwinds."

"I can't wait to hear it," Dad says, sniffing his recently delivered beer and then taking a small contemplative sip.

Dad, unlike Mom, isn't a classical-music buff. He loves to hear me play, but he can't really tell the difference between Vivaldi and Bach.

"Do you have any solos?" Mom asks. "You must if it's so challenging for the woodwind section."

Time for another long drink of my ice water. *Technically, yes*, I practice saying in my head. *I do still play the opening flute solo for* On the Waterfront *Suite I, but just not sitting first chair. That's Ella's place now.* I don't think Mom will care about this technicality. When I put my glass down, our waiter comes. I shut my eyes to stop the brain freeze, then I order a burger with sweet-potato fries. If Mom is mad about my food choice, she doesn't say anything. Sweet-potato fries usually win her over anyway. Plus, she's distracted herself by pulling out a packet of Clorox wipes, which she uses to wipe down the table in anticipation of our food.

Dad is already surveying the menu for his next beer selection.

"So, Zo . . . Zora," he says, putting the menu down. "What's new? What's shaking? How is it hanging? Do you feel like you had a productive summer?"

Before I can answer, my eyes lock onto the shape of Jasmine Baker entering the patio with a girl who looks like she's in elementary school. *What is she still doing here? The workshop was, like, two weeks ago.*

I try to slide down into my seat, but she notices us (the only other Black people in the restaurant), waves, and starts to walk over.

"Who is that?" Mom asks, sitting up straighter.

I really thought I'd deal with the dance-class confession at checkout on Saturday, but it looks like it is going to happen now. I scan the patio for an escape, but soon Ms. J. is at our table.

"Hello, Zora!" she says. "I saw you over here and just wanted to come say hello. Is this your family?"

Mom slaps me softly on the back of the neck, which I know means don't be rude, sit up and introduce us to this person.

"Yes, ma'am," I say. "These are my parents, Dr. Carla and Dr. Douglas Johnson."

"Oh, just Doug and Carla are fine!" Dad says, standing up to shake Ms. Jasmine's hand.

"And you are . . . ?" Mom says, as she, too, shakes Ms. Jasmine's graceful hand.

"I'm Jasmine, Jasmine Baker. I taught a dance master class at Harmony Music Camp a couple weeks ago."

There's no running now.

"Oh, yes." Mom's eyebrows go up. "I think Zora mentioned something about the master class offerings this year. I didn't realize you'd be one of us—well, what I mean is you don't see a lot of Black dancers who make it."

I sink down into my chair again. Mom is so embarrassing.

Ms. J. continues as if it's nothing. "Well, that's what they want you to think." She winks. "But there is quite an active Black dance community in Detroit, and gigs like this one help with exposure. Plus, I used this as an excuse to bring my daughter, Kenya, on a mini-vacation; we've been staying at a local bed and breakfast nearby."

Ms. J. is even more beautiful in the sunlight, wearing a flowy white sundress and a pair of gold earrings in the shape of triangles.

"I just want to let you know that Zora is a very talented dancer. She was the highlight of my workshop, very expressive and original with her movements."

"Well . . . well, yes," Dad says, catching Mom's pursed-lip look just as I do. "Zora has a lot of talents."

Next to me, Mom is folding and refolding the napkin in her lap.

"Thank you. It was a really good class," I manage to squeak out. "I learned a lot."

"Yes, well, I don't want to keep you all from your lunch, but I just wanted to come over and say hello. I told Zora about the dance troupe I run, and I hope you'll consider having her audition this September, if you're willing to make the drive from Ann Arbor. Nice to meet you both!"

Then Ms. J. squeezes my shoulder and glides away to her table. Mom and Dad each send her off with a polite "Nice to meet you too."

I exhale a big breath, and then peer at my parents' faces.

Dad picks up the beer menu again. Mom is still smoothing her napkin.

"So you took that class anyway? I thought we were going to revisit the idea," Mom begins.

"You lied to us? ZoZo, that's not like you at all," Dad says now.

"I didn't mean to lie. I just really wanted to take that class. I miss dance . . . I can pay you back. I promise."

"This is not about the money," Mom says. "This is about distracting yourself with something that, quite frankly, isn't going to get you very far. Zora, you chose flute, remember? We asked you what you wanted, and you decided flute was the more practical option. You remember how the dance world treated you. Why you'd want to put yourself back into that, I just don't understand."

"Now, Carla," Dad says, "let's hear her out. Maybe we've been too—"

Mom holds her hand up and Dad shuts his mouth. She never lets him finish.

"We've spent all this time and money on your passion for

flute and now you want to dabble in dance again? Well, I'm sorry, that's just not going to work for us. You need to finish what you've started. Johnsons do not quit."

I feel a stinging all through my body. A swarm of anger. "*YOU* DECIDED!" I yell, standing up and noticing a few heads on the patio turn.

"Oh no," Mom begins, "You better fix your attitude right now."

I stay standing and take a take a breath. Then I lower my voice, but keep my tone firm.

"You decided, Mom. About dance. I loved it, and sure, I don't have a 'ballerina body,' whatever that means, but that's not important to me. All I know is that I was seven, and those girls made fun of me, and I felt like I had to do what you said. You guys push me so hard on flute, I don't even know if I like it anymore! It's not fun, and you know what"—*Might as well let it all out*—"I failed at reaching my goals this summer, okay? I know you're going to ask me, so might as well tell you now. When you see me at the showcase on Friday, I won't be sitting first chair. Your perfect daughter is second chair. So if you're ashamed of me, I'm sorry. But I'm barely a teenager! I don't have it all figured out yet, and maybe there are other things I want to try. Maybe you don't know me at all."

For once, Mom is speechless. Our food arrives. I sit down,

trying to hold back tears as our plates are placed in front of us. I'm definitely not hungry anymore.

"Excuse me," I say. "I need to use the bathroom." Then I rush away before anyone can stop me.

I don't know when I started to hurt myself; I just know that it was little by little. In moments when I feel like the world is spinning out of control, when I can't seem to put everything in its place, I go back to it like a habit. Some people bite their nails so far down that they bleed. Some people pick at their skin or pull out their hair. I scratch and hit and pinch. I'm not trying to die—I'm just trying to feel something. I'm just trying to snap myself back into my body. I've gotten so good at it, sometimes I don't even realize it's happening.

I don't hear Mom come into the bathroom after me. I'm in the last stall, slamming my right hand into my left bicep like a hammer. *Smack, smack, smack, smack.* The sound is loud in my ears, and it echoes through the empty bathroom.

"Zora, is that you? What's going on in there?"

Smack, smack, smack, I answer back, tears dripping down my face. Each hit is a breath. Each hit is a sting, a way back to the present. And I can't stop.

"Zora— Are you— Oh, my baby girl. Please stop that. I'm here. Please unlock the door."

"I don't want you to see me," I choke out.

"Zora. I am your mother. I love you. No matter what. Please, please open the door."

I punch my arm hard one last time and let out a deep sob. Then I slide the lock over, and Mom is right there with me. She pulls my sleeve up and inspects the tender spot, pulls me into a hug, and kisses me on the forehead.

I go limp against her. I am so tired.

"Zora girl. I am so sorry. I didn't know." Mom pulls back with tears in her eyes. "I didn't know."

DRESS REHEARSAL

The next morning, I make my way with all of Junior Orchestra over to the amphitheater for a run-through of our showcase set. Stepping onto that stage never fails to impress me. The amphitheater is built to be great, with five hundred audience seats that slope down toward the stage in tiers. The stage is covered by a big red metal roof, but all the seats and sides of the theater are open to the outside, and the backdrop of the stage looks out onto Lake Harmony, glistening in the sun.

High School Orchestra gets to rehearse here every day, but we only have this one morning to get used to the acoustics and build our confidence.

I make my way over to my seat and start to warm up.

"Hey, Zora." Ella has joined me and is running through our solo. "Do you think you could help me with this one part?"

Since yesterday's lunch with my parents, and the fact that it's hard to keep my sore left arm up to hold my flute, I feel like the last person who should be giving help. After I calmed down in the bathroom, we went back to the table and ate our food in exhausted silence. Mom let me take

Ginny back to the car while she and Dad settled up the tab. Then we all took a walk to get some fresh chocolate–peanut butter fudge, and sat on a bench in the town square to talk. Mom helped me tell Dad about the hitting, and it was hard to open up to them more about it, but they listened and tried to understand. When we get back to Ann Arbor, we're going to go to family counseling. Mom even said she'd take a look at the dance troupe Ms. Jasmine had mentioned. We're definitely not a perfect family, never have been, but yesterday felt like a step forward.

"Please? I'm really nervous, and you always seemed so calm when you were sitting in this chair," Ella continues.

"I'm nervous all the time," I tell her. "I'm just a little too good at hiding it."

"Well, I think I'm going to puke. This stage is huge, and my moms are going to be sitting front and center recording me on Instagram Live so my whole extended family back in Maine can watch."

"I know how that is," I say. "You'll do great. And even if you mess up, it's okay—everyone messes up."

Andi walks by just as I say this, and I give her a small smile. She ignores me.

"Now, what part do you need help with?" I ask Ella, and she runs through her sections a few times, then I give her pointers.

"All right, get settled everyone." Mr. London steps to the

podium. He looks tiny up there against the rows of empty amphitheater seats. "Good morning, and welcome to our last rehearsal before the big night. I know we're not used to being on this stage, and it's a little distracting, but it's important that we stay focused today. We're going to run through our full set as many times as we can in the next three hours, so let's get started."

Everybody knows that dress rehearsals are a mess, but this one is really bad. It's like we all forgot how to listen to one another. As we get further and further into it, someone is always out of tune or coming in at the wrong bar, or forgetting the correct bowing. Mr. London starts and stops us so often I get whiplash from moving my flute up and down, up and down. When we finally get to the *On the Waterfront* Suites, Ella and I keep it together for our flute solo, but Andi struggles alongside Channing during the trumpet duet. We all know she can play this part like nobody else, but it seems like she's lost her nerve. The fifth time we start the piece, I want to turn around and give her encouragement, but I'm not sure she wants to hear from me. Plus, Mr. London has already yelled at two kids in the bass section for having a side conversation and threatened to keep us here through lunch if it happens again.

Three hours later, Mr. London closes his scores and puts down his baton. "That was not our best showing," he says, "but I know you all will rise to the occasion tomorrow. I urge you to use your sectional rehearsals this afternoon to really work on some of the errors we heard today. You all are very talented, and it's been an honor to work with you this summer, but sometimes it's easy to slip back into old habits when nervous. Take a deep breath, get some rest, and let's show up tomorrow ready to make your families proud. You're dismissed."

I turn around to look at Andi, but when I do, I see that she's deep in conversation with Joanna. Then I watch as Andi nods, packs up her things, and rushes away with Joanna in the direction of the main lodge.

"Ready for lunch?" Julie says as I meet her, Jori, and Beks at stage right.

"Um, you all go ahead. I need to run to the main lodge for something really quick. Save me a seat."

When I get to the lodge, it's mostly empty and there's no sign of Andi or Joanna. I pretend to inspect the bulletin board, then ask if there's any mail for cabin four.

"Nope, nothing for cabin four today," the counselor on office duty says.

"Thanks. I guess I'll just walk over to the dining—"

Joanna leads Andi out of a door that connects to the back office.

"Andi, I'm so sorry. I'm sure everything will be fine with your aunt and uncle. We'll get everything figured out."

Andi's face is blank, and her shoulders droop.

"I have to head to a staff meeting, but why don't you go get some lunch. Then we can chat later about getting you a ride home."

Why does Andi need a ride home?

"My parents and I can probably give you a ride," I blurt out.

"Zora, I didn't see you there," Joanna says. "That's a very kind offer, but I'll need to speak to your parents about it. And of course Andi's family."

"I know."

"Well, I need to go to my meeting. But we can make the calls later. Right now, Andi could use a friend. Are you headed to the dining hall?"

"Yes. We can go together if you want?" I say, looking at Andi tentatively.

Andi's eyes meet mine for a second, then she scowls.

"Is it okay if I walk with you to the dining hall?" I ask.

"I guess."

"Good. Good," Joanna says, holding the door open for us. "See you later, girls. Andi, don't you worry. Everything is going to be all right."

Our feet make a soft swishing noise as we head toward the dining hall. I stay quiet and walk next to her, watching my sandaled feet get in sync with her black high-top Chucks while we move along the dirt path, across the main camp street, and toward the smell of chicken fingers.

"Are you okay?" I ask, finally.

"I don't know," Andi says. "It's been a weird morning."

"Is your aunt okay?"

"I think so. She and my uncle can't come, though. To the final showcase. They just called me. That's why I was with Joanna."

"Why not?"

"My aunt got admitted to the hospital last night. The baby's not due until August, but I guess there are complications."

"Oh. I didn't know she was pregnant."

"Yeah. I'm going to be a cousin."

"It makes sense if you're bummed they won't be there tomorrow. You worked hard."

"You know, maybe it's better they don't come. I played like trash today in rehearsal. They don't need to see all that; plus, this baby is more important than me. I'm just some kid they got stuck with."

"Don't say that. Dress rehearsal was hard for everyone. But you're going to kill your solo. I know it."

Andi stops walking just as we approach the dining-hall entrance.

"Why do you care all of a sudden? You don't need to give me a ride home just because you feel sorry for me."

I gulp. "That's not why—I thought maybe you just needed someone."

"Well, thanks for walking with me, but I don't get you, Zora. You don't want me all in your business, but you're always trying to be in mine. I'm good. I don't need you either. In fact, I don't need anyone. So, can you just leave me alone right now? My head hurts."

"All right, but . . ."

"I'll see you later."

With that, I watch Andi run into the dining hall.

I stand outside for a few minutes. My left arm throbs, and so does my heart.

FINAL MIXER

"*C*an I stay here? I just want to chill and listen to music." I'm trying not to hear Andi's conversation with Joanna, but I can't help it. I'm in the back of the cabin, dabbing on some lip gloss in the small hanging mirror, when Joanna takes Andi aside in the corner to reason with her. Andi is still half in uniform—her bare feet are jammed into her Nike slides, and she's wearing her khaki shorts and the soft Miles Davis T-shirt she likes to sleep in.

"It's not an option, Andi," Joanna says. "Everyone has to be in the rec hall during the mixer. You don't have to dance, but you will have to come with us all. Division is going to be empty and you can't be unsupervised."

"But you know me, Joanna. All I'm going to do is listen to music on my bunk. I'll probably fall asleep."

"Look, Andi. It's final. We're all leaving together in fifteen minutes, so please get ready. I'm sure you'll have some fun when you get there. There's going to be a cotton-candy machine!"

In the mirror, I watch Andi's lean frame crumple a little, and I fight the urge to run over and give her a hug. To pull her close like I did at the lake and tell her it's all going to work out.

"Fine," Andi says now, walking away and back into the cabin chaos.

I feel the same, I want to say to Andi. This is the first year I'd rather skip the mixer, but I know better. Julie and Beks attacked me with excitement as soon as I walked into the cabin after dinner, and I've been helping them get ready ever since. Good thing I had my outfit picked out, because now I'm just on autopilot. I add a last dab of lip gloss and head back to my bunk. Andi is staring at her shelves and running her soft brush through her hair slowly.

"Don't know what to wear?" I ask.

"What?" Andi says, turning to me, her face softer than it was this afternoon.

"Everyone makes a big deal about getting dressed up, but it's still pretty casual."

"Nah. I'm good," she says. "I'll figure it out."

"Well . . . ," I start, biting my tongue a little. "Whatever you pick, I'm sure you'll look good. You always do."

Before she can respond and tell me to go away, I grab my sandals off my shelf and head toward the front of the cabin. *Super-awkward move, Zora. She doesn't want your help or opinion.*

"Julie, Beks!" I call, "I'll meet you outside."

I sit on the front steps of the cabin and start pulling on my sandals. Every cabin in division is bursting with noise as campers rush around getting ready. The air smells of every kind of fruity body spray you can imagine, and I'm glad that I skipped that trend. Instead, I take out a small tube of coconut lotion and begin to rub it into my ankles, elbows, and knees.

Someone stomps out on the steps behind me.

"About time," I say, expecting Julie, but when I turn around, I see it's Andi. Andi, wearing her high-top Chucks, a pair of black jean shorts, a black button-down, tucked in, with black-and-white piano-key suspenders that would look corny on anyone else but somehow work with her all-black-everything style. I must be staring because she crosses her arms and says, "What? Are the suspenders too much?"

"No! I like them. You look . . . nice."

Andi shrugs and looks away. "I guess if I have to go to this thing. Everyone else was getting dressed up, so."

"You'll fit right in."

"Cool."

"Cool."

Say something else, Zora.

But before I can, Joanna's holding the flaps of the cabin open and ushering girls out to line up. "Stars!" she yells. "Your ball awaits. Let's go go go go! Put the lip gloss down, spray your final spray of perfume, and back away. It is mixer time."

And then we are on our way.

I'm always impressed with how transformed the rec hall looks for the final mixer. We walk in and there are dangly fairy lights hanging from every corner in the room, giving off a soft glow. This year someone has even hung a big silver disco ball in the center of the room. It sends sparkles all over the walls. The music is already playing loudly, a BTS song, and there is a line of about ten kids posted up waiting for cotton-candy cones.

"This is magical!" Jori says, grabbing me and Beks by the hands. "Let's get some snacks."

"Wait for me!" Julie says, pushing through the crowd in the doorway to get to us.

We load up our plates with cupcakes, popcorn, and chocolate kisses and then find a small table to sit at. We watch the room fill, but unlike at the opening mixer when everyone was already hyped up from the competition, nobody is dancing. Everyone is standing around the edges of the room, swaying and two-stepping. Some of the boys from cabins five and six are having a competition where they try to throw pieces of popcorn into each other's mouths. So immature. I scan the room to locate Andi, but I don't see her anywhere. I hope she's not just sitting on that sad couch watching Ping-Pong games like last time.

"I'm going to see what's going on in the game room," I tell the girls, and they nod, distracted by a new cabin of boys that's just arrived.

I hear the Ping-Pong balls hitting back and forth over the three tables before I even enter the room. When I walk in, I do a quick scan, but Andi is not here either. I'm about to go back upstairs when I hear someone call my name.

"Zora!"

It's Christopher.

"Hi, Christopher."

"Are you looking for Andi?"

"I . . . um . . ."

"Because she's upstairs. She wants to dance with you."

I shake my head. "No. I don't think so. She hates dancing, and she hates me right now."

Christopher shakes his head furiously, and throws his arm over my shoulders. "Let's walk and talk, shall we?"

But he doesn't wait for me to respond.

"I know she seems mad, but she's really just afraid you don't like her anymore. I thought she was mad at me too, or at least didn't want to be my friend, but that's just because of some things I went through with kids at home and with my family. Andi's loyal and kind; I know that now. She just needs to know you'll be there for her."

"But, how? I keep trying to talk to her, and I keep messing it up."

"You'll figure it out," Christopher says. He leans in to whisper in my ear, "Actions speak louder than words, darling."

Then Christopher dances away from me, down the hallway toward the Ping-Pong room.

When I get back upstairs, the dance floor is a little more crowded; in fact, in the middle of the floor I see Julie, Beks, Jori, and Channing all dancing in a tight circle as a clean version of a Cardi B song starts to play. They are jumping up and down and mouthing the words to one another.

"Zora!" Julie screams. "Get over here!"

I smile and give them a motion that signals I'll be there in a second. Then I do another quick lap around the room.

Just as I am about to give up, I see her. Andi is standing by the cotton-candy machine, kind of hidden. She's swaying side to side, watching the room, and maybe Christopher is right—she does look like she wants to dance. *But with me?* I guess there's only one way to find out.

I know what I have to do.

I run over to the DJ stand and tug on DJ B's shirt. He leans down, and I whisper my request into his ear. He scans the tracks on Spotify, and I point to the one I want. I run back over to where my friends are and join them on the floor, jumping up and down and shaking my hips to the end of the Cardi B song. Might as well get all my jitters out, because I know what's coming next.

"All right, campers!" DJ B says over the fading notes of

the song, "we've had a request, so it's time for the first slow dance of the evening. Grab someone you like, and let the smooth notes of this throwback track take you someplace special. This song goes out to Andi Byrd, from Zora."

"Zora!" Jori yells, as she, Julie, and Beks all turn to me. "What is happening?"

My heart is pounding in my ears. It's time to reveal a little of mystery-me.

"Remember how I didn't want to dance with any boys?"

"Yeah," Jori says.

"Well, I . . ." I glance in the direction of Andi, who has come out from behind the cotton-candy shadows and is staring at me.

Jori gives me a huge hug and pulls back with a smile. "You do you, Zora!"

Beks just stares at me with her mouth open, and Julie looks back and forth between me and Andi as if she's never considered the option.

Before any of the others can say anything else, Jori shoos them all away. "Let's go, nerds. If we want to dance with any of these boys *or* girls, we're going to have to ask them ourselves."

I take a deep breath as Bobbi Humphrey's voice sings "Rainbows, rainbows . . ." from the speakers. Andi is still staring at me, and I can't tell what her exact expression is, but it's too late now. I walk over.

"Is this for real?" she asks, pointing to the stage as if Bobbi Humphrey herself is there, singing and playing her flute.

"I know. It's stupid. But . . . well, let's dance?"

I take Andi's hand, and she doesn't pull away. We join a collection of five or six other couples on the floor, including Jori, who has grabbed a tall guy from the percussion section named Clark, and Julie, who has asked Sam to dance, after all. Julie gives me a surprised thumbs-up and then leans her head on Sam's shoulder. He is, of course, wearing a T'Challa T-shirt.

"I don't really know how . . . ," Andi starts, standing awkwardly in front of me with her one hand in her pocket.

"Just follow me." I face her and put her hands on my shoulders, and then I put my hands on her hips. I step slowly to the right, and then to the left, and I nod at her to do the same, mirroring my feet.

She does, and before I know it we settle into a comfortable rhythm.

"You can get closer," Andi says after a few beats. "I think I got this."

So, I pull her in closer, until our cheeks are touching, and it feels like we are no longer in the rec hall. I close my eyes and enjoy the warmth of her skin on mine. I think about that image of us I had when she first played me this song on the Fourth of July. The two of us in a speeding car, a beautiful blue sky, our hands stretching out the windows, letting the air snake over our palms and fingers.

"Andi," I say, pulling back to look her in the eyes.

"Uh-huh," she says, swallowing nervously.

"I'm sorry. I'm sorry I'm such a mess, but I do care about what happened at the lake, and you. It meant everything to me."

Andi's arms relax on my shoulders, and she steps a little closer. "It did?"

"Yes, I liked being in the woods with you. I like being around you."

"I like being around you too," Andi says.

"Good." I grin.

"Zora?"

"Yes?"

"Thanks for asking me to dance. You're really good at this."

I think I might melt. But instead, when the next track comes on, I take Andi's hand and pull her into a new circle with the rest of my people. And then we all get silly, jumping up and down like popcorn in a pan, screaming along with the track, dancing our butts off all the way into the night. And Andi is the loudest of us all.

A ROOM
FULL OF LOVE

I love the way a concert hall feels right before a show. It's the night of the final showcase, and I am still full of energy from last night's mixer. In fact, I don't even mind that I'm sitting second chair, or that my parents are the front row of the audience, next to Ella's moms with their phones fully charged and ready to record my every move. I don't even mind that ever since I asked Andi to dance, some of the campers are gossiping about me, trying to figure out if I've always been into girls or not. I don't really care. For once, I'm just trying to be me.

The concert hall hums with noise, and I stand in the back-stage wings for a moment just soaking it all in. I can hear everything. A cough drop being unwrapped in the front row, the chattering of families making their way to seats in the audience, and then of course everyone onstage, warming up, plucking and playing bits and pieces of their parts. For once, I am wearing the same color as Andi; in fact, every-one is. Our concert attire, a sea of all-black dress clothes.

"Thank god!" Andi had joked this morning as we all shook out our concert attire. "Finally, a color I can get down with."

After the mixer, Andi and I had held hands on the walk back to the cabin. When we got to the door, we let go and shyly made our ways through the bedtime routines. But just as the cabin was getting quiet, and right before Joanna turned off the lights, Andi poked her head up over the side of my bed and handed me one of her AirPods.

"Some good-night tunes," she said. "Sweet dreams, Zora."

"Sweet dreams, Andi."

And we drifted off in our bunks, connected by the soft voice of Esperanza singing "You are black gold, black gold" into our ears.

I don't know if Andi is my girlfriend or just my friend, but I'm not afraid to be myself around her anymore.

Speaking of Andi, where is she?

I run my eyes over the trumpet section, but she's not there. We're twenty minutes from starting, and this is a huge night for Andi since she's playing the trumpet duet with Channing. She was in the practice huts almost all day, but I haven't seen her since dinner.

I should get onstage and warm up, but instead I turn back around and head into the greenroom. It's mostly empty, except for everyone's cases and bags, thrown all around on the floor.

"Zora!" Mr. Wright says, peeking into the room. "You need to be in your seat. We're starting soon."

"I know. Have you seen Andi?"

"Isn't she onstage?" Mr. Wright asks.

"No."

"She had a phone call in the main lodge, so I sent her over there. But that was about thirty minutes ago. Let me check and see if she's still there. Why don't you head onstage. I'm sure she'll show up."

I nod as Mr. Wright leaves, but I have no intention of going back onstage without Andi. Instead I make a beeline for the bathrooms.

"Andi, are you in here?"

No response.

I walk in and check all the stalls. Nothing. But then I hear a sharp inhale and see her, crumpled up under the sinks. Her head resting on her knees, her shoulders heaving.

I sit down next to her and reach out my hand. "Andi, it's me. Just keep breathing."

I've never seen her like this, but I know enough to see she's not okay, to know she's panicking.

"Andi, did something happen?"

I rub her back and try to even out my own breath alongside her.

After a while, her shoulders relax and she scoots closer to me.

"Andi, what's wrong?"

"The baby's here. Too early. She's four weeks early and her lungs are not fully developed. They're taking good care of her but—" Andi's voice breaks into a sob.

"Oh, Andi!"

"Uncle Mark called—he already felt really bad they couldn't be here, but he sounded extra upset. The baby is stable, she's going to live, but he sounded so worried. Star, she's still so small and needs help breathing."

"Star?"

"That's her name, short for Augusta, after my mom. At first I was mad they were going to name her that. But I get it now. The best parts of my mom can live in baby Star." Tears come fast when she says this.

"Is your aunt okay?"

"Yes, she's going to be fine. When I got the news, I just lost it. I know I haven't even met baby Star yet, but I want her to be strong and healthy . . . I don't want to lose anybody else."

I pull Andi into a hug. The lights in the bathroom flicker—the ten-minute warning that the concert will be starting soon.

"Listen, we needed to be onstage, like, ten minutes ago. Do you think you can play for her?"

"For baby Star?"

"Yes, and for your mom, and for Aunt Janine. I know

this is going to sound weird, but I've seen you play. When you're really into it, it's magic, like you take people somewhere else with your songs. What if you try to do that tonight? During the piece and especially your duet? What if you focus on sending love and strength to baby Star with your notes?"

Andi is quiet and I hold her tighter. "Your uncle said Star was stable. That's good. Play for her and maybe she'll hear how much you love her already?"

"I can try," Andi says finally.

"That's good. I know it sucks that your family won't be here. But I'm here, and Christopher is here, and Joanna. And my parents. We got you."

"Promise?"

"I promise. Let's wash off your face and then we'll go up together."

I pull Andi onto her feet and give her a hug.

We are stronger already.

Seven minutes later, Andi and I walk onstage. I squeeze her hand before we make our way to our sections. The bright lights of the concert hall blare down, but neither of us has time to waste. I run a few scales, but barely finish before the lights are dimming and the first-chair violin is walking onstage to tune us all. Then Mr. London steps onto the podium and the whole audience bursts into a round of polite applause. I sneak one last look back at Andi. She's sitting second chair, with her trumpet propped on her knee, her shoulders tall and confident. I smile at her and mouth "You got this!" Then Mr. London lifts his baton and we begin.

I know there are almost a hundred other people onstage with me and Andi, but it doesn't feel that way. It feels like it's just the two of us. In fact, when I look out into the dimmed darkness of the audience, it almost looks like the Lost Lake. A moonless, dull body of water with its attention drawn in our direction. I play my parts as strong and clear as I can. When it's time for Channing and Andi's duet, I close my eyes and sit back in my chair. Andi's trumpet answers me back just as strong and clear as I called out to her on my flute. I let her transport me, and the rest of the hall, into a room full of loss and love.

CODA

Harmony Music Camp

The roof of my amphitheater is vibrating
The wide-awake notes of trumpets
Wafting through the air like a prayer
Behind the orchestra, past the stage
Lake Harmony is a dark-blue canvas
Streaked with the sun's final orange

As the horns grow stronger—more urgent
Full of feathers and mourning and hope
Not a soul in the audience looks away, or coughs
Or shifts in the hard plastic seats

I have felt so many kinds of goodbyes
Songs full of letting go, or moving on
Songs that outgrow themselves
And tumble away into sand

But this is not one of those
This is a ringing *snap*!
A call to the air
This is a music full of lift and life
This is a goodbye that is also
Full of beginnings

So full that if you look hard enough
You'll see what Andi does not see, only feels
In the dark soaring behind her eyes

Baby Star reaching toward the sky
With a tiny, strong hand
Her newborn voice full of breath
    And fierce song

And a hawk   rising up from the lake
    A ghost mom
    Aimed at the stars
Feathers so black and full of light
    They vanish into a brilliant tomorrow

AUTHOR'S NOTE

I am a Black, queer woman who grew up in mostly white spaces. As a young person, I often made myself small— kept hidden the parts of me that I was scared of or knew might scare others—and instead sought to be perfect in everything I did. I was terrified of disappointing those that I loved. Like Zora, I sometimes turned to hitting or pinching myself when I felt out of control, and like Andi, I have experienced a lot of grief and still to this day live with chronic anxiety. While I wanted this book to focus on camp adventures, music, and Andi and Zora's romance, I also wanted to write a book that honors how complicated it can sometimes feel to grow up. One thing I wish I'd realized when I was young is that I wasn't alone in my feelings or struggles. I wish I'd been taught that asking for and seeking out support is not a weakness, but a strength.

So, dear reader, if you are hurting yourself, if you are making yourself small to please others, or living with depression or anxiety, please know you are not alone. Please know that I love you, and that the bravest thing I have ever done is reach out for help when all I wanted to do was hide. Reader, you are beautiful, and talented, and full of stories, and the world needs your voice in it. I hope you find joy, love, and adventure in this book, and in your life, and I also hope that you'll ask for support if you need it. Here are a few resources that might be a start:

THERAPY FOR BLACK GIRLS

A national space developed by Dr. Joy Harden Bradford to present mental health topics that feel more accessible and relevant to Black women and girls.

website: therapyforblackgirls.com

THE TREVOR PROJECT

A national organization "providing crisis intervention and suicide prevention services to lesbian, gay, bisexual, transgender, queer & questioning (LGBTQ) young people under 25."

website: thetrevorproject.org

phone/text: 1-866-488-7386 (for self-injury, suicide, or other crisis support)

THE LGBT NATIONAL YOUTH TALKLINE VIA THE LGBT NATIONAL HELP CENTER

"Free and confidential peer support for the LGBTQ and questioning community ages 25 and younger."

website: glbthotline.org/talkline.html

phone: 1-800-246-7743

email: help@LGBThotline.org

Stay safe, and sing often. You are loved.

Mariama J. Lockington

ACKNOWLEDGMENTS

A second book is a marathon, not a sprint, and writing this one during a global pandemic added an extra challenge. Some days it was a welcome distraction to get lost in Andi and Zora's love story, and other days all I could manage to get done was take care of my basic needs. Along the way, I was grateful for the support, understanding, grace, and motivation of so many people who believed in this story.

Thank you to my father, David, who lent his classical-music expertise to the manuscript when I had questions.

Big love to the Raynors, who read this book as a family in its messy draft form and provided me with feedback, love, and confidence. Special shout-out to Molly Raynor for reminding me of all the magic/awkwardness of summer camp and helping me add extra camp flare to the book.

Thank you to Callie Violet for inspiring me with your love of dance, and bringing me joy with your smile. Ray and Camille—you celebrate me at every turn, and make me feel so loved. It's an honor to be your chosen family.

Thank you as always to my editor, Joy Peskin. You always know just the right questions to ask to make my characters and plots stronger, and you have truly been a wonderful creative partner to me.

I'm also grateful to have a whip smart, caring, and vital guide in my agent, Jane Dystel. Thank you for pushing me to be my best and know my worth.

The artwork on this beautiful cover was created by Tonya Engel, and I'm so grateful to have Andi and Zora rendered so well. Your work is stunning. Thank you.

All my thanks to my early authenticity readers Meadow Sweet and Trisha de Guzman. Your attention to and care with this story and my characters made it stronger.

There are so many friends and chosen family members that held it down for me while I was drafting this book—providing feedback, encouragement, vent sessions, and reminders to breathe along the way. Big thanks to Nikkey Blackman, Lauren Cagle, Yomaira Figueroa-Vásquez, Yalie Kamara, Rajani LaRocca, Liz Latty, Ada Limón, Katy Clipson Mansino, Gillian McDunn, Lisa Moore Rameé, Clare Rittschof, Karen Strong, José Vadi, Jasmine Warga, Starla Whittaker, and Lauren Whitehead.

Vanessa and Henry, thank you for being my home and my heart.

Lastly, a huge thank-you to my readers. None of this is possible without you, and I never want to take for granted what an honor it is to be able to share stories with you. Thank you for allowing me to live my dream, and for reading my work with open hearts and minds.